To sweet
Colleen
Love

THE COFFINS

A Roanoke Island Archaeological Supsense Novel

Published by FIVE RIVERS PRESS

Copyright © 2017 by Deborah Dunn

This is a work of fiction. Names, characters, places and incidents are either the product of the author's imagination or are used fictitiously, and any resemblance to actual persons, living or dead, business establishments, events or locales is entirely coincidental.

Printed in the USA.

Interior Format
© THE KILLION GROUP INC.

THE
COFFINS

A ROANOKE ISLAND
SUPSENSE NOVEL

DEBORAH
DUNN

In love and gratitude, I dedicate this
book to my three grandchildren:
Raeglan and Khyber Briere, and our youngest,
Baby Bear (Barham Dunn)

HISTORICAL TIMELINE
OF THE
ROANOKE COLONIZATION

1584   A reconnaissance voyage is sent to the Atlantic coast of North America under the direction of Philip Amadas and Arthur Barlowe, charged with assessing its suitability for habitation. Wanchese, a Secotan, and Manteo, a Croatan, are taken back to England for a year. Fifteen soldiers left behind.

1585   A colony of 107 men, under the military leadership of Ralph Lane, directed by Sir Richard Grenville, arrive on Roanoke Island. The fifteen soldiers left behind have vanished. They stay for a year. In a confrontation with the hostile Secotan, their King, Wingina, is beheaded. Manteo remains faithful to the English. Wanchese vows to seek revenge.

April 1587   Sir Walter Raleigh directs one hundred and seventeen men, women, and children, led by Governor John White, to board the *Tiger* and set sail for Virginia. The party includes John White's pregnant daughter, Eleanor, and her husband, Ananias Dare.

July 22, 1587   Just off the northern coast of what

is now North Carolina, a storm churns up strong currents, blowing *The Tiger* onto Roanoke Island, a hundred miles south of their intended destination, Chesapeake Bay. Their captain, Simon Fernandez, a rogue Spaniard hired to transport them, leaves them stranded there without provisions, as most were lost in the storm.

August 18, 1587   Eleanor's daughter is born, strong and healthy; first English child born in America. She is baptized with the name, Virginia Dare. Manteo is given the title, *Lord of Roanoke,* in honor of his friendship to the English. Wanchese remains hostile.

September 1587   Food is scarce, there has been a drought that year. One of the colonists, George Howe, is found face down in the shallow marsh with an arrow in his back. Frightened, they vote among themselves to commission John White to return to England and convince the Queen to help them. With great reluctance, White leaves his daughter and his tiny new granddaughter, promising to return by winter.

But once there, instead of helping, the Queen confiscates his ship. The Spanish Armada is approaching and she must arm a military fleet. It will be three years before she allows him to return to Roanoke Island.

September 1590   John White finally returns, only to find the Fort eerily deserted, all trace of the colonists vanished, even their houses. Except for the skeleton of one guard, there is no sign of a struggle. White's papers, buried in the ground, have been vandalized. There is only one clue, the word "Croatan" carved on a post of the palisade. He believes that this is a sign that Manteo has helped the colonists move inland. For weeks he searches up and down the Outer Banks without success. He does not have the resources to search inland. With winter looming he boards his ship and returns to England. He retires to a cottage in Ireland.

Fourteen years later he disappears.

PROLOGUE

March, 1587
London, England

SHE HURRIES DOWN FLEET STREET toward Charing Cross, eyes darting to and fro. Frightening enough to be out on the streets of the city at this hour alone, but what if her husband wakes and finds her gone?

Witchcraft, Ananias said. *Dabbling in the black arts like your dead mother, God rest her wretched soul. Don't ye understand by now that the so-called "gift" ye claim is truly the Devil's work? Did losing our son teach you nothing?*

How can a man accuse his wife of such things? She should never have listened to her father.

Come with us Ellie! Marry Ananias! Help us build New Eden! You're the daughter of John White, the future Governor of Roanoke. Don't you want a husband and children? Don't you see this is the will of God?

So, caught up in the excitement she married Ananias Dare, one tile and stonemason of no acclaim, in a brief ill-planned ceremony at St. Martin's at Ludgate. And as if fate had surely decreed their union nine months later she birthed a grandson. Within a fortnight her husband was elevated to the status of *Captain Ananias Dare* and conferred with a coat of arms, as if he was entitled. Plans to mount a voyage to America the following spring began in earnest.

On some level, she supposed she never believed it would happen. John White, Governor of Virginia? As likely as turnips turning into whores!

But on and on and on he had spun his tales of riches, fame, and glory. Like everyone else she forgot he'd been gone most of her childhood, off on his adventures, only coming home when he had need of her. Ye gads it was like he was the Pied Piper of Hamelin himself, no one could refuse him. Even the queen had succumbed to the pictures he had drawn of the New Land and his romantic stories. How could his own daughter refuse him?

But to her shock not only was he named Governor; Sir Walter Raleigh procured a ship and stores. Whole families started signing up for the voyage, all thrilled to be leaving the squalor of London, convinced their fortune lay in New Eden, sure they were following the Lord's calling.

Still, cocooned as she was in the warmth of new motherhood, her father's plans seemed foolish and unreal, far away and unimportant. Surely, she could convince her husband to leave her behind, at least for a while anyway. *Why not?* He was allowing his son John to stay so that he might finish out his apprenticeship. She could stay, be a mother to John, bear her child in safety. Would it not be madness to force a new mother on such a dangerous voyage?

Her father would come to his senses, she was

sure of it.

At least she had a babe in arms to distract her. Entranced by his sweet gurgling laugh and rosebud mouth, she managed to pretend all was well in her world. Used to the coughs and colds that had wracked their lungs all winter, she'd thought nothing much of it when he developed a bit of a rasp in his breathing, only administering a small dose of elderberry syrup, wrapping him snugly in his bunting.

Eleanor sat rocking him by the meager firelight, her head nodding, trying to remain vigilant. When he had fallen into a fast sleep she gently lowered him down, only to awaken in the middle of the night to an uncanny, chilling quiet. *Too quiet.* Her baby lay in his cradle, bonny cheeks like marble, tiny bud of a mouth blue, body cold and lifeless.

Rocking, rocking, rocking. Rocking to bring him back to life, wearing grooves in the wooden floors. She held onto him for days, willing him to come back to her. Forcing her husband to build a roaring fire to keep her child warm, still she wouldn't put him down. No food passed her lips, not even a bit of warm broth. When Ananias finally wrenched him from her arms, she'd gone mad, tearing out bits of her hair, biting her lips until they bled. And though the doctor said it was likely a weak heart, Ananias blamed it on the elderberry.

But in her heart, she knew it had been the fog. It was the fog that had stolen her baby.

Yes, that was it! The fog had stolen her child, wrapping its skeletal fingers around his tiny throat, choking him to death with phlegm. Now that same horrid March fog had returned, slithering up the dark moldy alley by the tile shop, sliding down the chimney, creeping up the stairs. What if those icy fingers were wending their way up the gangplank and onto the ship even now? What would she do without her cures, stranded in the middle of a vast ocean and only the one doctor (such as he was), with nothing to ease their fevers and coughing, no way to protect her unborn child?

She tried to speak of it to Ananias, but he only turned a cold shoulder to her, peevishly forbidding her to leave the house, reminding her yet again of the devastating consequences of the elderberry syrup she had administered to their son.

But the only regret she had was that she hadn't given it to the child sooner. And now she is pregnant again, only three months along.

For months she obeyed, watching with growing unease as her stores dwindled before her eyes. But that very night a dream awakened her, a dream so clear and profound she laid rigid, eyes wide and unblinking. Helpless, tied to a ship's rail, she watched as crows lifted each passenger, already weak and frail from illness, toward the sky, bodies like tiny little scarecrows dangling from orange beaks. The nightmare only ended when the largest crow lit on her shoulder and began pecking at her eyes. She awoke choking.

Surely this was a warning. Why else would she dream so vile?

Compelled, she rose, pilfering a few six pence out of their money bag—*what need had they of coins in America?* —trembling as she tied her cloak strings, slipping down the stairs through the white mortar dust and out the front door onto busy Fleet Street, face hidden under her hood.

Once outside the city walls she set her foot away from the cart path to Charing Cross, striking out instead across an open field. Though the frosty stubble made the going tricky, it was better than the prying eyes of merchants in their trundling wagons churning up ruts in the rainy slime, their oxen dumping fresh steaming piles of manure, and the scores of unwashed streaming into the city in the foggy light of morn.

What if someone recognized her, whispered to her husband?

Despite a light rain the main square was filled with the hustle and bustle of trade—monks selling bones and relics, potters, weavers and bakers—all hawking their wares. After wandering around in circles, she finally spotted the grizzled old hag with rotted out teeth camped in a broken down oxcart by the road. Reeking of fungus, mold and onions, the woman stretched out her dirty palms, the gleam in her eyes uncomfortably knowing and something that bordered on scorn. When Eleanor dropped the coins into her hand she snatched them quickly, secreting them away in the folds of her shapeless woolen garment. Without a word she picked up a clutch of small cloth bags tied with ragged string, sneering when Eleanor took them from her and one by one held each bag to her nose, sniffing deeply, making sure they were fresh and potent.

Muttering a prayer for protection, forcing herself to blend in with the crowd, she slogged her way back up the mud and clay road and back onto crowded Fleet Street, fretful that her errand had taken longer than it should. Sidestepping the slick puddles of piss and offal, dodging the cripples and drunkards grabbing at her cloak, she was almost home when her foot slipped on a stone, body tumbled forward. Instinctively one hand reached out to cushion her fall, the other clutching at her belly, the herb basket flying out of her hands onto the cobbles a few feet in front of her. Before she could right herself she watched, horrified, as a pickpocket on the sly ran over, grabbed the basket and took off down the street waving it in the air in triumph, turned a corner and disappeared.

In shock, she slumped to the ground, too devastated even to weep or cry out for help, too discouraged to rise, gazing in disbelief at her empty hands and the beads of watery blood on each palm. Then, remembering her baby, she clutched her waist with a gasp, prayed in panic. Tears rolled down her cheeks as she sat sobbing in the street, a great unwashed sea of humanity flowing around her like a river rushing its banks.

Shuddering, she lowered her head into her hands. Not only did she lose her precious herbs and potions, but now she would have to explain the missing coins to Ananias and why she had stolen away from their bed. And the bruises! There was no way she could cover them!

Weeping, covered in mud, she forced herself to rise. She would have so much explaining to do, and packing—*oh sweet Jesus in Heaven*—she'd almost forgotten they were leaving tomorrow! Brushing the mud off her skirts, she began her weary trek back home.

New Eden. It had to be better than this wretched

hell, this place the world called London. Trees arching overhead like a living cathedral and rivers flowing with milk and honey, her grandfather said. *And the sassafras!* A sure cure for the dreaded syphilis that plagued all of Europe like the flies, the frogs, and locusts had once plagued Egypt.

Perhaps the Lord truly was taking her away from this foul city with its deadly fog and filth for her protection, taking her to His Promised Land.

But those pictures, those strange depictions of wild creatures with writings on their skin, bird skeletons entwined in their coal black hair and worse, women whose breasts swung naked, exposed to the sun! Those pictures frightened her, made her skin crawl.

Manteo will help us, he said. Manteo dressed like an Englishman, spoke English, professed his faith in God. *The Croatan will teach you about their herbs and healing* he claimed. In return she would teach them English ways.

Perhaps her future really did lie in the new land. Surely in New Eden Ananias would see that her gift of healing was being used by God, her second sight a blessing. Perhaps he would stop blaming her.

Didn't the Bible say that God gave His children every herb-bearing plant for their good use? And what if her mother had cast a spell or two every now and then? They were only meant for good.

On and on the voices of her father, her husband, God, the devil and his minions of demons raged inside her head, back and forth, back and forth, anxiety mounting.

Then out of nowhere, an insight, like the sun breaking through the mist in the glen. Her heart slowed. She took deep breaths and waited. Sure enough, an answer came floating up from the depths of her mind. A Scripture, Matthew 9:17, taught to her when she was a child:

Nor do people put new wine into old wineskins; otherwise the wineskins burst, and the wine pours out and the wineskins are ruined, but they put new wine into fresh wineskins, and both are preserved.

Yes, the answer had been there all along!

Excited now and flushed with new understanding, Eleanor hurried on her way. Hadn't the Israelites been instructed to take nothing with them when they left Egypt to follow Him into the Wilderness? And hadn't the Lord provided everything they needed? The herbs she had bought from the old woman were like the old wine! Everything would be provided for them in their new home!

If she was obedient, surely, He would let her children live.

Her daughter *had* to live.

And it would be a daughter, she was sure of it, the first English child born in America, God willing, despite her husband's insistence that the child she was carrying was another son. How she knew she couldn't say, only that she did, a knowing beyond understanding. And she would be named Virginia after the Virgin Queen, their Benefactor. They would baptize her with the silver cup presented to her father by Sir Walter Raleigh, the very same cup Grenville had used to trick the savages into surrendering their village, thus proving English domination of the New World!

Eleanor's heart swelled now, not with worry but with pride, her fears seeming silly in the light of her new understanding—that by not trusting her father she was truly failing to trust in the Lord. He would never let anything bad happen to her. Her father loved her even if he had stayed gone all those years. No longer would she be poor Eleanor, orphan daughter of a man who cared more about drawing pictures of savages than of his only child, or wife of a husband who married an old maid to elevate himself in the world.

She would be Goodwife Dare, daughter of the Governor, mother of Virginia, future Queen of New Eden!

New Eden, where she would be allowed to plunge her hands into the moist virgin soil without censure, dig up her roots, plant her seeds, dry, pound, and carefully mete out the powders — comfrey, bee's balm, wormwood and rosemary for ailments of the head and lungs, curling fern fronds like tiny fairy wings, juniper berries, milk thistle, dandelion, mint, and wild fennel for the bowels and gums. Seeds of tansy, marigold, basil, thyme and oregano from Spain for the garden she would grow, treasures that would quench the burning throat, cool the fevered brow!

God would give her an anointed garden and He would provide the seeds she would grow!

But out of nowhere came a voice—a gentle voice but loud and clear, ringing with authority, thrumming inside her head:

This voyage is doomed!

As quickly as it had left her only moments before, fear flew down her throat, flapping its black wings, beating against the cage of her ribs. If it hadn't been for the child she was carrying, she might have thrown herself into the river headlong.

Stop! She screamed out loud, standing in the middle of the street. Taking deep breaths, she forced herself to calm, willed her heart to slow. Gathering up her shattered wits, steeling her resolve, she raised her fist and cried out:

"Get thee behind me Satan! I won't listen to your lies anymore!"

She shuddered, nauseous with the effort. She drew a deep breath, forced herself to calm.

Now, that was better.

She would go home, confess her folly to Ananias, beg his forgiveness, and repent to the Lord. She would recant her mother's witchcraft, ignore those horrible dreams and visions and that voice in her head prophesying doom. Tomorrow they would board the ship and all would be well.

All she had to do was trust in the Lord and obey her husband.

Gulping in air, shivering, she closed her eyes, lifted her pale face toward Heaven.

The fog swirled around her, stroked her hair with its bony fingers; whispered its dark knowledge in her ear.

You are Eleanor Dare, mother of Virginia. The world will remember your name.

CHAPTER ONE

A NDREA WOKE WITH A GASP, heart hammering in her chest.

Only a nightmare, okay? Only a nightmare…

Shivering, she pulled the covers over her head. It had seemed so real.

She is lost in a dark, foggy forest. A baby is crying in the woods somewhere. Terrified, she runs toward the sound. But just as she thinks she has found it, the crying suddenly stops. The baby vanishes forever.

The same terrible dream, three nights in a row. Every night a baby dies and somehow it is all her fault. She wrapped herself tighter in the covers, cocooning herself in the dark, the pitiful cries of the baby still haunting her.

Stop kidding yourself Andrea.

The baby is her lost career, her dreams of being an archaeologist. No big mystery there. She closed her eyes, blocking out the thought. Reaching one arm out from underneath the covers, she rummaged for her phone on the bedside table, holding it close to her face to check the time.

Crap! It was already nine o'clock. She was supposed to be on the road by now! Still groggy, disoriented, she lay there for a second, a part of her still reliving the dream.

Then she heard the doorbell chime.

Great. The landlord again. What was his problem? She'd told him she'd hand over the key by noon last night.

She jumped out of bed, stubbing her big toe on the bedside table, the sudden stab of pain jolting her fully awake. Muttering, hopping on one foot, she grabbed a pair of jeans off the end of the bed, pulling them on underneath the oversized white t-shirt she'd gone to bed in. As she struggled to get dressed, the bell chimed again.

"I'm coming, I'm coming!" she yelled, hobbling out of the bedroom into the kitchen door. She stuck her eye to the peephole. *Thank God.* Totally forgetting the pain in her foot, she flung open the door.

"Doc," she smiled. "Come on in!" She extended both of her hands, kissing him on the cheek. If there was one person she didn't mind seeing this morning it was Doc, her graduate mentor for the last two years.

Not that he was anything to look at. Stout and balding, neatly trimmed white beard, thin maroon sweater vest and paisley bowtie, he wore the same "professor" outfit he always wore, even on the hottest days of summer. And the one person, aside from her mother, who hadn't turned on her when she needed him most.

"I couldn't let you leave without seeing for myself how you were doing," he whispered, eyes shining.

"I'm fine," she fibbed, then made herself busy in the room. She turned on a lamp, picking a sweater up off the back of the couch, then laid it back down. If she looked at him, she would start crying, and that would only upset him more.

"Andrea, I've been worried about you…."

She finally turned to face him, her smile crooked with the effort not to burst into tears. She waved at him to sit down. "Don't go getting sentimental on me okay? Let me keep my dignity, at least." Then, seeing the expression on his face, she softened. "Really, I'm fine."

He sighed, shook his head. "I can't stay long anyway. And I know you must have a lot to do. He reached into his pants pocket, pulled out a small box, and thrust it toward her. "But I wanted to give you this before you left, as a memento of the dig up in Massachusetts last summer. You were such an immense help."

She took it from him and peeked inside. Carefully she pulled out a copper coin pendant dangling from a thin silver chain, marveling as it glittered in the lamplight. Gasping, she held it closer. "Oh my goodness, a 1787 Horned Eagle!" A spread eagle was stamped one side, a very dignified figure of a Native American Indian on the other. "You really shouldn't have," was all she could say, her voice cracking.

"I only wish I could do more my dear. I feel so helpless…."

She met his eyes. They both knew he was talking about.

"I know," she finally answered, resigned. "But we've talked about this. It wasn't worth risking your tenure. No sense in both of us losing our careers, now is there?" She held up the necklace, her smile tremulous. "Can you do the honors?" Quickly, so he couldn't see her face, she turned her back to him, tossing her hair forward.

He lifted it over her head, careful not to tangle it in her hair, stubby fingers working at the clasp. When he was done, he patted her on the shoulder. She whirled, locking him in a bear hug.

"It's beautiful. I'll cherish it forever. Stay in touch, okay?"

He held her at arm's length. "You too, child. You too." He patted her on the cheek and then turned and walked back out the door.

Andrea stood alone in the apartment, fingering the necklace. She gazed around the shadowed living room, remembering the day she had moved in, so full of hopes and dreams, so sure she was on her way to becoming a world-class archaeologist. She had been about to start her graduate classes, thrilled to be in Williamsburg. Now she was leaving in disgrace, moving back home to live with her mother in Charlotte.

Well, too late for regrets now. What was done was done. It was time to get a move on. But at least Doc had come to say goodbye. It helped to know someone here cared.

Swallowing the lump in her throat she rounded up the last few items that needed loading, grabbed the comforter and sheets off the bed, and stuffed everything in a garbage bag. One final look around to make sure she hadn't forgotten anything before she slung her knapsack over her shoulder, then she picked up her keys off the counter and, dragging the garbage bag by her wrist, headed out the door, slamming it shut behind her.

(

Two hours later she exited off Hwy. 58 onto I-95. Tanked up on fresh coffee, she was cruising along just fine.

Then she happened to look in the rear-view mirror.

Crap! She should have known cops would be crawling all over the interstate, especially on a Friday. And not just any Friday; Memorial Day weekend. How many times had her mother reminded her this past week?

She pulled over, praying that he would keep going. If she got a ticket, how was she going to pay fines and court costs? She barely had enough money in the bank to pay for gas. And she sure as heck wasn't going to borrow it from her mother. Having to move back home with her tail tucked between her legs was hard enough.

But no such luck. Her heart sank as she watched him slow down and pull over about a hundred yards behind her. After what seemed like ages he opened his car door, languidly extending one long leg out after the other, in no great hurry. Tall and lanky, a bit paunchy, middle-aged perhaps, old enough to be her father anyway. Should she pretend to be rushing toward some disaster or throw herself on his mercy and tell him the truth?

But then again, her life *was* a disaster. And wasn't it the truth that had gotten her into this mess in the first place?

She shook her head. *Enough already.*

When he finally got to her window he tipped his hat, scanned the inside of the car, pallid face an unreadable mask. He was cool, she had to give that to him.

"May I see your driver's license and registration, ma'am?" he asked, voice firm but soft.

For a second her mind went blank, then she panicked. Shoving aside boxes and bags to get to the glove compartment, she pawed through the contents. Papers, bills, and bank receipts scattered everywhere. Where in the hell was the registration?

There! She handed it over to him, then turned and grabbed her knapsack off the floor, fumbled around until she found her wallet, slid her license out from its plastic sleeve, and passed it over to him, dry-mouthed.

He took it, stared at it a moment, then flipped it over and back. When he looked up at her again he squinted, moved his face in closer.

"Andrea Warren?" he asked.

"Yes sir," she answered.

"Heading home to Charlotte?"

She nodded, this time too eager. "Yeah, I just finished graduate school. I never got my licensed changed…."

He glanced down at the license again, then back up, his expression still guarded. Her heart thudded. She braced herself to be ordered out of the car.

"Busted out tail light, that's all. Bad news with this fog rollin' in, okay? You get that fixed when you get back to Charlotte, you hear?" He handed her a pink slip of paper. "This here's a warning ticket. If you get stopped again, just show this. But don't wait too long. Next time you might not be so lucky." Then he tipped his hat again and turned on his heel.

But, just when Andrea was about to relax, he stopped in mid-stride, snapped his fingers in the air; turned around and came back.

"I *knew* you looked familiar. Aren't you that girl who blew the whistle on that developer over near Williamsburg? The jerk who tried to get you to shut up about that old bone pit? An ossuary I think they call it. Saw it in the paper…"

She blinked at him, mute, then gave a slight nod.

"I knew it!" he exclaimed, slapping the window frame. "I remember thinking that sure took some guts. A lot of sacred cows in the university systems these days, a lot of politics if you know what I mean. Trust me, I know how it works." He hitched up his pants, then leaned in closer. "I'm a history buff myself. Sad to me that folks seem to care more about their golf courses and planned communities than they do preserving the past." He leaned back out, swept his arm in an arc.

"Here we are almost sitting right on the Great Indian Trading Highway. Ran all the way from the coast of Virginia down into Georgia for centuries. I-85 got built right on top of it. Don't people realize that once our history is gone, it's gone for good?" He leaned close in again, stared at her. "After all, don't know who you are unless you know where you come from, now do you?" Then his eyes softened, his voice dropped a notch. She could have sworn she saw him wink. "Don't give up now, you hear."

Andrea felt her face flush, her mouth drop open. Before she could answer he tipped his hat once more, took a few steps back, professional mask dropping into place again. "And watch that hot foot of yours, okay?" Then he turned, strode back to his car, got in and drove off.

Andrea sat there, her eyes wide, giddy with relief.

The Great Indian Trading Trail? She'd written her thesis on the Algonquian Indian, for Pete's sake! And to think she'd just gotten a roadside history lecture from a highway patrolman, of all people. Wonder what he would have done if she had told him she was part Indian? He'd probably have wet his pants!

Then she heard his voice again, in her head.

Don't know who you are if you don't know where you come from.

Tears sprang unbidden. He was right. How could she know where she was going when her whole damn life was a mess? No wonder she was having nightmares. The last few months had been like a bad dream itself, her days filled with detectives trying to catch her in a lie, making her feel like a criminal instead of the one trying to stop a crime. Systematically demoted from choice assignments on local archaeological digs to washing old bottles in the lab, her credibility called into question, talents minimized. And all because she had dared to expose the truth, dared to fight big money.

But it got worse. There were the rumors the scandal had generated, like her childhood all over again. People whispering, avoiding her eyes when they passed her in the hall.

Heard her Daddy killed himself, drove himself crazy....

And in the end, it had all been for nothing, all her truth-telling, her high-minded archaeological ideals. Like prehistoric monsters, massive iron machines rolled in, teeth crushing everything in their paths. Those precious bones she'd fought to protect were stored in a box somewhere, the sacred ground they'd come from filled in and covered with sod. Any future knowledge the earth might have yielded lost, sacrificed forever on the altar of commerce. Advised to skip graduation ceremonies, she received her MA in Anthropology in the mail, along with a letter advising her not to talk with anyone about "the incident," not if she ever wanted a career in her chosen field in the future. And, as if they enjoyed pouring salt on a wound, the next day she was served gag orders to drive the point home.

But even that wasn't the worst—the worst was how her fiancé, Chad, had treated her, as if his career would be fatally tainted by association with her, although at the end, it was she who had broken it off. What did it matter that he was the most promising doctoral student the school had seen in a long time? How could she marry a man more interested in saving his own ass than anyone or anything else, including her?

She glanced down at her left hand on the steering wheel, so bare now. What good man would betray the woman he claimed to love?

Of course, Doc thought she'd been too hard on him. *Maybe*. But she was tired of betrayal and emotional abandonment. After all, hadn't her father done the same thing?

At least that's what her mother claimed.

She shook her head, forcing her mind back into the present. These thoughts were doing her no good. She gazed around her, noticing pine forests banked each side of the interstate. So many questions haunted her, and all of them about her father. Surely others must have known him. Who then?

She closed her eyes, listening to herself breathe. Finally, still undecided, she turned the ignition, easing back into traffic. Within minutes she pulled into a rest area. Inside she washed her face and hands, pulled a spare t-shirt out of her knapsack, throwing it on over her dirty tank top. A quick brush of her silky brown hair and a smear of lip gloss and, *there*, she almost felt human again.

She leaned over and stared into the mirror, turning her head back and forth to examine herself from different angles—the cut of her jaw, olive skin, wide-set deep brown eyes. Raking her dark silky hair with long, tapered fingers, she tossed it back, and for the thousandth time wondered: Do I look like him?

Then she blinked, startled. For a second she could have sworn someone else's eyes stared back at her, dark as obsidian.

Great. Now she was seeing things. She grabbed up her knapsack, glancing at her image sideways. No strange eyes looking back at her this time, thank goodness.

Breaking into a trot she headed back to the Jeep. Inside she yanked open the creaky door, slid onto the hot cracked leather seat, and retrieved her old North Carolina map out of the side pocket.

If you don't know where you come from, you don't know where you're going.

As she gazed at the outline of the state on the map, she realized she never really looked at it in its entirety before. Its narrow length stretched from sea to mountain, one end pointed out into the ocean, the other dipping in a slope all the way down into Georgia. Miles and miles between Charlotte and the Outer Banks, that was for sure, a good six-hour drive unless traffic didn't slow things down. She studied the small chain of islands on one end, like a string of beads, tracing them with her index finger.

What did she have to lose?

She stuffed the map back into the side pocket and started the car, heading toward the exit. At the stop sign she hesitated for a moment, undecided.

Charlotte was three hours to the west. The Outer Banks three hours to the east.

It was now or never. She turned east, toward the Outer Banks.

It was time to face her demons.

CHAPTER TWO

AN HOUR LATER SHE WAS in a pawn shop in a seedy strip mall just off I-95.

She almost changed her mind when she saw the old man standing behind the counter, silver hair styled into a helmet, hooded eyes cold, thin lips downturned. He reminded her of a large toad.

"How much is this worth?" she asked, dropping the ring on the counter. It rolled around like a juggler's act in a circus before it fell over, tinkling as it landed.

He picked it up between his pudgy liver-spotted fingers like it was a dead insect, flipping his jeweler's glass down over one eye without speaking. When he looked back up at her his face was deadpan.

"Two thousand and final," he stated, voice flat and raspy.

"You know it's worth at least ten, don't you?"

He grunted. "Not to me. Take it or leave it."

She hesitated. Should she take her chances somewhere further down the road where she'd get more for it or unload it here, a place she would probably never see again?

She took the bills in hundreds.

Walking back to the car she felt lighter, free almost. Two thousand dollars was a lot of money, enough to tide her over until she got a job at least. But then her steps slowed, her throat tightened. That ring had symbolized all her hopes and dreams. No amount of money would ever be enough to replace what had been taken from her.

Stop it, Andrea. Focus on your mission.

Back in her car she checked the map again. If she stuck to her plan to exit off the interstate and take Route 158 the drive was another three hours from this point, unless she ran into heavy traffic or fog. Of course, going that way was crazy—a whole lot easier to pop down I-95 to Rocky Mount then hang a left on Hwy 64 straight into Manteo, and certainly a whole lot faster. But that route was an emotional landmine that would take her right over the Alligator River where her father's body had been found. She wasn't quite ready for that, not yet anyway.

No. Better to take the winding backroads via Elizabeth City into Kitty Hawk. She would find a cheap motel, get a good night's sleep, walk on the beach and clear her head. Maybe by then she would have the courage to circle around to East Lake. She would spend the day asking around, then head home to Charlotte from there.

She cranked up her car again, glancing at the Weather Channel on her phone, glad to see that high pressure off the coast had stalled the rain clouds inward. If she was lucky it might hold long enough to give her at least a few hours of sunshine tomorrow.

Then she remembered: *Her mother.* She punched

speed dial.

"Sweetie, what happened? I was getting worried?"

"Hey, listen, I hate to disappoint you, but I got to thinking. Who knows when I'll get back this way? If you don't mind I'm going to head down to the Outer Banks and take a few days to explore. I don't know when I'll get the chance again...."

The silence on the other end was palpable. Then, "Well, what can I say? You're a grown woman."

Yes, I am, she wanted to say, but didn't. She couldn't count the times her mother had used that same tone of voice through the years, effectively shutting Andrea down, keeping her from asking questions.

Well, those days were over.

"Listen, Mom. I am not doing this to hurt you. This is something I need to do for myself. I don't expect I'll do more than check out a few places. Maybe this will help me put it all behind me...."

The continued silence on the other end spoke volumes.

Unable to stifle it any longer Andrea blurted, "I know suicide was a shitty thing to do. But he was still my father. I promise I'll be home soon, okay."

Her mother sighed, started to say something then stopped, then started again, this time sounding resigned.

"Andrea, I love you. Whatever you find out, please know that if I kept things from you, it was only to protect you. Just be careful, okay? People may not like you poking into their business."

Andrea stared out across the ugly parking lot, throat tight. Big fat drops of rain began to spatter on the windshield. The wind had picked up.

"I understand. I'll call in a few days, okay?"

Then, as if an afterthought, her mother's voice changed again, her tone ominous.

"Andy wait. You aren't going looking for those coffins, are you?"

Coffins?

"Mom, I have no idea what you are talking about. All I want to do is see what my father's life was like, say goodbye. I never got to do that you know."

A tiny silence. "Well good then. Like I said, be careful. Come home soon. I love you."

"I love you too."

The line went dead.

Drained, Andrea sat, trying to get her bearings. She hadn't meant to sound so resentful. But every word was true. There was so much she'd never been told, everything shrouded in secret. She didn't even know how her father had killed himself. Not that she had ever asked. If she went to his funeral, she didn't remember it.

But then again, she was only four when it happened.

Four years old. It was like that child was still trapped inside of her, crying to be let out.

Her search for a coffeehouse nearby came up cold, so she settled for the McDonald's across the street. Inside she placed her order, but they had to brew a fresh pot. While she waited, she scanned the place, empty except for a young woman sitting in a booth off to the side staring blindly out the window, dabbing at her eyes with a tissue. She didn't look a day over sixteen, despite the swollen mound poking out under her too-tight t-shirt.

Andrea walked over to her and smiled.

"Hey, I don't mean to pry, but is there anything I can do?"

The girl's head bobbed up, her pink face eager. "I need to call my aunt in Murfreesboro. Can I borrow your phone?"

"Sure." Andrea handed it over, watching as the girl tapped the keypad with her forefinger, trying not to stare at the chipped purple nail polish or the ragged bloody hangnails. She stepped away, turning to watch the parking lot so as not to appear nosy. Thunder rumbled in the distance. An empty food wrapper tumbled across the parking lot toward a dark, rundown house. An employee brought her coffee to her. Finally, the girl hung up, motioned Andrea back over.

"I forgot she switched shifts," she murmured, handing the phone back, crestfallen. Standing there, belly hanging over the waist of her tight Juicy Couture jeans, the girl looked so impossibly young, so worn down with life already, Andrea was moved. Then she had an idea.

"Hey, I'm headed toward Murfreesboro if you need a ride. Car's kind of crowded, but I can make room in the front seat if you don't mind."

The girl blinked once, suspicious. "I can't help with gas if that's what you're thinking," she blurted, cheeks flushing.

Andrea smiled. "We're good." She turned on her heel, motioning for the girl to follow.

They ducked in their seats just as the downpour started, brushing the drops off inside as rain pummeled the car. Andrea cranked the engine and pointed the car out onto the highway. At first the girl was quiet, but when they stopped at a traffic light she piped up.

"You moving?"

Andrea hesitated, her smile wry. "In a manner of speaking. I just finished grad school in Williamsburg. Headed home to live with my mother in Charlotte until I can afford a place of my own. But I decided at the last minute to take a quick vacation on the Outer Banks." Then, her voice bright. "That's enough about me. What's your name? You live here in Roanoke Rapids?" she asked, just as the Jeep rumbled over the wide railroad tracks into Weldon, a typical eastern North Carolina town that had seen better days.

"Crystal," the girl answered, voice flat. "Yeah, I did live here, with my boyfriend. But he got mad and dumped me. Drove off with my pocketbook in the truck." Her head turned to gaze out of the window, palm of her left hand moving to her belly.

Andrea could feel the heat rising in her neck. "Where's your mother?" she asked, an edge in her voice.

Crystal snorted. "Mad at me for getting knocked up." She turned her head away again. "She wouldn't even let me sleep on the couch." She gave a small harrumph. "Not that I'd want to anyway. Her new boyfriend gives me the creeps. Little too friendly, if you get what I mean, especially when he's drunk…."

Andrea flushed. The way the girl described her life was so casual.

Oblivious, Crystal kept talking. "You must be smart. What did you study in college?"

Andrea brightened. "Well, my undergradu-

ate degree was in Sociology and Anthropology.
My graduate degree is in Anthropology with a
concentration in Archeology," she answered, not
expecting much reaction. But to her surprise the
girl's face lit up.

"I *love* those programs on the History Channel, you know like *The Curse of Oak Island*. I can't
wait until they find that treasure chest." She turned
to Andrea, leaned in a bit. "Have you ever found
anything valuable?" Then, without waiting for an
answer, "They think those Knights Templar or the
Masons put lots of treasure on that island and boo-
by-trapped it so no one could get to it."

At first Andrea didn't say anything, hating to
throw cold water on the subject. But what the
heck? She was an archaeologist. It was her job to
set the record straight.

"I hate to tell you; most digs aren't that
dramatic."

Crystal's face fell a bit. "What do you mean?"

"Well, a lot of the work is tedious. There's a lot of
paperwork, applying for permits, making sure we
don't harm the environment. If the site is on state
or federal land that can take a very long time. We
can't just go in and dig where we want, not unless
the land is privately owned and we have the owner's permission."

"They're digging lots of holes on that island.
Really deep holes." Crystal made motions with
her hands.

"Well, that's a unique situation I think. Most digs
here in the U. S. take place close to the surface.
We lay out a grid of squares over the entire site,
marking it off with stakes and string, like laying out

the foundations of a house. Then the soil on each square is removed in small increments and screened for small objects like potsherds, iron, or preserved wood. Once each square is flat and level we photograph and map the stains and other discolorations, going through the soil teaspoon by teaspoon. Then we are required to fill it all back up again so it looks as much like it did when we found it. It can be grueling and very time-consuming, and hard on the back and knees. Not to mention the snakes, the heat, the flies, and other creepy-crawly things."

She glanced over at Crystal, gauging the girl's reaction.

"What do you do if you find a ring or something?" she asked, apparently unfazed.

"Well, a ring was found, up at Buxton, on the Outer Banks. A brass signet ring. They think it was from the early colonial period. It's in a vault in the Special Collections at East Carolina University. My father was an archaeology student at that school, but he died long before it was found."

"That's crazy!" she crowed, all ears now.

"Yeah, but remember, real archaeologists aren't so much interested in finding treasure as we are learning about how people from a different time and place lived. We get excited at old trash pits. It's the things people throw away that tell us who they are—what kind of dishes they used, what they ate; the old broken things that give us clues about their daily lives. And it's important we thoroughly document artifacts before they are removed. The context of a discovery is vital. Artifacts in and of themselves don't tell us anything."

"Yuck. Old dishes sound boring." She turned her

face to the passenger side window, as if the cows they were passing were of greater interest.

Andrea sighed. "Well, I'm sorry to burst your bubble, but it does get boring every now and then, especially when the conditions are hostile, like the desert or swamps. But that is where we often find our best information. No one else bothers to look in those areas."

The girl's sudden shallow disinterest bothered her on some level, why she couldn't fathom. *Maybe I should have been a teacher after all, like my mother,* Andrea thought.

By then they were passing over the Roanoke River. Andrea glanced off to her side, appreciating the sweeping vista, the glistening of the sun on the rocks, and the rapids that gave the area its name. She thought about Crystal's romanticized view of archaeology. With at least another thirty minutes' drive ahead of them she had to think of something to fill the time. She tried again.

"History isn't something dead, Crystal. And people are more important than gold or silver. Those people and what happened to them made us who we are. That is the real treasure." She paused, pointed at Crystal's stomach. "That little girl in your belly is the result of thousands of people who came before her, who lived, had babies, died, suffered, loved, and fought wars. See that river down there? Thousands of people have traveled that river for centuries. It was as important to them as the interstates are to us. Who knows what bones are down there—slaves, Indians, white men. Could be the graves of some of our ancestors. I'll bet you didn't know that the Roanoke is famous for being one of the major trading routes used by all the various Indian groups on the eastern seaboard all the way inland to the foothills. Back then this river led to Occoneechee Island."

"Occoneechee Island? Where in the heck is that?"

"Well, the island was once in the middle of where the Roanoke and the Dan River converge on the N. C. and Virginia state line, but it was flooded over when they built the dam. For thousands of years Indians from all over traveled to that island from a five hundred–mile radius, meeting once a year to trade slaves, furs, copper, beads, and baskets of corn. It was one big party that lasted for weeks."

The girl's head shot up. "Slaves? I just thought that was black people."

Andrea smiled, glad the girl was paying attention. "Indians kept slaves too; stole women and children from each other. Life was pretty brutal back then."

"They never taught us this in school," her tone disbelieving.

"No, they don't. It's sad, but most high school history curriculum focuses on white history. But thank goodness that's changing. It's interesting but I believe there is going to be a resurgence of interest in Algonquin history. DNA tests are showing that a lot of people descended from the old colonial families are not only part Indian, but have African ancestry too. Like me, I'm part Indian on my father's side. That's where I'm going now, to the Outer Banks, to research my own ancestors."

Crystal's eyes lit up. "Shut up! You're kidding me! I'm a registered member of the Haliwa tribe. You know where Hollister is?"

Andrea chuckled. She had finally gotten through to the girl.

"I've heard of it, I think. That means you might be descended from the Occoneechi or Eno Indians yourself, maybe the lower Virginia Indians like the Pawmunkey, or the Tuscarora even, if I remember correctly. A lot of those tribes intermarried, or stole each other's women. They regularly paddled this river looking for trade or hunting. They paddled down that river we just drove over. Have you studied your tribal history?"

Crystal sat back, more subdued now, but engaged. "No. My Mama ran away from Hollister before I was born and wouldn't ever take me back. Growing up she wouldn't talk too much about where her folks came from. I think she wanted everyone to think I was white, because I look like my Daddy. I didn't meet my grandparents until she lost custody of me and they took me in. They wanted me to go to the tribal school there but I didn't fit in." She looked away, subdued.

"What did you do?" Andrea asked, already knowing the answer.

"I dropped out, went to live with my boyfriend."

"Where was your father when you were growing up?"

"She wouldn't tell me. Said he was bad news. I found him later though."

Andrea sighed. "Yeah, my mother wouldn't talk too much about my father either. That's why I'm going to the Outer Banks…." She let the statement hang, then changed the subject. "Listen, you ought to read up on it. There's blue-eyed Indians up your way I hear. An English explorer by the name of

John Lawson reported he saw Indians with blue eyes, way back in the early 1700's."

"Really? I guess I missed that part in school."

"Well, you seem like a smart girl. Maybe you can go back to school after the baby is born."

"I doubt it." Her voice went flat, sounded tired. "J. T. can't keep a job; he probably ain't going to pay child support. He's the one that wanted me to keep it, now he's done run off and left me high and dry. My grandparents are too old and broke. My Momma is too strung out…." She frowned, picked at the leg of her jeans.

"What happened to your father?"

"He got caught for selling drugs and went to prison. I go and see him every now and then." She shrugged, like it was no big deal. Then, "What about those Lost Colonists? What do you reckon happened to them?"

It was Andrea's turn to shrug, surprised at the sudden change of subject. "We don't know. Most of the researchers think they probably split up, got massacred by the Indians, or intermarried."

Crystal's eyes lit up again. "Did you see that Dare Stone show? That was spooky!"

Andrea laughed. "Sorry, but no, I really don't watch a lot of television. Remember, I've been in grad school. But if I remember correctly there's a lot of controversy surrounding how that stone was found. Could be a fake; could be real. So far no one has proved anything conclusively. I'm a skeptic, that's for sure."

"Are you going to help dig somewhere soon?"

Andrea felt a pang, then sighed. "Maybe one day perhaps. But if I get a job teaching I won't have the time. I would love to be on a dig some-where though. That's my first love. I worked on one up in the Chesapeake area during my graduate internship, and on another up in Massachusetts last summer. I wanted to work in Jamestown, but that didn't pan out. A team up there found the bodies of the four main men who settled Jamestown back in the early 1600's. That was big news."

"But what about that baby, you know, Virginia Dare? Do you think she lived?"

Andrea couldn't stop herself from rolling her eyes. "Well, I know this is not what you want to hear, but the likelihood is pretty slim Crystal."

Crystal turned, facing the window again, pout-ing. As the miles passed, her head began to nod. It was obvious, at least for now, the subject was closed.

Relieved, Andrea drove on in silence, traveling through vast flat open fields filled with rich bot-tomland planted with long straight rows of new green corn bordered by piney woods. The bushy heads of new peanut plants stretched for miles and miles regular as cabbages in a garden.

A lonely ribbon of blacktop stretched out in front of her, for the most part empty except for a tractor or a farm truck, or the occasional school bus. Progress was slow and plodding. It was good to have another warm body in the car, even if the girl was sleeping. She looked like she needed the sleep, that's for sure.

Her thoughts drifted to the baby again. What would happen to it—a single mother, a father not in the picture?

Like me.

Passing through the tiny hamlets of Jackson and Seaboard, she forced herself to shift her thoughts to the difficulties she might encounter ahead. Where should she start? She had always been told her father had no known living family, none her mother knew about anyway. Her grandmother had died of breast cancer when he was young, her grandfather dead of liver cirrhosis within months after his son, according to her mother, too drunk to even care.

She always wondered if there was more to the story, especially the first time they received a mysterious Christmas card from a woman who claimed to be an Aunt Polly. The postmark was Columbia, a small town she knew was about forty miles west of Manteo, about twelve miles from the infamous Alligator River on whose banks her father's body had been found. The cards were always yellowed with age, no doubt bought by the box from a dollar bin.

Her mother never offered to share them with her, just took them off to her bedroom where she never saw them again. When Andrea pressed for answers she shrugged her off, saying the cards were from a crazy old lady in the community who everyone called Aunt Polly, that's all. Over time they stopped coming. Andrea assumed Aunt Polly, or whoever she was, must have died.

It was on her fifteenth birthday she finally got up the courage to ask a more important question. How had her father died? And when her mother said one word—suicide—Andrea had been too stunned to ask for details.

It took months for her to get up the nerve to

broach the subject again. Had her father suffered from a history of depression? Her mother blushed, then gave a vague answer about the lack of medical knowledge back in the eighties.

But her answer only angered Andrea. How could her mother not have known her father was depressed? And if she did, how could she have left him? Or perhaps it was the breakup of the marriage that caused his downward spiral.

Then, a more horrible thought. *What if I inherited those genes?* And worse than that:

Why didn't he care enough about me to fight for me? Wasn't I good enough for him?

Even now she wasn't sure she wanted to know the answers. Instead, she did what she'd always done. She pushed her questions down inside, closed the door on them, embarking instead on a relentless quest to prove her worth to the world. No challenge was too great, no triumph too small. Any sort of competition, club, award, honor to be had, she won them all.

But overachievement didn't begin to describe Andrea Warren. She was a fiery star, set on a path to implode.

Of course, no one ever saw the tears, the clumps of hair in her brush, the diet pills, the late nights studying until she thought her eyes would pop out of her head, stomach knotted in a ball. Instead she pulled it off, landing a full scholarship to her hometown university, UNC-Charlotte, finishing with the highest GPA in her class. When she won a partial scholarship to graduate school, her mother was ecstatic. The only thing Andrea felt was relief. Perhaps now she had earned a right to the air she breathed.

But by then The God of Perfection had become impossible to please. In her eyes, nothing she did was ever good enough.

It helped to get away from Charlotte. She could forget her questions, the ever-present gnawing sense of inadequacy. Archaeology was not only a distraction, but the passion that gave meaning to her world.

Then I screwed that up too, she thought.

She shook her head, forcing herself back into the present, rolling down the window a bit to get some fresh air. By then they had reached the edge of Murfreesboro. She reached over, gently nudged the girl.

"What?" Crystal jerked upright, startled.

"I need directions to your aunt's house."

Within a couple of miles she stopped in front of a little brick ranch in an older part of town. Crystal hopped out, then turned around and leaned in.

"Thanks for the ride." Then, a shadow passed over her face. "I need to ask you something. When you talked about my baby you called it a girl. How did you know that?"

Andrea went blank, the hairs on the back of her neck prickling. "I don't know. Just a lucky guess I suppose."

"Well, you're right. I had the ultrasound last week," she blurted before swinging the door shut, waving. Somewhere in the backyard dogs barked, apparently excited by a couple of young black boys cutting through the yard, pants hung so low their navels and briefs were exposed. As she drove off she could hear Crystal calling out to them, excited, already forgetting her ride.

☾

By the time she made it back onto her route, the sun was low in the afternoon sky. Thank heavens the tortuous single-lane now opened into a brand new four-lane. According to Google Maps it would take her all the way into Elizabeth City. With any luck she'd get to the Outer Banks in time to see the sunset on the water.

Not that the country she was passing through didn't have its charms. Beautiful antebellum homes dotted the landscape like sagging old beauty queens sitting in a nursing home, ragged and forlorn. Skirting the Great Dismal Swamp, she marveled at the thought she was traveling over land once claimed by the most powerful Indian nations on the eastern seaboard—Occonneechi, Chowanoak, Weapomeoc, Yeopim—Andrea could tick their place names off like ingredients in a recipe written in a foreign language.

She stopped for gas near twilight, her neck stiff, shoulders burning. In a diner across the street from the station she wolfed down a dry barbecue sandwich with coleslaw and fries, got a refill on her Coke, paid up, and headed back out the door. Then on through Camden, Grandy, Harbinger, and Point Harbor…one more hour and she would be there. Why in the hell had she thought taking this route was a good idea?

Exhausted, she rolled into Kill Devil Hills around nine o'clock and checked into the first cheap motel with a Vacancy sign she found, a garish cinderblock painted pink and aqua with the dubious name,

See-A-Horse Inn. The dark musty box of a room smelled of wet towels and stale cigarette smoke; not that she cared much at that point.

When she dozed off her sleep was fitful. Once again she dreamed of the crying baby. But this time she was in the Dismal Swamp, fighting off snakes and alligators.

`

CHAPTER THREE

SATURDAY MORNING DAWNED BRIGHT AND warm, pungent with the tang of salt in the sunny breeze. A long walk dodging the surf and gulping in the fresh air did wonders to make up for the lack of sleep. She packed her few toiletries and checked out of the dump, hoping to never see the place again.

Standing at the end of Jennette's Pier she drank in the ocean view like an addict, feeling the blood rush in her veins. The sound of the giant wind turbines hummed overhead, vibrating with an energy that made her feel like she was on the back of a great sea creature. When she finally reached the end of the pier, she was surrounded by nothing but ocean. It was like standing on the edge of the world. She wished she could sprout wings and fly.

Was this what it felt like to be standing on the bow of a great ship headed out to sea, like Rose on the *Titanic* or Eleanor Dare on the *Tiger*? An amazing span of blue sky arched above the blue-green swells, no sound except the gulls, turbines, wind, and the swoosh and boom of the pounding surf against piling, a thundering heartbeat in the womb of mother earth.

She could have stayed out there for hours, but she was getting light-headed from too much sun and lack of food. Taking one last look around her she walked back to the parking lot, then crossed the street over to a little restaurant.

It was a homey place. Pine-paneled, walls filled with pictures of fishing charters and celebrities, it had that old salt and fried seafood smell typical of beach diners. All the tables were full, so she headed to one of the two empty seats left at the bar, noticing right away that the waitress barely greeted her. Even more annoying was the tall, lanky man with dark hair that sat down beside her. She'd been hoping for a bit of privacy. But at least he smelled good and was clean-shaven.

Andrea watched as the two flirted. The girl had a crush on him, that was apparent. Guess some men liked that look—spiky bleached blonde hair, small diamond stud in the nose, eyes heavily ringed with mascara. She handed Andrea a menu with one hand as she wiped the counter with the other, not smiling or offering a greeting of any kind to her, in stark contrast to the attention being lavished on the man. She thought about asking for a booth, but then decided it wasn't worth the trouble. Scanning the items on the menu shoved at her, she picked the first thing she saw, then signaled to the waitress, finally getting her attention.

"Coffee. Two eggs and toast, please. Add a tall orange juice if you don't mind…" she ordered, forcing herself to smile. The waitress nodded but still didn't look at her, scratching out the ticket in about two split seconds, turning and slapping it on the cook's window. Grabbing an empty white mug, she sloshed hot coffee into it without offering cream or sugar. But when it came to the man sitting next to Andrea, she was all smiles again.

Andrea tuned them out as the waitress took his order, focusing on her coffee, looking around for the cream. The waitress made herself busy at the end of the counter.

Frustrated, she tapped the man on his arm and pointed toward the cream. He reached over and retrieved the pitcher, placing it gently in front of her, then turned to look at her.

"Thanks," she murmured, avoiding his eyes.

"You from around here?" he asked.

She shook her head. "Just passing through."

"I thought you looked familiar, that's all."

The waitress drifted back, hovering, way too interested in the conversation.

She sighed, put her coffee down. "Well, I'm sure we've never met because I've never been here before. But I've been told I look like my father. He was a local, from East Lake. He died in 1985 so I doubt seriously you ever met him." She cradled her coffee cup, her head down. Had everyone in the entire world seen her picture in the newspaper? Embarrassed, she lifted the cup, hiding behind it. Thank God, the annoying waitress had left to go wait on another customer across the restaurant.

"I didn't mean to pry." he offered, turning to her.

"You caught me on an off day, that's all. I'm really tired…." she finally muttered.

His hazel eyes were probing, but he didn't say anything. Finally, their food arrived. They ate in relatively companionable silence until they were both almost finished. He seemed interested in something going on out in the parking lot, but from her seat she couldn't see a thing. Finally, he turned back to her and grinned.

"I still don't know your name…."

"My God, you don't give up, do you?" she retorted, putting the cup down with a clunk.

"Nope, I don't, not when the subject is so interesting. But it's pretty obvious I've struck out this time." He smiled at her, winking. He pushed his plate away and stood up; threw a couple of bills on the counter. The scent of pine, or maybe cedar, wafted toward her. She had to admit he smelled good.

"Listen, be careful, okay. Nice to meet you, even if you are having a bad day." And before Andrea could answer he strode over to the cash register, paid his bill, and left.

Her face flushed. She toyed with her food, the empty seat beside her like an accusation. Had she been that rude? She hadn't meant to run him off. She ate the remainder of her eggs in silence. The waitress finally returned, surprising Andrea when she leaned in and whispered.

"Sorry if I ignored you when you walked in. Scott's an old friend of mine and well damn, just like that I became invisible." She lifted the coffee pot. "Here, let me pour you another cup."

Andrea gave a slight smile, waved the coffee away. "Nah, I'm wired enough as it is. I'm just not in the market, that's all. A bit burned around the edges by men these days if you know what I mean." She balled up her napkin in her fist, dropping it on the plate for emphasis.

"Don't I know…?" the girl agreed, rolling her

eyes. "Actually, I shouldn't have acted so silly. My boyfriend was watching me like a hawk." But then her face softened. "But Scott's different. He really is one of the nice guys."

"Well, I'm not going to be around long enough to make friends, so he's all yours. Hope it works out for you."

"Fat chance," the girl replied, a funny look passing over her face. Then, "You know, I overheard you say you father was a local from over in East Lake. I've got friends from there. Some of them claim to be descended from the Indians and the Lost Colonists. Know anything about that?"

Andrea pushed her plate back. "Not really. Even if there were descendants around here, it would be almost impossible to prove."

The waitress handed over the ticket as she picked up the plate. "Well, it's still an interesting mystery if you ask me. Good luck finding whatever it is you're looking for…."

Andrea slid off the stool, grabbed her knapsack and headed to the cash register to pay her bill. Outside, the heat and misty salt air was like walking into a steam bath. She stopped for a moment to soak in the rays, inhaled, exhaled; stretched her neck, forcing the knots to loosen. When was she going to get comfortable being around people again?

She sighed, thought of a million other things she'd like to do instead of the one thing she'd come down here for, the one thing she couldn't put it off any longer. She gazed over at the beach with longing. Finally, she got in her Jeep and headed across the bridge.

She didn't see the SUV that pulled out behind her.

CHAPTER FOUR

THE DRIVE OUT OF MANTEO to the mainland was extraordinarily beautiful, water,
marsh, and sound stretching far as the eyes could
see. But when she got to East Lake it was nothing
like she expected. Nothing was there.

Not a store, a stoplight, not even a school. Only
a few houses, most looking empty and forlorn.
The few paved roads didn't seem to lead anywhere except to public boat accesses, or clusters of
mobile homes. Other than a small white church,
and a tiny cinder-block community center, all she
could see was farmland, its huge fields intersected
by long, straight gravel roads, bordered by canals
and swampland.

Disappointing was an understatement. She had
come so far! She had counted on there being stores,
service stations, or businesses where she could ask
questions of locals. She couldn't just walk up to
houses and knock on back doors. No wonder her
mother never talked about East Lake. There had
been nothing to say.

She thought about calling her Mom to ask her
if she'd made a mistake, but when she reached for
her phone she couldn't find it anywhere. Then it

hit her. She'd left it on the counter at the restaurant. *Crap!* Now she'd have to go all the way back to Manteo.

She slowed, looking for a place to turn around. That is when she noticed that one side of her car was lower than the other, the tire on her right front side making a bumping sound. *Oh no!*

She managed to get as far as River Road and turned in. Rolling to a stop, she threw the Jeep in idle and got out of the car, stomach churning. Sure enough, the front left tire was losing pressure by the minute.

She shivered with anxiety. What in the hell was she going to do out here in the middle of nowhere? With no phone, she had no way to call a tow truck. She sure as heck wasn't going to flag a stranger down.

Of course, things could have been worse. At least she'd made it across the sound bridge. Not that her situation here was much better, black canal on one side, asphalt on the other, cars whizzing by bumper to bumper, none of them bothering to slow down at all.

Think, Andrea, she told herself, taking deep breaths. Wracking her brain, she remembered one or two brick houses she'd spied through the trees in passing, but they were a mile or two back down the road. It was way too far to walk back to Manteo, and she had no idea what lay up ahead, toward the Alligator River.

She was so upset she didn't pay any attention to the white Dodge Ram that passed by her until it began turning around, pulling in behind her. Right away she recognized the grin. What was his name again?

Scott! She didn't know whether to laugh or cry. Thank God!

"Something I can help you with?" he called out to her, climbing out of the truck.

"Flat tire," she said, pointing toward her car.

"Roger that. Got a spare in the trunk?"

Without looking at him she nodded, opened the back end of the Jeep, pointing at the spare tire inside, buried under all her belongings, bras and panties hanging out of paper bags, wire coat hangers sticking out at odd angles. Everything but the kitchen sink.

"I know, I know. I'm moving," she winced, flushed with embarrassment. "Here, let me take this stuff out of here."

"Let me help," he offered, and to his credit he had the good sense not to say anything.

Finally, tugging and sweating, he managed to reach inside and pull out the tire, drop it on the ground and roll it up to the front of the Jeep, while she stuffed the rest of her things back into the car. She had to admit he was efficient, even providing the lug wrench and a jack from the tool box in the bed of his truck.

Maybe he really was a nice guy, like the waitress said.

Oh, what the heck.

"I'm Andrea Warren. Most people call me Andy. I've just finished grad school in Virginia. I was moving back home to Charlotte when I got the crazy idea to turn around and come back here for the weekend. That's why all my junk's in the car," she chattered, getting more embarrassed by the minute.

He didn't say anything, just kept changing the tire, only glancing at up at her every now and then, squinting in the hot morning sun. Sweat had begun to roll down the side of his face.

"My father was from East Lake. He died when I was four. Thought I'd see it for myself. Am I crazy, or what?" She tried to laugh, but faltered, looking up into the sky.

Scott rocked back on his heels, swiping his forehead with the back of his forearm. "Nothing crazy about that. By the way, I'm Scott McWilliams."

She smiled, began to relax. "Nice to meet you, Scott. And I really mean it this time. Sorry I was so rude this morning."

He shrugged. "No apologies necessary. I could tell you had a lot on your mind. Glad I could help you. Not exactly a safe road. If the bears don't get you, a tourist will," he joked.

There it was again. That smile.

"Well, it didn't help I left my cell phone at the restaurant this morning so I'm pretty much stranded out here."

His eyes widened. "Well damn. You really are a damsel in distress. Now all I need is a white horse. Or does a white truck count?" he joked, laughing.

While he tightened the lug nuts on the spare, Andrea made small talk. When he was finished, she rummaged in the backseat for a towel. As he wiped his hands down, she wondered if she should offer to pay him. Would he be offended? He really had saved her life.

But his answer caught her off-guard. He cocked an eyebrow, seemed to consider, then grinned. "I'd rather you pay for dinner tonight. Columbia? 6 pm?"

Crap.

"Sure. Where?" she finally answered, trying not to wince.

"The Rusty Bucket. It's a restaurant on Main Street. A friend of mine owns it." He stood up, began packing up to leave.

"Okay. See you at the restaurant then," she called out.

As he got in his truck she hopped in her Jeep, yelled her thanks again, waved goodbye, then pulled out onto the highway toward Old Ferry Landing. When she looked in her rearview mirror he was gone.

❦

Old Ferry Landing was a peaceful enough place, its air of isolated abandonment not as frightening as it was lonely, even beautiful in its own way. Situated in the curve of a cove, it overlooked the wide expanse where the Albemarle and the Alligator converged, a public boat access now. She wondered briefly when the state ferry system had stopped running here. Had her father chosen this spot to die because he had happy memories here? Or had he been so eager to be done with his life he no longer cared?

A few solitary cypress trees dotted the shore, strands of silver-grey Spanish moss hanging from scrubby branches waving in the late morning breeze. A derelict shrimp boat sat over on the other side of the narrow inlet in a thicket of tall pines, marooned on dry land. Monolithic old wood pilings crusted with barnacles and green slime flanked each side of the concrete boat ramp, as if they were guarding the place. When she walked out onto the small wooden pier, dragonflies darted over the surface of the water. Below them, crabs skittered in all directions, seeking shelter in the brown mud.

She surveyed the landscape, noticing a small path winding down an embankment toward the water. Within moments she found herself on a narrow beach, hidden from the world. The Albemarle Sound stretched out in front of her. To her left lay the mouth of the Alligator River. The bridge going over it to the mainland crawled with tiny cars, like ants from where she stood.

The water was choppy, the sky arched over it a clear blue. Foam bubbled up on the brackish sand, washed up to the edge of her boots. She stood on the spot wondering what her father had been thinking, if he was thinking at all, or simply staring off into the water just as she was doing now. Then words floated up from somewhere inside of her.

Keep going.

She shook her head, annoyed. Recurring dreams, eyes in the mirror, voices in her head? She was a scientist, for heaven's sake. She didn't *do* supernatural stuff, not even when she was a teenager. She quit going to sleepovers in the seventh grade when a girl she thought was a friend brought out a Ouji Board and insisted she summon up her father. She'd called her mother to come get her, then cried herself to sleep that night.

But, in the end, she accepted she was different. Those girls read the *Twilight* series, she read *National Geographic*. Those girls had fathers; she didn't. She pretended it didn't matter how her father died.

Now she walked up the narrow beach in the direction of the bridge, stepping over ropes of gnarled black roots, dodging small rogue waves. A couple of hundred yards further down the beach gave out, turning into marsh. She found herself on a small, sandy knoll hidden away from the world.

She stopped, breathed, scanning her surroundings, relieved that she felt nothing except a bit of nerves, but she figured that was probably normal. After all, she had dreaded this moment for years. Not knowing what else to do she forced herself to concentrate on the sounds—waves hitting the beach, the cawing of crows. The earth hummed beneath her feet, sunlight beat down on the top of her head. It was so peaceful she started feeling a bit drowsy, breathing in, breathing out, eyes closed.

Then, like a surreal dream sequence, it played itself out in her head. She heard the gunshot, smelled the awful stench of gunpowder. A body thudded to the ground. Her heart knocked in her chest at the sound. Looking down she saw the waves turning a rusty red, pink froth on sand. She started getting nauseous.

Stop it, Andrea, she told herself. It's just your imagination running wild.

But then she began to feel strange, an uncoiling in the pit of her stomach, as if something asleep in her belly had been disturbed. It began to glide upward, form a ball in her chest, wrap around her lungs until she could hardly breathe. As she gasped for air, it wound its way into her throat, turned into a black pool behind her eyes. She felt as if she was about to explode.

Then she did.

"You selfish bastard!" she screamed at the top of her lungs, shaking her fist at the sky.

The rage kept coming, as if from some bottom-less pit. And with it came all the horrible things she had ever wanted to say to her father in person, all the ugly accusations, all the bitterness of a lifetime.

But even as she ranted, something inside her shifted. She began to realize how self-absorbed and childish she sounded, how pathetic. How could she see herself as a victim when it was her father who was suffering so much he wanted to die?

Only because she had chosen to see things that way.

She closed her eyes. It was truth and the truth was so simple. Why hadn't she seen it before now?

But there was more. For the first time in her life she realized it was she who had been trapped on this beach for years, not her father, reenacting his death all these years. Her father was long gone. Too busy being a victim to consider his pain, she hadn't stopped to think that perhaps he had been beyond all hope, beyond all reason.

The thought made her so sad.

But for the first time in her life she was no lon-ger angry, and that was a wonderful feeling. Finally the nightmare was over; at last the crying baby had been found.

A soft breeze caressed her cheek. The wind sighed, as if in understanding. Slowly, a few at a time, the birds started singing again, as if a great storm had passed. She opened her eyes. Wiping her face with the backs of her hands, she forced herself to look down at her feet. No blood this time, no scary images. Only rubble, stones, and bits of sea glass.

But *there*, something different—a piece of bor-derware, so old it had been worn down smooth. An untrained eye would have assumed it was sim-ply a piece of clay rock, weathered down through the ages. But the flat regularity of it, worn mark-ings, and a bit of a curved lip told a different story. Probably the edge of a small pot from the colonial period.

How perfect that she would find it in this moment.

She raised it to her lips, tasted the salty brine, felt the warmth of a thousand suns, and for a moment, it was almost as if a hand reached out to her across the years, touching hers. Then the voice again.

Let him go.

This time she did not allow herself to question the wisdom, or where it might be coming from. All she knew is that it felt good and right, even sacred somehow. Starving for light she lifted her face, breathed in the briny air; smiled into the sun.

"I'm sorry, Daddy. I'm sorry you were in so much pain," she whispered. All she heard was the rustling of the trees, the tiny slap of waves, the cries of gulls in the sky.

She breathed a sigh, slipping the potsherd in her pocket for safekeeping. She gazed at her surround-ings one last time. Realizing how fast the tide was rising, she scrambled up the bank, took a shortcut through a patch of brush and briars that led into the woods, and found her way back to the parking lot to the Jeep.

She left Old Ferry Landing for good.

❦

"Thought you'd be back," the cashier joked, handing the phone to her.

"Thank you!" Andrea crowed, reaching to take it from her.

"Don't thank me. Bobbi found it on the counter right after you left this morning."

"I'd like to thank her. Is she still here?" she asked, scanning the room.

"Nah, already left for school. Something you need to tell her?"

"No, just give her my thanks." She reached in her bag and handed the woman five dollars. "Would you give her this for her trouble. I don't think I tipped her enough this morning."

"Sure thing." The woman smiled and took the money. "Come back again now, okay?"

Relieved, Andrea walked outside, looking up at the sky. She had wanted to walk on the beach but the wind was whipping sand everywhere and rain-clouds were gathering inland. After checking her weather app, she decided to spend the afternoon at Fort Raleigh over at the northern tip of Roanoke Island.

She drove back over the bridge to Manteo, following signs that pointed to the Fort Raleigh National Historic site, a few miles down. She turned onto a narrow asphalt road at the entrance, following it as it wound through the woods. Ancient live oaks dotted the landscape on each side of her, extending their branches outward, almost as if they were dancing. Patches of light moved in and out of the shadows as the clouds scudded overhead.

This place is magical, she thought, smiling.

She parked at the Visitor Center, a long low wood and glass building designed to blend perfectly with the environment. The sidewalks were filled with families, kids and strollers, a runner or two, and older couples holding hands. Climbing out of the car, she walked up to the museum, noticing the name on the building right away: The Lindsay Warren Visitor Center.

Huh? That's ironic. Wonder if they were related in some way?

Once inside, she made a beeline to the bookstore. The titles on its shelves were like a syllabus in one of her courses—Kupperman, Miller, Stick, Quinn, Oberg, all authors she'd read, for the most part anyway. She couldn't help noticing the lurid graphic posters featuring dancing Indians advertising *The Lost Colony* Outdoor Drama plastered everywhere.

Browsing, she picked up a small book for children, *The Legend of the White Doe*. From what she read on the back, the story was based on a local legend that Virginia Dare had been adopted by the Croatan Indians, loved by all, but hated by Chico, a jealous Indian sorcerer who enchanted her, turning her into a white deer. She was mistakenly killed when Wanchese, a great warrior, shot her with a silver arrow given to him by Queen Elizabeth when he visited England. He was horrified when, at the very moment of her death, the spell was broken and she turned back into a beautiful girl. Wanchese ran into the forest never to be seen again. The people mourned. To this day locals claim to still see a white deer roaming in the Roanoke Woods.

Andrea smiled as she put the book back down. *No thank you.*

She continued along, fingers tracing the book spines on the shelves. So many books written through the years. What was it about the story of the Roanoke colonists that elevated it to such mythic status, inspired people to write about it in every imaginable form?

The story certainly had all the elements of a Greek tragedy— the brave, though perhaps naïve young mother, Eleanor Dare, and her husband, Ananias. Then there was Eleanor's father, the artist John White, bent on colonizing a New World despite the dangers to his family.

And the baby, Virginia, lost to the world.

Sobered by the thought of the baby, she wandered over to a rack filled with laminated copies of the roster of men and women on their ship, the *Tiger.* Running her forefinger down the small print she murmured the names: Harvey, White, Scott, Edwards, Gibbs, Jones, Dare, even to her surprise, a Warren. Not that this meant anything, not in this part of the world anyway. Warrens were everywhere, even on the building outside.

Still, all those people—men, women, and children—vanished off the face of the earth within three years, no trace of them anywhere. Would anyone ever find out what happened to them? Not likely.

Then she spied a short archaeological history of the excavation of Fort Raleigh. And what in the world was this one, something about Beechland and the Lost Colony? Flipping through it, a few passages caught her eye, especially when the author seemed to be suggesting that the colonists, or at least some of them, migrated to an area near East Lake. Something about some coffins being found.

Coffins? Near East Lake of all places. Hadn't her mother mentioned something about coffins?

She looked out of the window toward the mounds where the old fort had been, grassy knolls now, live oaks dotting the trenches of the old fort ramparts. If she used her time wisely she could walk the perimeter of the fort, locate the palisade boundaries, figure out where the digging had been conducted and still have time to head to the beach for a couple of hours if the sky cleared.

She could at least pretend she was still an archae-ologist.

Smiling, she hurried to the counter, paid for the books, and headed into Fort Raleigh.

☾

She spent the rest of the afternoon there. It felt so good to simply stroll through the trees, sit on a park bench, and enjoy life for a change. She had always been stuck in classrooms, head down peer-ing into a microscope, or digging in the ground. Now with no career, she had nothing to really strive for, no specific goal to reach. For a fleet-ing moment, she wondered what would it be like to live here on Roanoke Island, even become a park ranger. Maybe they'd let her pitch a tent, she thought, amused.

Well, that might be a bit of a stretch, but at least she could get a motel room for a few nights. There was still so much left to see. She would have to cancel her dinner plans with Scott, of course, but he would probably understand.

Then she remembered she had forgotten to ask him for his phone number.

Well, she couldn't just not show up, though the thought was tempting. She looked at the time. If she hurried, she wouldn't be late. Maybe she could stay someplace in Columbia, then come back in the morning.

Sighing, she brushed the sand off her jeans and headed to the Jeep. Rummaging around, she managed to salvage a wrinkled sundress, then, following the sign that led to the public restrooms, went inside, threw the dress on and freshened up a bit.

By the time she passed over Alligator River Bridge the sun was setting in the west, sparkling on the water. Gulls swooped and dove, circling around the car. As she passed by the road to Old Ferry Landing she felt at peace, realizing that she wasn't frightened of the spot anymore.

The bridge itself seemed ancient, one of those old concrete draw bridges, complete with a bridge tender in his tiny glass cubicle, mariner's flag waving gaily at the top. Just as she reached its apex, the warning bell rang. Traffic came to a stop as the crossbar began to lower and the bridge slowly rotated open.

She got out of the car and leaned against the hood. Gulls dove around her head looking for a handout. In the distance she could see white sails leaning into the breeze, shining in the sun. She wasn't quite sure, but as it approached it appeared to be an old periauger, fashioned after those most likely used by the English settlers. Wonder who owned such a fine reproduction? That thing must have cost a mint.

Looking east she could see the beach where she stood only hours before, her thoughts in such a dark whirl. She crossed her arms, gazing out over the water. She could almost see the spot where she had been standing.

Strange now, how free she felt.

A short while later the boat passed, the bell clanged an "all clear" signal; traffic started moving. Reluctant to leave, her gaze swept the panorama one last time before she got back in behind the wheel.

Within a few miles she reached the outskirts of Columbia, surprised that the entire business section was only about three blocks long, a postcard for small towns on the water. It even boasted an Arts Center overlooking the marina, some cool handmade pots and art jewelry on display in the window.

A block down she popped into a cozy little antique shop, drooling over a few nautical items and some old maps of the area. She moved in closer to look at a map of the eastern seaboard from the 1800's, but when she saw the price tag she frowned.

Maybe someday, she thought.

Stepping back out onto the sidewalk, she spotted Scott walking toward her.

"What? No finds today? That's one of my favorite places."

She smiled, stepping alongside of him. "Well, it would be mine too if I had the money. But remember, I'm fresh out of grad school and don't have a job."

The restaurant was charming. The hostess greeted them with a smile, speaking to Scott as if he were an old friend as she ushered them toward a table at the window. Within moments a pretty young waitress wrote down their drink orders, brought a beer for Scott, a glass of Riesling for her, suggesting the homemade clam chowder to start.

"Cheers…" he offered, tipping his beer against her wine glass. "Thank God for flat tires," he intoned, flashing a grin.

"And here's to princes in white trucks who come along and fix them," she countered, smiling back at him.

As they sipped, her eyes scanned the room, appreciating the exposed brick walls, the simple elegance. She was surprised at how relaxed she felt, how rested. And so far, no red flags. On the contrary, she was beginning to enjoy herself.

"You already know a bit about me now, don't you think it's time to tell me about yourself?" she ventured

"Well, let's see. I'm forty years old, healthy, have my own teeth, and can make a mean apple pie. Anything else you'd like to know?"

"Well, I know your age, that you live somewhere near Edenton, and what else? Oh, let's see, I figure you like to fish. I saw the gear in the back of your truck."

He grinned. "What else do you need to know?"

"For a start, what do you do for a living? And oh, do you just happen to have a few skeletons you're hiding in those big old closets?"

Slow down on the wine girl.

"Oh that. Yeah, well only a few, but I make sure

that I only bring them out on Halloween. But since you insist on being serious, here you go," he answered. He took a long swig of beer as if preparing, then leaned forward on his elbows, gazing at her as he spoke.

"I graduated from UNC-Chapel Hill with a degree in political science in 1997, thinking I might follow in my father's footsteps, get my law degree, and go into practice with him. But he died of a heart attack my senior year in college. My mother remarried within a few years and now lives in Raleigh, is a diehard Methodist, and does a lot of mission work." He stopped, toyed with his napkin as he dropped his voice a notch lower.

"I married my college sweetheart shortly after graduation. She was a student at UNC too. We continued living in Chapel Hill while I interned in the state legislature. Jennifer was a rookie in a downtown Durham investment firm. We were married a couple of years when she had to start traveling a lot, meeting clients in New York, or at least that is what she told me at the time. One of her clients had offices in the World Trade Center. She was up there the day the planes hit." His eyes clouded over. "Her body was never found."

Andrea frowned. *A widower?*

"Scott, I'm so very sorry. It must have been awful."

He leaned in, dropping his voice lower. "I never told anyone except my mother. She's the only one who knows. But the truth is my wife was having an affair with that so-called client in New York, a frat brother of mine from college. Can you believe they actually met at our wedding?" He shrugged and looked down. "He was her first big client."

Andrea didn't know what to think, much less say. She was deeply sad for the man, flattered that he trusted her but, on the other hand, uncomfortable. Why was he confiding in her? Or was that just a way to charm her so he could get her into bed?

But, then again, she had shared her own past. And she *had* mentioned skeletons. She just hadn't expected such a doozy.

In the brooding silence that followed, their clam chowder arrived, offering a needed distraction. Andrea stirred her soup but didn't taste it, waiting for him to continue. She didn't have to wait long.

"The irony is that he was at another meeting across town that day. While my wife was being blown to pieces he was making deals that were securing his fortune. He didn't even have the balls to attend her memorial service."

His face had gone pale, his eyes flat and tired looking. She held her breath and waited, instinct telling her to keep quiet.

"You know the most awful thing? How do you grieve someone you thought you knew, then find out how much you didn't? I thought we were a happy couple. Obviously, I was wrong."

She nodded. "That would be tough. I didn't tell you earlier but my father committed suicide. At Old Ferry Landing. That's where I was going when I had the flat tire…."

"Oh my God, Andrea, I'm so sorry."

Sighing, she gazed off across the room. "I was a child, so you'd think it wouldn't have affected me that much. But it did. Like you, I thought we were a happy family, then like that, my father disappeared, my mother became someone different. I've spent most of my life angry at both of them. But today I finally realized how silly it was for me to keep seeing myself as a victim. Standing where he died was so different than I imagined. He was a sick man with problems. End of story. Maybe your wife was unwell too."

Scott sat still, considering her words. When he spoke again his tone was introspective.

"I don't know. Maybe. Something to think about anyway."

"What did you do afterwards?"

"I wallowed for a while. I had no desire to be part of the collective grieving. I didn't want to tell the truth and smear her name, but I didn't want to see her glorified as a hero either. Given the circumstances coming back to where I grew up seemed as good a place to start over as any, especially since we didn't have any shared memories here. At the time my grandmother still lived in our old home place out in Belvidere. I set up camp with her for a few months."

"Doing what?" she asked, relieved to be on safer ground.

He shifted in his seat, rubbing the palms of his hands on his khakis like he was brushing off dirt. "I fell back on my old loves, carpentry and restoring old houses. Edenton was perfect for that at the time. The other was researching the history of the area. It's pretty intense around here, you know."

"I can only imagine."

"Then the economy crashed and remodeling went down the tubes. I was out of luck. But thank God, a cousin baled me out. She inherited an old plantation house needing work. She offered me a deal. I could live in the house for free if I restored it for her."

She nodded in encouragement.

"By the way, the owner is Roberta McWilliams, the famous romance writer who's had all of those movies made from her books. A real interesting person, but has her own set of demons, if you know what I mean. She has no desire to live in the house; too many bad memories."

"Is Roberta supervising you closely, or do you have a lot of freedom?"

"She lives in Europe so I don't see her much. Mainly uses it as a tax write off so I pretty much have free reign. I teach a few online classes through the College of the Albemarle to augment my income."

"Wow," was all Andrea could muster.

He burst out laughing. "Well, that was honest." He paused, head ducked. "Sorry if I'm running on. You are easy to talk to and I've had a lot bottled up for a long time."

"I get that," she answered, smiling.

He grinned. "Okay, I'll shut up. It's your turn now."

"Well, there's not much to tell," she said, though a part of her wanted to tell him everything. Instead, she launched into a spiel, hoping that if she talked fast he wouldn't hone in on the details.

"Awarded a full scholarship to attend UNC-Charlotte in History and Anthropology; MS in Anthropology with a concentration in Archae-ology, hot off the press from a snooty grad school in Virginia this past May. Like I said, I was moving back home to Charlotte when I decided to take a side trip here first. No big deal, but some things went down in Virginia that left a bad taste in my mouth for the politics of archaeology. By the way, there was a fiancé who fell along the wayside in the process, so now I'm reconsidering my options, trying not to rebound…." She stopped to take a gulp of wine. "So, how's the house restoration going?"

His look was probing but, to her relief, he took her hint.

"Well, the kitchen is finished and there is a new master bathroom, but other than that it's going slow. The house was built in the late 1700's, you know. That's a long time in house years. A lot of layers of paint, ugly wallpaper, and all basic systems had to be refurbished. By the way, it is true what they say about old houses—you get one thing finished, another needs redoing."

Andrea sighed. "I wouldn't know. All my mom could ever afford on a teacher's salary was a small brick house in Myer's Park. It's tiny, actually; nothing to brag about."

"Myer's Park? That neighborhood is gorgeous!"

About that time their dinners arrived: broiled tuna for him, shrimp and grits for her, both looking and smelling delicious. A refill of her wine glass, another beer for Scott, and she finally truly relaxed, their silence companionable, past the awkward *boy meets girl* phase that Andrea had always hated.

"Are you going on to Charlotte from here or staying around for a few days?" he finally asked.

"Hmmm, I was going home, but after today I'm thinking of heading back to the beach. I need the rest. And I know this sounds farfetched but

I'd like to learn a bit more about my native heritage here and the history of the area. Supposedly I'm descended from the local Indians through my father's people."

His eyes lit up. "Which tribes?"

"Now they are collectively called the Hatteras, the Mattamuskeet or the Machopungo, depending on who's asking. Further back they were the Croatan, Secotan, the Chowanoak and the Roanoke. They were all part of the Algonquians, a large loosely related group of native Americans with similar language and culture who were somewhat nomadic, traveling all up and down the coast between Florida and New York. Some were peace loving agrarians, others were aggressive, living off their spoils. They were here for thousands of years, long before the English came along."

"How do you know so much about the Indians?"

"Because I wrote a thesis on them in grad school. I'd like to get my doctorate."

"Wow, a smart woman."

"Not so much. I just studied hard. You're probably more of an expert on the history around here than I am."

"Not as much as you might think. Regional architecture has been more my thing, and I'm largely self-taught," he responded, his tone diplomatic. Then, "You know, evidently the Indian women around here were knockouts. The word Perquimans means *Land of Beautiful Women.* I'd like to show that river to you sometime."

Andrea blushed, caught off-guard. Undeterred, he continued.

"You know; I've got a ton of artifacts up at the house I've been collecting for years; bowls, arrowheads, tools and stuff."

Well, she had to hand it to him. He moved fast.

"Sorry, but I came here to research my genealogy, not to hook up with anyone." She looked down at her plate.

He shrugged, folded his napkin.

"I'm not trying to hook up with you, Andrea, at least not in that way. I'm not ready yet either. It's just that there aren't many women who can talk about this stuff, and you seemed interested, that's all. I am sorry if I offended you… yet again."

"No, it's me who is in the wrong, Scott. You've been nothing but kind to me all day," she offered, clearing her throat. "But like I said I'm fresh out of a broken engagement to a very popular doctoral student in Williamsburg. Considered quite the catch, until I found out otherwise. We were to marry in September. Everything crashed and burned when I blew the whistle on a situation I thought was unethical. Our relationship was collateral damage. Google my name. I'm sure you'll read all you want to know." Her vision blurred. "And by the way, this thing with my father is heavy," she said, then drained her wine glass, setting it down with a clunk.

There was an awkward silence. When he finally spoke, his voice was kind. "No apology needed." Then, out of nowhere, that electric smile again, like lightening striking at night in an open field. "By the way, I already Googled you. I must say I was impressed. It took a lot of guts to do what you did."

She was speechless. *He knew already?* She didn't know whether to be relieved or pissed off. She started to say something, but then the moment passed.

He didn't seem to notice one way or the other. "You know, if you need a place to stay tonight my friend owns that bed and breakfast across the street, as well as this restaurant. We are old friends. She'll give you a price break. And the offer still stands to show you my artifacts tomorrow, or we could go out on the boat. I promise I won't hit on you, okay?" He laughed and winked.

Lord, the boy's persistent. But she'd already made up her mind.

"Scott, I'd love to see them. But another time, okay? I came here in search of my father, and I can't afford to get sidetracked. I'll call you in a few days, I promise."

He nodded, shrugging. For a second he reminded her of a small boy, endearing and vulnerable.

"Actually, you don't know how therapeutic this has been for me. You know, you're not only the first person I've confided in, you're the first woman I've really been interested in getting to know since my wife died. Most of the women around here are knee deep in babies or aren't into men." He chuckled in a way that took the insult out of his words.

"The bed and breakfast sounds wonderful Scott." And she meant it.

"Can I interest you in dessert then? Coffee?"

"No, I couldn't eat another bite. I think I'll have to call it a night, okay?"

In spite of her insistence he refused to let her pay

for dinner. Outside he walked her across the street and up onto the porch. A quick brotherly kiss on the cheek, then he handed her his business card. She couldn't help noticing that good clean soap smell again, more noticeable now in the humid night air. As she watched his retreating back, she almost regretted her decision not to spend the day with him tomorrow.

Almost, but not quite.

Inside, the inn was cozy without being cheesy, more like someone's home. She was given a key to the front door so she could come and go freely, and told to help herself to hot coffee and pastries in the dining room in the morning.

She climbed into bed and tried to read, then, unable to focus, checked her email. Nothing interesting there. She sent a text to her mother, telling her things were going fine. It was still rather early so she turned on the small television, found an old movie, watching until she became drowsy. At last she switched off the light, slid down underneath the covers, and for the first time in weeks she slept through the night.

CHAPTER FIVE

GROGGY, SHE WOKE TO THE sound of bells pealing from the steeple of the little Methodist Church on the corner. She had forgotten it was Sunday morning. Stretching and yawning, she climbed out of bed, filled with a sense of well-being.

Donning her standard uniform - black t-shirt, slim-cut jeans, and old leather boots- she caught a glimpse of herself in the old-fashioned full-length oval mirror in the corner of the room, medium-height, slender but not unhealthily so, at least not like she used to be, flat in the chest, but not quite. A thin gold chain was her only jewelry. Smearing on lip gloss, she grabbed her backpack and almost danced down the stairs.

Coffee was on the sideboard as promised. She poured herself a cup, then popped a pastry in the microwave. As she waited she noticed a Sunday edition of the Wall Street Journal on the dining room table, its bold headlines jumping out at her.

NEW DISCOVERIES MAY ANSWER
A FOUR HUNDRED YEAR MYSTERY
ABOUT THE LOST COLONY!

Interesting. Pottery from the early 1700's, made

using techniques from both the English and the Algonquian. Right away Andrea knew that was important, perhaps a sign that the two groups might have intermarried, borrowing from each other's store of knowledge, merging their skills in successive generations.

She scanned the article, trying not to care.

Who was she kidding? She'd give her eye teeth to be in on that dig, even if she had to work for free, and probably would there now if she hadn't messed things up in Williamsburg. Now she wouldn't get close to it, not in a million years.

As her mood soured, an elderly couple walked into the dining room. Trying to be friendly, she offered the newspaper to him.

"Thanks," he responded, "but I read it up in our room." Then, sounding irritated, "What's all this fuss about the Lost Colony anyway? Sounds like a bunch of crap to me."

Beside him his wife nodded, mirroring his sour expression.

"Well, it's not only important, it's a breakthrough," she explained, taken aback by his rudeness. "A patch was found on a map drawn by John White, the man responsible for bringing the first English colonists here. It's in the British Museum. It seems to point to the presence of an old fort where the colonists might have gone, not too far from here. That's a big deal."

He cut her off. "I can read. What they aren't saying is how much it's going to cost the taxpayers, not to mention the developers who own the land. A damn shame is what I say, just to look for a bunch of arrowheads and pots. Won't change history, will it?" glaring at her as if it was all her fault.

God, what an ignoramus!

"Sir, I don't mean to argue, but the benefits of archaeology are enormous, especially for those locals who've never been able to confirm their oral histories. That's got to count for something."

"Just another excuse they'll use for a free hand out," he retorted, pouring his own cup of coffee.

"Excuse me, I'm descended from the Indians who lived here. And I've never gotten a handout in my life!" she spat.

He waved her off. Chiming in, his wife simpered, "Well, we went to see the Lost Colony outdoor drama last summer. Those Indians seemed rather vicious."

So, that was it. Bigotry. She was only wasting her time.

"Still think it's a lot of hoopla over nothing," the old guy added in a huff, the set of his jaw letting her know the subject was closed.

What an old windbag.

"Well, hope you enjoy your drive back to wher-ever home is," Andrea replied. She picked up her cup and her backpack and made her retreat, grate-ful to put the ill-tempered couple behind her.

She walked down to the gazebo overlooking the Scuppernong River, not as wide or impressive as the Alligator, but more mysterious. The water seemed darker here, almost black. Spotting a nice wooded trail winding off around the bend, she set out for a short hike, hoping to get some exercise.

But it wasn't just the exercise. She needed to work off some steam. Memories were resurfacing, memories she must have been suppressing all these years, hiding in the back of her mind.

She thought she remembered living in one of those houses on Main Street, though which one she wasn't sure. Her father had played "horsie" with her, helped blow out candles on her birthday cake when she was four. She remembered those candles vividly, and her first pair of cowgirl boots, bright red. She wouldn't even take them off to go to bed.

And vaguely she recalled the sound of a mower in the yard outside of her bedroom window, gauzy white curtains moving gently in the spring breeze. Her mother had come in and scolded her for not napping, while her father smiled and waved at her outside her window, making monkey faces until she couldn't stop laughing.

The most vivid memory was falling asleep on his shoulder, being tucked in at night when he was home. The smell of swamp, tobacco, and aftershave. No wonder she felt at home here.

Home. Was that what she was feeling? She had to admit that so much of it—the trees, the salt air, the way the light glistened in the trees in the late after-noon—felt so familiar, comforting in a way, despite the tragedy. She stopped and stared out over the water.

This had been her home as a child, she was sure of it. Technically of course, she was born in the hospital in Greenville, at least that is what was on her birth certificate. But at some point they moved here, though how she knew this was beyond her.

There were other things she remembered too, sad things. Like going to visit her grandparents, then never coming back. She had cried and cried for her father. But, as the days slipped by, gradually the memory of him dimmed. Then one day she was taken into the garden and told he was gone for good. By the look on her mother's face, she knew it was best not to cry.

Well damn. That was a revelation. She'd have to remember to call her mom tonight and get confirmation. What if she had walked right by the house she had lived in? Bet it was still here.

Excited, she made her way to a white lattice gazebo in the small park by the Town Hall. Stretching her legs out in the sun, she pulled out a sandwich the innkeeper had packed for her, took a few bites, then realizing she wasn't hungry, tossed the rest to the gulls. She was deep into the Fort Raleigh book she'd stored in her backpack when she heard a familiar voice.

"I thought I might find you here."

Scott. She'd been concentrating so hard she hadn't even noticed him walking across the grass. She shielded her eyes from the sun, leaned her head back and looked up at him.

"You tracked me down." She grinned to take the sting out of the words.

"Well, not exactly. I had to go to Fairfield to pick up some old flooring a friend of mine ripped out of a house he tore down. I figured you'd gone for a walk. Need a cup of hot tea?" He handed her a thermos, warm to the touch.

She took the cup from him, cradled it in her palms. "Thanks. I keep forgetting it's not summer yet."

"How's the research going?" He sat down beside her, leaned back on his elbows.

"Well enough. I'm remembering some things

about my childhood. Good memories." She held up her book, using her fingers as a placeholder. "This is interesting. It's about the excavations at Fort Raleigh, and what's been dug up through the years." She turned it around so he could see the cover.

"You know, I've not paid much attention to Fort Raleigh, or seen the play either. I've been so focused on architecture. There's been a flurry of activity in Edenton around the Dare Stone in the last few months. I suppose I should brush up on that part of history. What do you suggest I read?"

"Well, the quintessential authority was David Quinn, but he's dead now. His research was impeccable, but he pretty much insisted that they all went *en masse* to the Chesapeake area and were massacred up there by the Powhatan. I prefer Miller's book, *Roanoke*. It's easier to read, like a novel. She's convinced the colonists dispersed, a few families going to live in major Indian villages up and down the Albemarle and Pamlico Sounds—you know, Damonsekepeuk, Aguasococ, and Chowanoak, which would explain how Eleanor could have ended up in your neck of the woods. She's convinced that seven colonists survived and were taken captive."

"Really?"

She stopped, saw the expression on his face. "I'm going on and on, aren't I?" she offered, wincing.

He grinned, winking at her. "Yes, but I like to hear you talk. I love your passion. It only makes me realize how much I've taken for granted living here." He sighed, looking off across the water. "So, do you think the captives survived?"

"Who knows?" she shrugged. "There were reports of sightings through the years. A French explorer claimed that seven English people, including a young woman, were forced to work in the copper mines."

His eyes widened. "Geez, that's hard. I think I'd rather be killed than taken captive."

"Yeah. Me too." She sighed and looked around her. The topic was sad.

"What about the recent archaeology? Are there any digs going on now?"

"Well, I'm more familiar with the Chesapeake area than here, but as far as I know the research up at Hatteras Village is ongoing. Now there's Salmon Creek. I think more digging is planned."

"What about around here. Anything found around here lately?" he asked as he busied himself fishing trash out of his cup.

She paused, glancing at him out of the corner of her eye. "Why do you ask?" she finally answered, on guard for a reason she couldn't quite put a finger on.

"Oh, no particular reason. I've heard legends off and on…"

"Here? In this specific area? I'm sure there are lots of stories, but nothing important going on that I know about, specifically not about the Roanoke colonists if that is what you mean. That was more my father's interest than mine. Besides, you're probably getting bored."

"Not really," he replied, shrugging, then, "I was thinking about running into Manteo for an early supper. Most of the restaurants are closed on Sunday but Poor Richard's is open. I usually go on

Sundays. My fishing buddies hang out there. And I need to check on my sailboat." He paused, then added, "Want to go?"

Sailboat? The man was full of surprises.

Twenty minutes later she was enjoying the scenery on the highway when he turned onto a wide gravel road. He turned to her, grinning.

"Don't worry. I'm not kidnapping you. I just want to show you the bears. At least I hope I can." Then suddenly he pointed, excited, "See, right there!"

She leaned forward, staring. A mother bear with a set of twins waddled along the ditch bank in front of them. "Scott! That is so incredible!"

Edging his truck as closely as possible, Andrea snapped pictures with her phone, holding her breath, afraid they'd get scared and run off. Sure enough, it wasn't long before the bear herded her two charges back into the woods.

"That was amazing. Thank you so much! Gosh, I hope I got some good pictures." Then, surprising herself she slid over and pecked him loudly on the cheek. "That was so much fun! And they are so cute!"

He grinned. "They may be cute, but they're still dangerous. A grown bear can run as fast as this truck. At least they can't see us very well. It's safe so long as we stay in the truck."

"They're blind? I didn't know that."

"Not totally, but their eyesight is poor. They rely on their sense of smell."

"Interesting…thank you for bringing me here."

"I love showing off the bears. They're a local tourist attraction. There's a ton of them around

here. Eastern black bears are protected on the refuge, but they are very amorous, especially in the
winters, so we see a lot of babies this time of year."

"Amorous bears?" she chuckled. "Sweet that
they have twins."

"Yep, pretty common I'm told."

They went on a mile or so, but no more bear
sightings. Scott turned the truck around and
headed back to the main road toward downtown
Manteo.

"Do they ever wander into civilization?" she
asked.

"Well, if they do I've never heard about it. They'd
have to cross over the Roanoke Sound. They have
all they need here."

Ten minutes later they were pulling up to Poor
Richard's. Typical waterfront bar, Sunday night
football on the television, low lights hanging over
small tables, a row of regulars perched on stools.
A couple of Scott's friends were there, but other
than checking on the score and a question about a
truck for sale he didn't linger. Instead, he sat down
with her and shared small talk about the town until
their food arrived. By the time they emerged it was
almost twilight.

"My sailboat is docked right over there," he said,
ushering her toward a beautiful all-white sailboat
tied up in a slip next to the boardwalk.

"Gorgeous. I didn't know you were a sailor."

"Well, I wasn't until I married Jennifer. But her
boat was nothing like this. I sold it after she died.
That and her life insurance allowed me to upgrade.
I sold our condo in Raleigh too. Otherwise I
wouldn't be able to afford the maintenance, much

less the docking fees. I plan to sail for a year once I've finished remodeling the house." He turned to her. "Do you sail?"

"I can't say I have that much experience, but I can bail water with the best of them," she joked.

They strolled down the waterfront a bit. Scott point out the historic houses, elegant old bed and breakfast inns, and several galleries and high-end shops, most of them closed. When they passed by the Manteo Bookshop he informed her that he knew the owner, opening the door for her as they stepped inside. While he and Scott chatted, she browsed, her eye drawn to a new book she'd not seen before titled, *The Head in Edward Nugent's Hand*.

Hmmmm. That had to be about the beheading of Wingina, killed in a skirmish by English soldiers, then presented as evidence of conquest. The fly said the book had been written from an Indian perspective. How had she missed that one?

Stepping up to the counter to pay for it, she spotted Scott outside in a heated conversation with someone on his cell phone. She tried not to let her curiosity run wild, but by the look on his face the conversation was not pleasant. Not wanting to interrupt, she wandered around a bit more, only joining him when it seemed safe.

"Is everything okay?" she asked, trying not to sound intrusive.

He snorted. "Just pissed. The lumber turned out to be dry rotted, that's all."

He was quiet as he drove the forty miles back to Columbia. When he escorted her to the door of the Inn, he squeezed her shoulder, watched as she made it back inside, then drove off as if he couldn't get away fast enough.

That was strange. He seemed to be enjoying himself, but after that phone call his mood changed.

Oh well. She'd call him tomorrow. Clear the air. But then again it was likely they'd never see each other again anyway, so what did it matter?

Still, she was disappointed. She'd been having fun with him.

Back in her room she changed into her baggy nightshirt and settled down to read in earnest. Content, she spent the remainder of the evening reading what was left of the Fort Raleigh book, thumbed through the book about Wingina, then started in on the thesis about Beechland.

The more she read the more intrigued she became, especially by the author's theory that the colonists had been deliberately hidden, sequestered away so they would be unseen by the Spanish or jealous factions in the English court who would sabotage their mission. He claimed the colonists had been outfitted with provisions and allowed to leave England in exchange for finding gold, precious metals, and valuable crops for the Queen, particularly sassafras, thought to be a cure for syphilis back then, worth its weight in gold.

Well, that was news. She'd never heard of the sassafras theory before.

Then there were stories too, mainly oral family histories. The narrative was compelling even if there was little in the way of proof. Something about some coffins being found and lost again.

Was that what her mother had been talking about? A good possibility. Surely her father would have known about the legend. But, then again, there were probably lots of coffins in the woods around here.

By the time she finished reading, it was almost bedtime. Realizing she hadn't eaten anything since her meal with Scott she grabbed some fruit, nuts, and a pastry in the kitchen, heated it in the microwave. As she ate she watched PBS.

Gosh the house was quiet. The only other guests, the couple she'd talked to this morning, had checked out that afternoon, thank heavens. The innkeeper was long gone. She made one last trip to the bathroom and crawled into bed early, plugging her phone into the charger. As the house settled in for the night, so did Andrea, sliding under the down comforter, grateful for its luxurious warmth.

As her eyes grew heavy her mind drifted toward thoughts of Scott. He really had been kind to her, even if he had gotten moody toward the end. But, what did it matter? Her life was too complicated right now for anything more than friendship, especially with someone who lived so far away.

She sighed, going back and forth in her mind. Finally, she settled on a compromise. She would call him after she spent Monday morning doing research. She really did want to see Edenton. And hadn't she read that Salmon Creek was not far off Hwy. 17 at Merry Hill? It was a straight shot from there to Charlotte.

But then she remembered, Scott taught classes on Monday afternoon.

Darn.

She switched off the reading lamp and pulled the comforter over her head, feeling her body relaxing, releasing tension.

She was about to drift off when the phone vibrated, then chimed like a bell, an all-too-famil-iar combination that could be only one person. Startled, she sat back up and shook herself awake. Why would her Mom be calling this late at night?

It was not her Mom, but her Aunt Connie, her voice cold, disapproving.

"Andrea, your mother has had a heart attack and it's bad. Come on home now, you hear?"

CHAPTER SIX

NOTHING COULD HAVE PREPARED HER for what it felt like to be standing at her mother's bedside—tubes, IV's, and the monitors blinking off and on in a steady, syncopated rhythm. She stood there for what seemed an eternity before she realized that she was holding her breath, jittery as a feral cat, adrenalin making sounds in her head like a radio with too much static.

She'd driven straight through all night, stopping only long enough to fill up on gas and cheap road-side coffee. The trip had seemed to take forever, made worse when it became almost impossible to get through to her Aunt Connie to get fresh updates on her mother's condition. Either the cell phone connection was bad or it went to voicemail. The lack of information almost drove her crazy.

Exhausted, she pulled into the hospital parking lot at dawn, only to learn that she had gotten there too late to talk with the doctor, who'd already come and gone. What information she had her aunt carefully meted out, explaining that, though it had been a close call, the doctor was certain her dear sister would recover just fine. And oh, by the way, her phone couldn't get a signal in the bowels of the hospital. "Sorry about that," she cooed.

The only thing that kept Andrea from slapping her silly was remembering that her mother was still alive.

With nothing to do but think, she listened to the continuous beeping of the machines monitoring her mother's vitals, the bustle of the nurses coming in and out and the slow drip of the IV dripping sedative into that soft, pale forearm.

She stared at those arms, the arms that had wrapped around her as a child, held her when she cried, hugged her fiercely. She watched her chest rising and falling, eyes darting back and forth under her lids, as if scanning the horizon for someone she could only see.

When had her mother aged so much?

Of course, she'd not seen her in months, not since Christmas when she and Chad met her for lunch at a trendy downtown restaurant in Charlotte on Christmas Eve. They had been on their way to the airport to catch a flight to Vail where they planned to ski for the week.

She'd noticed then that her Mom had seemed a bit quiet and pale, but they had been in such a rush to make their flight that she didn't bring up the subject. Chad had pretty much dominated the conversation anyway so she really hadn't had the chance.

Now she could kick herself. How unkind and selfish she must have seemed, as if the only time she could allot was an hour simply passing through on the way to somewhere more exciting. They could have come the night before and stayed over, or bet-ter yet, invited her to go with them. Andrea was sure her mother had never been skiing. If nothing else, she would have loved sitting by the fire in the lodge. Her mother had never taken vacations, not that she was aware of anyway.

But if she were honest, she knew why she hadn't offered the invitation. Once she married she had planned to put this city, her mother, and her past behind her for good. Out of sight; out of mind.

No wonder her mother's heart had given out.

Leaning over, Andrea kissed her softly on the cheek, stroked her arm, and whispered, "Mom, you've got to pull through this, okay? We've got to make up for lost time…" She stood back up, watched as she took a deep breath and sighed. When her eyes finally opened ever so slightly, Andrea felt a gush of relief. Tears sprang unbidden.

"Hey baby… I was worried about you," her mother whispered, struggling to finish the sentence.

Andrea leaned down closer. "You just need to rest and be quiet, okay? We'll have plenty of time to celebrate later. I'm home for good now," she whispered, squeezing her arm.

Gradually her mother calmed, looked off across the room for a long moment, then turned her head toward Andrea. She was wide awake now, looking Andrea straight in the eyes, voice clear and firm.

"Listen to me sweetie. I need to tell you something."

"You shouldn't be talking right now," Andrea interrupted. "Please, rest! I know you love me. I love you too. I've been such a jerk lately. I promise I'll make it up to you, okay?"

"Andrea, listen to me. Please, it's important!" Her

breathing was becoming ragged, her face flushed.

"Mom, calm down, please! This isn't good for you. If you need to talk, go ahead, but promise me you won't get upset. I'm listening. What is it?" She was frightened now.

Gradually her mother quieted, then spoke, her voice measured and deliberate. "There is a trunk in the attic. I didn't want you to find it and be angry at me, in case something…something happens to me."

"Mom, nothing is going to happen." But before Andrea could finish, her mother lifted her hand, stopping her, raising her head slightly off the pillow, straining.

"Andrea, it's a trunk of your father's things: his field notes, his journals, his personal effects— everything. And the urn with his ashes, that's in there too." Her head flopped back down, her face pale now with the effort.

Andrea was stunned.

Her father's ashes in the attic? His journal?

"Please, please don't be angry with me," her mother pleaded, whispering now. "Promise me you'll try to understand."

"Mom, I'm not angry. We'll talk about it later."

But she was lying. She *was* angry, but now was not the time to deal with it.

"I was so mad at him. And then he died like that. I never could get the courage to open it. Your granddaddy put it up in the attic for me. He put the box of Aunt Polly's letters he found up there in it too."

Aunt Polly? She bit her tongue.

"I should have fought harder for him. I would

have if I had known he would take it so hard. But I hated East Lake so much and he wouldn't leave. He spent all his time with those old high school friends, Steve and Anna Lee. They were obsessed with those coffins, just like he was." She stopped then, staring blindly off into the shadows of the room as if she was seeing a ghost, then, her tone bitter: "That woman stole him from me."

Andrea froze, afraid if she moved or spoke she would shatter into a thousand pieces. When she finally summoned up the courage to speak, her voice was raspy with emotion.

"Look, Mom, I understand. It's all in the past. We'll sort this all out when you get well." She grabbed a tissue from the bedside table and wiped her mother's face. But her heart felt like a stone.

At least her mother seemed at peace now, though strangely distant, as if the truth she had kept bottled up so long had taken every ounce of her strength.

"Did you learn anything at East Lake?" she murmured.

Andrea shook her head. "Nothing that important. Everything I need is probably up in the attic anyway. We can take it down when you're better. Maybe we can spread Daddy's ashes together, take a trip down to the Outer Banks at the end of the summer."

Her mother nodded in agreement, sagged with relief. But then the monitor began zigzagging, alarms sounded, she began gasping. Andrea ran into the hall, screamed for help, then ran back to her mother's bedside.

After that, everything was a blur. Between the nurses, the doctors, the paddles, the absolute total

frenzy of coding there was no time to say goodbye.
Within moments her mother was gone.

CHAPTER SEVEN

SHE SAT IN THE LIVING room a week later, staring at her cell phone. How many times had she called her mother's landline in the last week just to hear her voice again?

Hello. I'm sorry I'm not here to take your call. Please leave a message and I'll get back to you as soon as I can. Hope you have a great day.

She couldn't stop herself. If she could still hear her mother's voice, she could pretend she was still alive.

She was about to dial the number again when the phone rang. She almost jumped out of her skin.

"Hello," she answered, rattled.

"Andrea, it's Scott McWilliams. Have I called at a good time?"

Good heavens. Scott?

"Hey there. Sorry I didn't get back up with you before I left town. A family emergency," she managed to state before her throat closed up.

"I was afraid of that. Hope everything is okay now."

"My Mom had a heart attack and died last Sunday night. I barely made it home in time," she answered, her voice shaky.

"Oh God, Andrea. I'm so sorry! I wish I had known. I could have at least sent flowers. When was the funeral?"

"Thursday. She was cremated. We buried her ashes next to my grandparents in Salisbury."

"So, what are your plans now?" he asked.

"My plans? Let's see, I've got to clean the house, settle the estate, find a job… the list is pretty end-less," she answered, her tone snarky. She knew she was being a bitch, but she couldn't help herself.

He was silent for a moment. Then: "I was hoping you would say you were going to take off a few weeks to get your head back on straight. If so I was going to offer you the guest house here at the Montrose to make up for my rude behavior that last night you were here."

She flushed, relieved he couldn't see her embarrassment through the phone. She took a deep breath and let it out. "Thank you. That's very kind of you," she finally answered. Then she paused, considering her words. Could she confide in him? She *had* to tell somebody.

"Scott, my mother confided in me right before she died, things she'd never told me about my father and how he died. I had no idea…." She stopped to staunch back tears, then spoke in a rush. "Like I said, I've got a lot to do here. I'll be back down that way soon. When I come, you'll be the first to know." She couldn't help that her voice sounded cold.

She could hear him hesitate, start to speak, then pause again. When he finally spoke, his voice was gentle.

"Well, I'm sorry if I intruded. I remember how

hard it was when my Dad died. He was a good man and I miss him terribly. Take care, okay. I'll be thinking about you. Call me if you change your mind."

Oh damn. She'd forgotten about his father.

"Scott, wait minute. I'm not blowing you off, okay. I just need some time that's all, and right now I need to focus on some things. I'll consider your offer, I promise."

"No worries. The offer stands whenever you are ready to take me up on it."

"Thanks. Enjoy this fine spring weekend. Go out on your boat. Enjoy life while you still can…."

"Same here, Andrea." And the line went dead.

She put the phone back in its cradle, brushing away tears.

Thank goodness, Henry jumped into her lap about that time, her Mom's ragamuffin Silky Terrier. He had been so miserable—not eating, shivering continuously, nails tapping endlessly on the hardwood floors as he searched the house room by room. *Where is my human!*

Same here, buddy.

Not that she got any answers. The house seemed so damned empty, so little of her mother left here now except a few sweaters and books stacked beside the bed. Her mother had never worn per-fume or jewelry, had no real hobbies. The only real personal items were a few cosmetics in the bath-room, the clothes in her closet, and of course, her purse. Credit cards, a driver's license, a few breath mints, a receipt from a recent movie that she had probably seen by herself. The scent of her hand cream lingering in the satin lining of the purse had almost been Andrea's undoing.

Her mother's one passion, aside from her child, had been her dog, adopted after Andrea had left for Williamsburg. Henry, the Wonder Dog, as her mother had fondly called him.

What would she do with him now? She didn't have the heart to give him away or take him to a shelter. There were no family members willing to take him. Every time she tried to pick the creature up, the poor thing trembled. How was she going to take care of a dog?

Not that he wasn't good company. And she really didn't have the heart to give him away. He was a piece of her Mama. And, despite what she had told Scott, she really didn't have all that much to do, thanks to her mother's penchant for organization.

That was an understatement, the woman had thought of everything. The house was deeded to Andrea free and clear to do with as she pleased, the mortgage paid off long ago. Per her instructions, included with her prepaid burial plan, there had been no flowers at the service in her hometown of Salisbury. All the food had been shuttled over to her Aunt Connie's larger home, where the family, what was left of them, gathered afterwards. Andrea had already finished writing the thank you notes. Nothing was left for Andrea to do but pack her mother's clothes and shoes up and give them to Goodwill, and even that didn't have to be done anytime soon.

Her mother had lived such a small, careful life.

But her heart had been big, how big Andrea had never realized before now. Hundreds had shown up for her funeral—present and former students, faculty, church members, neighbors—most of them strangers, at least to Andrea. They stood in line afterwards to express their gratitude for her mother's help, support, or patience. It was humbling for Andrea having to realize how little she really knew about her mother's public life, how much she had underestimated her accomplishments as a teacher.

The shocking revelation had been the insurance policy naming Andrea as the beneficiary. The agent had called her to let her know the money had been deposited that morning in a joint savings account at the State Employee's Credit Union where they had banked for years.

One hundred thousand dollars. She almost dropped the phone.

So now she didn't even need a job anymore, though she was still considering taking the teaching position, if only to have something to do.

But deep down she knew she couldn't. Those shoes would be too big to fill.

But what other options did she have? From where she stood, the horizon looked empty and meaningless. And then there was that stupid trunk in the attic, like a dark cloud hovering in the ceiling.

Not that she wasn't curious. Curious didn't even begin to describe her desire to know what her father's note and journals contained. *But ashes?* In the attic? That's the part she couldn't get around.

And those journals. What if he had written down intimate thoughts about her and her mother, or worse, revealed terrible secrets that would shock them all? That trunk could be a Pandora's Box, once opened never closed. And she sure as heck didn't want to open it alone. Not that she'd ever ask any of her mother's family to help. Her Aunt Connie was too nosy.

Without warning a wave of grief crashed against her so heavy it almost took her breath away. As if on cue Henry came clicking around the corner again, his tail dragging, ears drooping, eyes sad with longing. He hopped up on the sofa and stood on his little hind legs, gazing out of the picture window. He even yipped in excitement when a car the same color as her Mom's passed on the street.

Poor little guy. I know how you feel.

But as she watched him an idea started forming.

Her mother had told her that Henry loved riding in the car. Her father had loved the Outer Banks. She had promised her mother to scatter his ashes there.

She looked back down at the phone in her hand, took a deep breath and hit redial.

"Hi there…what's up?" Scott's voice was pleasant but guarded.

"Will your fine establishment allow me to bring a small dog?' she asked, trying not to sound so needy.

"It does, if said small dog hasn't been trained to attack," he responded

"Good, I'll be there sometime late tomorrow. And by the way, I'll need your help with an old trunk."

"Your room will be waiting for you. I'll even change the sheets."

There was one final test. She couldn't take the dog anywhere if he couldn't sit still in her lap, let her hold him.

"Henry boy, come here!" she invited, patting her lap encouragingly.

Puzzled, curious, he cocked his head. Then suddenly he bounded from the couch into her lap and started licking her face, his tiny tongue like a hummingbird. He was still shivering, but with excitement now. She stroked his silky ears; felt his warm, cuddly body.

"I love you, Mom," Andrea whispered out loud.

I love you too Andy.

The voice was her mother's, even if only in her head.

She sat stroking Henry until the warmth faded. Then she stood up, full of energy.

"We're going on a road trip boy. Come on, let's go pack!"

&

"A hotdog all the way and a large cup of ice water please," Andrea instructed the attendant at the drive-thru window.

"Awwww!" cooed the girl at the window, ducking back inside and emerging with a tiny dog biscuit for Henry. "You little flirt," Andrea admonished the dog, smiling.

As she had hoped, the drive seemed to have done its magic. For the better part of the trip he slept curled up on one of her mother's old sweaters, snug in his crate. Now, tanked up on fast food and fuel, she rolled down Hwy. 64 East through Rocky Mount, trying not to think about the trunk in the rear of the Jeep.

It had turned out to be more of a large wooden crate than anything, crudely made, flat on top with cracked leather handles. She had lowered it down the retractable attic staircase in the hall by tying a length of nylon rope she'd found in the shed to one of the handles. When it bumped against the floor she winced.

"Sorry, Dad," she whispered.

By noon she managed to finish packing the car. Locking the house tight, she swung by the lawyer's office to sign a few last papers and tie up loose ends, mainly handing the title of her mother's car and a bit of jewelry over to Aunt Connie. Then it was back on I-85 again.

Had it only been two weeks?

Finally, after almost five hours, she rolled off Hwy. 64 onto Hwy. 17 through Williamston, breathing a sigh of relief when she passed over the muddy Roanoke River. Breathing the swampy air made her feel like she was going home again.

A flock of wild turkeys strutted along the edge of the highway and a young doe bounded off into the woods. Sweet bay and dogwood blossoms dotted the forests like white stars, wedged in among towering cypress, dripping with Spanish moss.

This was ancient Indian land singing the song of the Albemarle.

In less than a half hour she was crossing over the Chowan River, wide and glittering, then turned right onto Hwy. 32 toward Edenton, passing a sign that claimed it was "The Prettiest Town in the South."

And it was, or at least one of them anyway. Wide brick streets lined with three-story historic houses, wide verandas overlooking Edenton Bay. She passed a sign that said she was nearing the historic Cotton

Mill district that seemed to be quaint refurbished bungalows, on past the city limits headed south toward the sound bridge.

A couple more turns on back roads and she was there, easy enough to find, standing at the end of a long row of elderly cedars, bent and twisted by time. The house itself certainly was imposing despite a bit of sagging on one side and its dire need of a new paint job. White with black shutters, two-storied, four-columned with a piazza, it opened onto the wide panoramic expanse of the Albemarle Sound in the background, shining in the late afternoon sun.

Whoa. She had imagined it would be grand, but not quite as grand as this. Scott must be more talented than she realized. No one would entrust a jewel like this to a hack.

She drove around to the back, parking under a massive oak tree towering over the yard, shade so dense no light could break through. Scott bounded down the steps to greet her, a wide smile on his face.

She had to admit she really was glad to see him, although Henry didn't seem quite convinced, growling and yipping his fool little head off. She hoped that all it meant was that he needed to go to the bathroom. She'd hate to have to kennel him after bringing him this far.

She noticed Scott seemed a bit more tanned and he'd gotten a haircut. Looked like he was already enjoying summer, and it hadn't even gotten here yet.

"Welcome to the Montrose," he exclaimed, "… see you made it in one piece," he intoned, hugging her sideways.

"Yep, we did. None the worse for wear," she answered, pulling away a bit sooner than necessary. She covered by placing her hands on her hips, looking around, and soaking in the view. Henry ran around the yard, sniffing and lifting his leg on anything that didn't move.

"Scott, this house is beautiful! I can see why you love it so much. The Montrose, huh?" She pointed in the direction of a dwelling in the backyard. "Is that the guest house?"

"Yes, and it's yours for as long as you like. I'll give you a tour of the big house, but let's get you settled in first." Then he pointed at the back of the Jeep. "Hey, is that the infamous trunk? It doesn't look that heavy." He paused, leaned over and peered inside. "By the way, I've made some pasta for dinner. A glass of wine and we'll be all set to have a go at its contents." He opened the tailgate, and without asking first, pulled the trunk out and began walking with it toward the cottage.

Slow down, buddy, she wanted to say, but didn't.

It was a low country cottage, shingled, deep porches gracing both front and back. The brick path that wound down the hill led up to double French doors, flanked by rocking chairs on each side and pots of ivy, all overlooking the sound.

The inside was even better than the outside, all creams, neutrals, and hardwood floors. Strategic lighting made the pale lemon walls glow. Heavy crown molding painted a soft white gave a luxurious feel to the place without being too overdone. A small brick fireplace was flanked by two massive club chairs covered in off-white linen slipcovers dominating the living room. A few primitive antiques were scattered here and there. A door to the right led to a bedroom housing a king-sized bed, complete with a comforter covered in the same linen fabric as the chairs.

She loved the muted creams and beiges with a pop of cherry red here and there. A large arch to the left opened into a kitchen boasting black marble counter tops and stainless-steel appliances. A screen door opening onto the back porch completed a quick tour of the space.

"This is amazing!" she gushed. "Such a little gem!" She headed toward the bedroom to get a closer look, then stuck her head into the bathroom. Thick white towels, French soaps, a bunch of fresh lilacs in a clear white vase. The man had thought of everything, all in exquisite taste.

"Roberta wanted a place to stay. She only comes down once a year to take care of business. Other times she lets friends or colleagues use it. There is some talk of a movie being filmed here, so it will come in handy then I suppose," his expression dubious. "But who knows if that will pan out. Sometimes my boss lady can be a bit dramatic. At least she's not one for cutting corners, thank goodness. You should have seen it before I started. It was a derelict."

"What was the guest house back then?" she asked.

"An office most of the time, I think. This was a working cotton plantation for a couple of hundred years, along with a lumber company and a fish hatchery. The Montrose family was quite wealthy, but a lot was lost during the Great Depression I think."

"Well, if the rest of the house looks like this Roberta certainly hired the right person to do the work," realizing too late how coy she sounded. But the awkwardness of the moment was broken when she heard Henry barking outside the door.

"Oh crap! I forgot the dog," she moaned, sprinting to the front door. On the porch, Henry jumped in her arms.

"Hey fellow! Good thing you didn't run off," she fussed, nuzzling the squirming dog.

"He'll be okay. Nothing much he can get into around here. But we do see a water moccasin every now and then so I'd advise you to keep him on a leash." Then, "Hey, I've got to check on dinner and uncork the wine. Bring Henry if you like, or leave him in the guest house. Whatever works for you is fine with me."

"Thanks. I'll be up in a bit. Let me get him settled in first," she replied, clipping the leash, putting him down on the ground again. Henry proceeded to shake vigorously, sneezed once, then began wiggling and sniffing at the foundations of the house.

That gave her an excuse to watch Scott from behind as he walked up toward the big house—typical Carolina boy that one, slim hips and tan legs encased in khaki shorts, spring green Ralph Lauren shirt, sleeves rolled to the elbow.

He really is nice looking, she thought. But the last thing she needed right now was to hop into bed with a stranger. No rebound boys for her.

"Let's go down to the water and look around, Henry!" she blurted, trying to distract herself from her thoughts. Henry bounded across the grass, happy after being cooped up after such a long drive.

It was a bit of a trek down the embankment to the pier but well-worth the trouble.

Shielding her eyes from the sun with a hand, she peered at the sweeping expanse, cypress and pine trees dark on the horizon. The sun's rays were warm on her face, but a chill spring wind had sprung up, quickly evaporating the heat of the day. She could see thunderheads piling up in the distance.

Andrea turned back to look at the house up on the hill. Partially hidden in the shadows of the old oak tree, its windows were dark, the dormers, peaks, and piazza stately but a bit forbidding. She shivered. Gooseflesh rose on her arms.

Then out of the corner of her eye she saw a curtain falling back into place, as if someone had been spying on her. The hairs prickled on her neck. *Scott?* Was he checking up on her?

That was strange. Maybe he didn't want her wandering all over the property. But if the pier was off-limits, he should have said so.

She gazed at the water, fatigue and self-doubt washing over her. Now that she was here, she was having second thoughts. If she were honest she wished she could simply skip dinner, curl up with the trunk and a glass of wine, and spend the night reading whatever she found in it.

She'd driven all this way because she didn't want to be alone when she opened it. And Scott had cooked special food for her. She could at least try to be cordial.

Okay. She would spend one night, clean out the trunk, go through her father's notes, then take his ashes to the Outer Banks. She would spend a few days at the beach then return to Charlotte as quickly as possible.

Glad to have an exit plan, she headed back inside. Scott had thoughtfully put out two small bowls for the dog, and after a quick feeding she tucked Henry away in his crate, where he seemed content to curl up and snuggle down for a snooze. She unpacked only what she would need for one night and turned back the covers of the bed. A quick hair brushing and a bit of lip gloss and treat for Henry, and she headed toward the door.

It seemed foolish to lock it this far out in the middle of nowhere, but she did it anyway, simply out of habit. No one ever left their doors unlocked in Charlotte. She made the walk up to the house in quick strides, not letting herself think too much until she got to the back steps and knocked on the screen door.

"Come on in," he called out. When she walked in Scott was standing at the stove smiling. He motioned her to sit down while continuing to stir something in a large stainless steel pot, steam rising to the ceiling.

"I thought maybe you'd taken a nap or something."

"Nah, Henry and I needed to stretch our legs. I saw you in the upstairs window by the way," she added, "I hope it was okay to walk out on the pier."

His stirring slowed. "Of course. Just watch your step. I haven't had time to check it out this spring. I'm not sure what you saw upstairs. I haven't been up there in a few weeks, but I'll check it out later," he offered, brushing aside the subject. He put down the spoon, opened the stove door to check on the bread, then slammed it back shut. "I'll give you a tour of the house tomorrow if you like, in the daylight. For now, let's tackle this pasta. I hope you like shrimp marinara, and if I remembered correctly, you prefer a dry white. Help yourself. The bottle is chilling in the refrigerator. I'll drain the pasta while you pour, okay?"

Plates filled, he brought out a salad, divvying it up between their two bowls, and tossing them with a bit of lemon juice, balsamic, olive oil, and sea salt with the flair of someone who was obviously comfortable in the kitchen. Then he pulled two small loaves of French bread out of the oven piping hot, quickly shoveling them onto a small bread board on the table.

"This looks incredible Scott," she offered, her mouth watering. She hadn't eaten anything since that hot dog at lunch.

"Well, since I didn't get a chance to pay my respects after your mother died, this is the least I can do now. Enjoy yourself."

"You've certainly gone above and beyond. The guest cottage is delightful, and this meal looks divine." She smiled, hoping that she had set the right tone.

"Your seat Madam," he offered with a flourish, and pulled out her chair.

"Be careful. Any minute now I'll expect a violinist to jump out of the pantry and start playing *Clair de Lune,*" she teased, unfurling her napkin with exaggerated flair.

"You've been through a lot. I am so sorry about your mother. She must have been a wonderful woman."

"She *was* a wonderful woman; although I'm not sure I always did a very good job of appreciating her while she was alive." She took a sip of wine to cover her eyes misting.

He stopped, gazed at her.

"Andrea, second thoughts after the loss of anyone we love is normal. At least you've got the trunk to look forward to opening. If you and I do it together, it won't be so bad," he said, winding pasta around his fork and popping a shrimp in his mouth.

Ah, there it was. *The trunk.* She took a deep breath and plunged.

"Scott, I hope you don't mind. But I really would like to unpack it by myself. I have no idea what's in there, and well, you know… I need some time to be alone with my Dad. This has been almost thirty years in the making."

"Well, I guess I'd want privacy if it were my father's secrets," he said, head down as he kept busy eating.

Secrets? But she let it slide, retreating to safer ground.

"Tell me more about this house," she said, finally taking a bite of the shrimp.

His face brightened. "The Montrose family came from a long line of wealthy Quaker merchants in Richmond who bought the plantation as a financial investment. Their only child, Mary Ruth, grew up spending her summers here, met and married my grandfather's cousin, John McWilliams." He stopped, tore off a hunk of bread and buttered it. "He was a fairly ordinary lumber man from over in Belvidere, and a Quaker too. There were a lot of

Quakers here back then."

"That's interesting, I don't know too much about the Quakers. So, Mary Ruth was the one with the money? Wasn't that rather unusual back then?"

He nodded. "Yeah, but her story is rather grim. Her portrait is in the upstairs hall, by the way, been in the same spot for years. She died giving birth to twins, Carolina and Charlie."

She grimaced. "That's so sad. What happened to the children?"

"Well, Charlie died when they were both four. Carolina grew up the only daughter and went on to inherit this place as a young woman. Her oldest brother was killed in World War I, and the other went off and became a famous artist. His name was Alexander Wadewright McWilliams. You may have heard of him…"

"A wildlife painter, right? Are those his paintings in the guest house?"

"Yes, and no," he answered. "Those are clever copies made after he died. The originals are in various museums around the country. Way too valuable to keep in a private home." He picked up the bottle of wine, topped off her glass.

"What about Carolina?"

"Well, her life was colorful, to say the least. She married and had two sons and a daughter, but she outlived both of her sons. She lived to be eighty-nine and died right here in her room upstairs. Roberta is the only one left of them all."

Chills ran down her arms. "Doesn't it bother you?"

He smiled. "Not really. I love this place. I hope to buy it if I can get my hands on the money," then gazed around the room before adding, "one day." He finished off his glass of wine, face unreadable.

"Good Lord. If you're not careful I won't sleep a wink tonight!"

"Oh, the Old Boogey Man Tree out there will watch out for you. That's the legend anyway. It's a tree that watches over children especially. Roberta won't let me cut it down. But I fear one bad storm and it will take out the roof." He gazed at her, then added. "You know, you and Carolina look a lot alike from what I've seen in family albums. She was half-Indian too, supposedly a direct descendent of Pocahontas. A real fighter, so I heard."

"Well, never say never, but I doubt if we are related. Pocahontas was a Powhatan's daughter, but one of many, from the Pamunkey, a lesser tribe up in the Tidewater region. I'm pretty sure my ancestors were native to the Dare County area."

He wiped his mouth, gazing at her. "There are so many legends around here, you know. I read one not long ago about some coffins being found near the Alligator River. Ever heard about that?" He dipped his head; studied his empty plate.

First the trunk and now he was asking about the coffins? *That was odd*. Well, she might as well get it out in the open.

"Strange that you should ask. I bought a book about it the last time I was here, before I left. I think the author is from around here somewhere. But I'm not convinced that his theories are provable. And, even if they are, I suspect they are long gone."

"Interesting." He continued eating, as if he'd run out of things to say.

"My father was looking for them when he died, I think. My mother warned me not to go looking for them myself, probably because she was afraid I'd get obsessed like he did, or maybe it's because she hated his family. I've never quite figured it out. I do know my grandfather was a big moonshiner. She detested him. Nothing I'm proud to admit, that's for sure. If that's the kind of people they are, I surely want nothing to do with them." She took the last sip of wine before adding, "And if you want to know the truth, I've always wondered if there was more to my father's suicide than a failed marriage. But then again who wouldn't be depressed with a father like that. I am trying my best to understand…."

Abruptly Scott stood, picking up his plate and carrying it to the sink. "He must have been a very troubled man." Then, before she could answer, "How about dessert? I've got a French silk pie in the refrigerator and a pot of coffee, decaf if you like."

But his offer sounded mechanical, too polite, as if he was only going through the motions. She took the hint, deciding to end the evening while she was still ahead.

"Sorry, I couldn't eat another bite. And if you don't mind, I'll take a rain check on that coffee until morning, okay? That long drive, you know."

"Not a problem. I'll walk you home. A few tricky roots and potholes you'll need to watch out for. Are you still going to try to open the trunk tonight?"

Her jaw clenched a bit. "No, I think I'll go through it in the morning after I've had a good night's sleep. It's been a lovely evening and the dinner was delicious. But honestly, I'm exhausted. I hope you don't think I'm being rude. Here, let me help you clean this up first." She stood up, gathering the rest of the dishes to take to the sink.

He shooed her with a wave of his hand. "Nah, nothing here I can't put in the sink to soak, then straight into the dishwasher." Then he turned, lifting a jacket off a hook on the wall next to the door. "Here, put this on. You don't want to catch a cold in the night air," placing it over her shoulders. She shivered slightly when his knuckles brushed her bare skin. Opening the screen door, he ushered her out onto the porch.

He had been right about the night air, a bit chilly now, especially with a damp breeze coming up off the water. She was grateful for the warmth of the coat, a vintage bomber jacket that had seen better days, soft and supple. Stepping up onto the porch he opened the door for her, then reached inside the living room, switched on the porch light. Then he turned toward her, lightly placed his hands on her shoulders, barely brushed her cheek with his lips, then took off striding toward the house, not looking back at her again. She stood a moment and watched as his lanky form mounted the back steps, shoulders slumped, not entirely sure she was glad she had ended the evening so abruptly now. He seemed hurt by her somehow.

Well, maybe it was just as well. This off and on moodiness of his kept her off kilter.

It helped that Henry was deliriously glad to see her. She bent down to the crate, opened it, and as he wiggled out, slipped on his leash.

"Come on boy." The dog trotted behind her out to the back porch, began his routine of sniffing around, testing and marking different spots as if he was guarding the territory.

She stood on the porch, breathing deeply of the soft spring night air, gazing at the panoramic bowl of midnight blue sky. She didn't remember how long it had been since she had really looked at the stars. They were so vivid they pulsed. A bright swath of light from the full moon shone down on the water like a highway straight up to heaven.

My God, it is so beautiful.

Here, with so few city lights, she could truly see the stars, clearer than she had in years. The Big Dipper, the Little Dipper, Orion, and Venus glittering low on the horizon. She breathed pine sap, cypress, briny water infused with the more primordial scents of fish, rusty iron, and layers of silt and mud. The slap of the waves against the pier was even more insistent, more rhythmic now, under the sway, the push and pull of the full moon.

But it was a lonely kind of beauty, no doubt about that. And now that the wine was wearing off she was jittery and, unfortunately, all too wide awake. She leaned her head against the white porch post, tears welling up in her eyes. Out of nowhere a wave of loneliness washed over her, dark and cold.

God knows, he was attractive enough and she'd certainly been impressed by his thoughtfulness and manners. But all that talk of ghosts and dying children had spooked her. It was almost like he was trying to scare her or something.

Had he changed his mind about inviting her? She sure had gotten mixed signals.

Whatever. She was leaving tomorrow anyway.

She stared out over the water. The stars continued to wink, taillights of a jet plane traveling slow and steady across the sky. She wondered about the people it carried, and for a fleeting moment wished she was up there with them, going somewhere.

Anywhere but here.

She looked across the water toward a mass of dark forest, deep, and impenetrable, amazed that there was so little development on this part of the sound, except a single light twinkling here and there. Would her ancestors have traveled these waters in their canoes?

Would their fires have dotted these banks? If she closed her eyes she could almost smell smoke.

But then she shivered, wanting nothing more than to be safely inside.

"Come on, hurry up boy." As if on cue the dog squatted, then shook. At a tug of his leash, he hopped up onto the porch, following her into the warmth of the cottage.

Once he was settled in his crate, Andrea locked the door, washed her face, and put on an old t-shirt of her mother's. The scent of her favorite shampoo hit her, almost doing her in.

As she feared, sleep eluded her. She was all too aware that she was alone in the big bed. It didn't help that Henry kept turning in his crate, unable to settle down.

She was a grown woman, for God's sake. Why was she acting like such a baby?

Frustrated, she looked at her phone. It was only ten pm—still early by her usual standards. She turned on the light, tried to read a book but couldn't focus.

Of course, all she had to do was hit redial on the phone. Scott would be glad to bring down a bottle of wine. *Maybe.* Either way it wouldn't turn out well, even if there was a chemistry between them. Besides he'd almost seemed more interested in opening the trunk than in her.

She sighed, tossing and turning. She finally got up, tiptoed over to the crate. "You lonely too boy?" she crooned. Opening the metal crate door, she scooped him up, stroking him softly to calm him. She took him back to her bed, where he curled up and nestled like a baby in the curve of her belly. Within minutes they were both nodding off.

The Old Boogey Man Tree watched over her from atop the bluff.

❦

She woke to the sound of soft rain pattering on the tin roof, a wet tongue darting at her face and a knock on the door. "Ugh…" she moaned, sliding further down under the covers.

Undeterred, Henry kept nudging and whining, relentless in his quest to get his new playmate out of bed. Giving in, she threw back the covers, dragging herself upright until she sat on the edge of the bed.

"Okay, okay! I get the message," planting her feet on the hard floors. Rubbing the sockets of her eyes with the heel of her palms, she stood, gingerly padding on bare feet to the living room, Henry tapping behind her.

Still in a sleepy fog, she padded to the door. Peeking outside, she saw a delivery service driving

off, but couldn't make out who it was. Grabbing Henry's leash hanging on the hook by the
door, she stepped out onto the front porch, surprised that the first thing she saw was a breakfast
tray, complete with a thermos, a carafe of orange
juice, and a basket covered with a pale blue linen
cloth. There was even a buttercup in a tiny bud
vase. Such thoughtfulness, especially considering
how the evening had ended the night before. She
couldn't help but smile. Maybe this was his way of
making it up to her. But a delivery service? That
was going way above and beyond.

Henry finished his business quickly, apparently
not too fond of wet grass. Hopping back up on the
porch he made a quick beeline toward the basket.

"Oh no, mister. Those are for me!" she laughed,
scooping him up in her arms, taking him to the
kitchen. She took a paper towel to his paws, then,
setting him down, poured a bit of kibble into his
bowl.

She retrieved the tray and took it to the bedroom, carefully setting it down at the end of the
bed. On a rainy morning like this all she wanted
to do was crawl back in and pull the covers over
her head. She was so tired. Then again, it could be
allergies. Sleeping in strange beds sometimes gave
her a stuffy head.

She poured a cup of coffee in the thick, white
mug she had found in the kitchen, doctoring it
with cream and sugar. A tentative sip revealed that
it was not only hot, but strong and smooth, just the
way she liked it. Sighing with pleasure she took
another sip, lifted the edge of the linen napkin, and
peeked underneath. The scent of sausage wafted

upward. Her mouth watered. The biscuits looked homemade.

Wow. He was going all out to impress her it seemed. But then again, maybe he is only fattening me up for the kill, she thought, chuckling.

Smiling, she started to pull one out, only then noticing the folded piece of white paper tucked underneath the basket. The handwriting was nice, almost like calligraphy, written on the catering service letterhead:

> *Unfortunately, Scott has been called out of town on business and won't be back until later today. He asked us to deliver breakfast on his behalf and tell you that the house is unlocked if you need anything. He will look forward to seeing you upon his return.*

Gone until tomorrow? That was cold. Why didn't he send her a text or call?

"So much for friendship," she murmured, dropping the note in the trash can by the bed.

If he was angry with her why did go to such lengths? But then again, maybe there had been an emergency of some kind. She couldn't jump to conclusions. Not yet, anyway.

Still. He had to have known how it would make her feel to leave her here out in the country in a strange place alone, with nothing but a small dog for company.

No longer hungry, she drained her cup, then carried the tray back to the kitchen. After tidying it all, she stuck the basket of biscuits in the refrigerator. Her stomach was clenched too tight to eat anything.

But who was she to complain? From Scott's per-spective, it was she that had been rude, coming all this way because she didn't want to be alone when she opened the trunk, then flipping the script once she got here. Talk about mixed messages.

Well, what was done was done. She stomped into the living room, grabbed the trunk by the rope and yanked it into the bedroom. At least there she would feel less vulnerable and exposed. She stood and stared angrily at it, as if daring it to move. Then she remembered the latch, and the cheap padlock holding it in place. *Crap!*

She ran through the kitchen scrambling through all the kitchen drawers, most of which were empty except for a bit of cutlery. Nothing in the pan-try but cleaning supplies and dish towels. The bathroom yielded nothing. The only thing in the bedside table drawer was a box of Kleenex and an old *Our State* magazine.

She stopped, considering her options. The only thing left to do was to go up to the big house. Scott *had* told her to get anything she needed. Before she could talk herself out of it, she grabbed her jeans off the floor, pulling them on under her mom's t-shirt. She thrust Henry into his crate then headed out of the front door and across the yard, up to the kitchen porch.

She was relieved it was unlocked, just as he had promised. She started searching, first in the draw-ers, methodically opening them one by one until she finally got to the last one next to the door.

"Aha!" A long flat screwdriver crusted with old white house paint—that should work!

She ran back down the hill and into the cottage, every nerve in her body stretched tight. Kneeling by the trunk, she inserted the screwdriver into the metal clasp and pried, twisting and turning until the palm of her hand burned and her shoulder ached. Finally, it popped off.

"Yes!" she shouted, sucking in her breath and throwing back the lid.

The first thing she noticed was how musty it smelled, and the next how little there was to see inside. The urn, innocuous enough, lay on its side, wrapped in what appeared to be clothing, beside it a belt, a cracked leather wallet, a couple of text books, a yellowed newspaper, and an old Dockers shoebox held shut with a rubber band. On top of it all lay a scratched up legal-sized tan leather Day Planner, the kind that had been popular in her father's era, before everyone got smart phones and computers.

Carefully she pulled the clothing away from the urn, trying not to think too much about its contents. Coarse-grained and crudely formed, glazed a muddy green with a few blood red and cobalt streaks dripping down the sides, it seemed typical of hand thrown pottery made in the seventies folk era, but with a dome lid sealing in the contents.

Slowly she turned it over, wincing when she heard the ashes inside sliding downward. There were initials carved into the bottom, but they were unclear. She turned it back over, gingerly placing it on the dresser.

Stepping back, she gazed at it for a minute, surprised at her lack of emotion. The cottage was quiet except for the sound of the rain and Henry scratching behind his ears every now and then.

"Hi Dad. "It's been a long time," she whispered. "I wish I had known you better…"

Nothing.

What did she keep expecting? That he would talk to her? Sighing, she turned her back on the urn, picking through the shirt and pants it had been wrapped in, then laying them out on the bed. Standard issue for a working man almost thirty years ago—khaki pants clean but frayed a bit around the cuff, oxford cloth blue shirt with a buttoned-down collar, and a purple and gold ECU Pirate pullover from his college days.

She stuck her fingers in the pants pockets, but came up empty-handed. Tossing them back on the bed, she picked up the shirt, sniffing the collar. Nothing but the smell of trunk, dust, and attic. She folded it neatly and placed it on top of the pants, then pulled out the wallet, a faded flat brown leather bi-fold, curled at the edges. When she opened it her father's face gazed back at her, laminated in perpetuity on his driver's license.

Caught off-guard, she stared back at him, heart thudding. He was handsome; she had to say that for him, even if he wasn't smiling. Square-jawed with short dark hair and deep-set brown eyes. The license gave his birth date as November 22, 1960.

Twenty-six years old. Certainly, too young to die.

Thumbing through the wallet she found a receipt from a gas station, a couple of dollar bills soft with age, and the stub of a raffle ticket of some kind, but nothing else. No pictures of his wife or child. Sighing again, she closed the wallet and laid it on top of the shirt.

What did you think you'd find, Andrea? A suicide note?

Well, at least now she knew what he looked like, and as she suspected, she was his spitting image.

Still, she was disappointed. She had hoped for so much more. Discouraged, she tossed the textbooks aside. Nothing promising there. She scanned the headlines of the old newspaper. Nothing there either. Shoving the books and newspaper over into the corner, she poked around the insides of the trunk for small items, her hand brushing against the coarse lining. Except for a safety pin and a loose Tyrell County library card with no name on it, the trunk was now empty.

She decided to get another cup of coffee and give herself a moment to breathe. She laid the clothes back in the trunk, but left the urn on the bureau, the wallet next to it, an idea forming in her head. The weather was clearing, the app on her phone predicting nothing but sunshine for the weekend.

Why didn't she just go ahead and leave? There was nothing to keep her here.

Yes! She ran back up to the big house, slipped the screwdriver back in the kitchen drawer, grabbed a pen she found and began scrawling a hasty note on a pad next to the toaster. A generic note of thanks and "I hope our paths cross again one day". The sort of thing couples say to each other when they want to be polite but both know the relationship is going nowhere.

She took one last look around the room. It was a shame she wouldn't get the full tour since this was likely the last time she'd ever get the chance. Even if the house was spooky, it was grand.

But then again, one last look couldn't hurt anything. Besides, he'd told her to make herself at home.

Slowly she tiptoed into the long hall connecting to the foyer. Unlike the kitchen, modern and updated, the rest of the house was like stepping back in time; dark, shadowy and dim. Still it was magnificent, even on such a rainy, gloomy morning. Wide heart pine flooring shone in the meager daylight coming from the elegant starburst beveled transom over the front door. Rich wallpaper depicting English hunt scenes graced the walls, stopping at the raised-panel wainscoting and thick chair rail, the wood sanded and stained a rich, warm brown. Wide pocket doors sealed off rooms on each side of the massive foyer. Her fingers itched to open it and peek inside, but just as she was about to touch the doors, out of nowhere a thunderclap, a gust of wind and the door to the kitchen slammed shut behind her. She whirled around and ran back, heart in her throat, skin crawling.

But when she crossed the kitchen and opened the door to the porch, a draft caused a piece of paper that had been tucked behind an old radio on the kitchen counter to dislodge and flutter down toward her feet. Bending over she picked it up and gave it a cursory glance. The only thing on it was a telephone number. She noticed it was Scott's handwriting. She felt herself go cold. The number was to her mother's house in Charlotte, her landline.

Big deal. He had called her on that number just two days ago.

But she had never told Scott her mother's name and that number was unpublished.

Calm down. There must be a logical explanation.

Her eyes scanned the kitchen. Right away she noticed the laptop over at a desk on the side wall. He'd closed the lid, but the pulsing power light let her know that it was only in sleeping mode.

She walked over to it, then lifted the screen. Maybe her mother's telephone number had been easy enough to find online, despite being unpublished. Everyone knew you couldn't trust the internet with your privacy.

It flared up and on. She held her breath, clicking on the button to open his Chrome browser, surprised when she saw he was still logged in to Google. She opened the menu in the upper right hand corner, scrolling down to click on the link to History. As she watched, a list of all the sites he had visited in the last few weeks glowed on the screen. She sucked in her breath and began reading, squinting at the screen.

At first there was nothing that alarmed her. A boat for sale on Craigslist, a site for building supplies, the Outer Banks Voice, evidently a local online newspaper. But then she stopped, her pulse quickening. There was a link to the Charlotte obituaries, with her mother's name as the extension.

Well, of course he'd read it online. Everyone did that these days.

But then she looked at the date. He'd read it the day after her death, before she was even buried.

How had he known her mother had died? She hadn't told him until he called a week later.

She kept scrolling. More architecture sites, Edenton local news, *pbs.org*—nothing out of the ordinary. Then something else—the newspaper

story from Williamsburg, the one about the whistle blowing.

So what? He told her he'd done his homework
on her.

But the deeper she scrolled, the more alarmed
she became. Old articles from her days back in
Charlotte, pictures of a couple of her professors,
her achievements and awards; then the final straw.
There in front of her was a picture of her at her
mother's funeral, albeit slightly out-of-focus, and
a screenshot of her mother's house from Google
Earth Live. She felt her throat close. *The son-of-a-
bitch was stalking her!*

She slammed down the screen, slipping the
piece of paper back where it had fallen. So, this
was how he treated women? No wonder his wife
had cheated on him.

Or had she? What if he simply hated all women?

Tiptoeing into the foyer she fished for light
switches, proceeding to turn every light on she
could find. She slid back the massive pocket doors
of the study, forcing herself not to think about
what she might find.

Bookcases full of old volumes, ledgers on the
large desk, an old roll-top desk over in the corner, and a big brown leather armchair that looked
inviting, though the leather was cracked and the
seat worn. A big oak grandfather clock in the
hall ticked away the hours. A fleeting picture of
a woman sitting in the chair popped in her head,
then vanished, her imagination in overdrive no
doubt. She had no idea what these people looked
like in real life.

Walking over to the desk, she saw a stack of

papers—bills, advertisements, fliers, that sort of thing. She tried the middle desk drawer but other than miscellaneous office supplies it held nothing of interest. The remaining drawers didn't contain anything special either. Most important, no weapon of any kind.

Except when she opened the top left drawer a newer framed picture of a woman stared back at her, and right away she figured she was looking at Jennifer, Scott's dead wife.

Her first instinct was to slam the drawer shut, but something about the way she was staring into the camera, right at Andrea, as if she wanted to tell her something. Mesmerized she took the picture out and held it under the light.

Jennifer was so beautiful.

Not that she was surprised. Scott had good taste in houses, he dressed impeccably, of course his wife would have been a class act too. Andrea stared at her green eyes, her long blonde hair. Had her death twisted him somehow, made him hate women?

What's your side of the story Jennifer?

The woman only kept smiling.

Chilled, she slipped the picture back in its dark space and slid the drawer shut. She padded across the room, toward a roll top desk over in the corner.

Boxes of checks, more pens, a dog-eared James Patterson novel and a few architectural plans rolled up tight and stacked, held together by a rubber band. *There! A tiny drawer.* Pocketed inside was an old-fashioned maroon leather address book with the name William B. McWilliams stamped in gold on the front.

Scott's father. It had to be.

She hesitated. But a quick glimpse wouldn't hurt anything. If there were questionable contacts—gentleman's clubs, racetracks, lots of women—wouldn't that tell her something about the character of both men? Tiptoeing back to the plantation desk she switched on the banker's light and held the book under the pool of light, carefully turning the delicate vellum pages, studying the tiny handwriting.

At first there was nothing. Then a single name that jumped out at her.

Steve Strayhorn.

The name rang a bell. Hadn't her mother mentioned her father's best friend was Steve? But there were lots of men named Steve in the world.

She stared at it again. Something about it bothered her though she couldn't put a finger on it. The address and telephone was for a listing in Norfolk. And out beside that a telephone number penciled in, and one word: *Talton*.

Puzzled, she kept leafing through the book. No names of women unless there was a Mrs. in front of it. No bookies, no cat clubs. Instead she saw listings for ministries, charities, and church offices. If his address book was any indication, the man was squeaky clean.

Then finally, there in the back:

Andrew Warren.

Her heart froze.

He had known her father?

Now she was truly frightened. Heart thudding, she slipped the address book back into the cubbyhole. A quick sweep of the massive formal dining room and what appeared to be a large guest bedroom, all pretty much in various stages of remodeling, furniture covered with canvas, paint cans, stacks of flooring, and piles of debris. Did she dare to check out the upstairs?

Why not? After all she hadn't seen links to serial dead girl sites or ways to kill and rape women on his computer. And it was not like he hadn't had plenty of chances before now. Last night would have been a perfect opportunity. Besides, if this guy was dangerous, she needed to find some evidence against him.

Then out of the blue her phone went off, echoing in the empty foyer. It rattled her, but not nearly as much as when she looked at the Caller I. D.

Oh damn! It was Scott.

"Well, there you are," she answered, trying to sound cool.

"Ouch. I deserved that. Listen, I'm sorry I had to take off on you."

"No problem. I didn't expect you to entertain me."

"Can you stick around, let me make it up to you?"

She closed her eyes, forced her tone to be civil. "Scott, that's tempting, but I think I'm heading on out this afternoon. It's raining, I've finished with the trunk, and I think it's time to spread my father's ashes. I need to move on."

"Now I feel really awful. It was too complicated to explain in a note and I didn't want to wake you up by calling too early. Tell me I've not messed up too badly."

Ah, yeah you have, she wanted to answer, but instead she played along.

"Thanks, Scott. But I need to get on back. I'll get a tour of the house next time, okay?"

"Are you sure you won't change your mind about leaving?" he asked.

"If I do, you'll be the first to know," her words so sweet her teeth hurt. She glared into the phone, trying to keep the coldness from her voice.

"Well then, take care. Keep in touch."

"Sure will. Hope your meetings go well. Take care yourself," she said, about to end the call.

"Andrea, wait. I need to…." and then there was a muffled noise, a clunk, and the line went dead.

The jerk hung up on her!

That was it. She was done with this place. She couldn't get out of here fast enough. She crammed the phone back in her pocket and ran back to the guest house.

Inside she went straight to the pantry in the kitchen and grabbed a heavy trash bag. She drained the glass of juice, retrieved a biscuit from the refrigerator, dropping the sausage in the trash can, stuffing the remainder in her mouth.

Back in the bedroom she put the shoebox in the trash bag, stuffing the planner and the wallet in her knapsack along with her mother's t-shirt. Shaky with nervous energy, she zipped it up and heaved it onto her back, checking her pocket to make sure her phone was still there.

She'd leave the trunk here, send Scott a text later, asking him to dispose of it and donate the text-books to the library or something. Of course, she wouldn't really say what she wanted to say—that she hoped someone would shove those books up his ass.

Back in the bedroom she looped the full trash bag over her wrist, tucked the urn in the crook of her arm, and with her free hand picked up the crate.

"Come on guys. Let's get the hell out of here."

CHAPTER EIGHT

AT FIRST SHE DISMISSED THE idea as impractical and way out of character for her.

But the more she thought about it, the more living at the beach for the summer made sense, especially as she drove over the long Albemarle Bridge, saw how the sun sparkled on the water. There was certainly nothing for her in Charlotte. Scott had seen to that.

Why not? After years of striving, studying, being so goal-oriented, it would be nice to enjoy long days reading, taking Henry for walks and playing in the surf. Who knew? Maybe she'd even get a mindless job of some kind, research a book, learn to fish. The possibilities were endless.

She opened the sun roof, turned up the radio to Mix 109.9. Yep, it was high time she had some fun, even if it was only temporary. She'd read about "bouts of euphoria" during the grieving process, but who cared? She'd deal with the crash later.

The irony didn't escape her when "Dust in the Wind" came on the radio.

By noon she was in Nags Head, parked in front of the first realtor's office she could find on the main drag. Housed in an old beach house with a wide wrap-around veranda it promised an array of properties, at least by the number of flyers on the showcase outside. She walked up the steps and into the cool air-conditioning, Henry on his leash.

"Hello. Can I help you?" the woman called out gaily. Deeply tanned, hair dyed dark red, fingernails painted to match, she wore a bright aqua short-sleeved tunic that showed her cleavage, so crinkly from sun damage it looked like an alligator hand-bag. Andrea cringed, trying not to stare. Instead she focused on the name badge the woman wore. *Loretta*.

"Good morning, Loretta. I'm Andrea. I was hoping to rent a beach house for the summer, on the water if possible. And I need a place that will allow a small dog – this small dog," she added, pointing to Henry.

Loretta's eyes widened. "Well, honey. I'm not sure about that. Most of our houses are booked by the week for the summer, the more reasonable properties that is. I might get you something in August." Her mascara-laden lashes fluttered up and down. She glanced out the window, checking out Andrea's battered vintage Jeep.

"I'm sorry. I really need a house now, like in the next few days at the latest. I'll pay in cash up front if necessary. I was hoping to stay until September, maybe even longer."

At the offer of cash, her eyebrows lifted, but she shook her head.

"I'm sorry, but the least anyone would consider would likely be six months and that certainly wouldn't be on the water. But you can try other realtors if you like. Free coffee and wifi while you look. I've even got a box of Duck Donuts if you want some. Best donuts on the beach. Already had three today," she declared, winking.

Andrea smiled. "Well, I'll pass on the donuts but the coffee is a good idea. Can you suggest other agencies?"

"Oh, just Google. We all work together down here. The Keurig is right back there in the kitchen," pointing through a door. About that time the phone in her back office rang, so Andrea was left to her own devices.

She found the sites quickly enough, scrolling through the listings of at least ten agencies, but Loretta was right. No short-term leases unless she counted the dumps. Most were monster three-story mansions in Corolla, one after another, or old beach box houses on cul-de-sacs in sketchy neigh-borhoods renting by the week. She was about to give up when Loretta, finished with her phone call, walked back out to the front desk, her face screwed up in concentration.

"You know, I don't know if it would appeal to you, but I've got a girlfriend with one of those vin-tage Airstreams parked down at a permanent site in Rodanthe. She usually comes down here every summer, but she is nursing her sister up in Balti-more and won't make it this year. Sister has cancer you know."

"Hmmm. What kind of shape is it in?"

"Aw honey, that little camper is the love of her life. Had it restored and everything, just as cute as a June bug. I'd need references of course. And cash up front, like you said."

Andrea sipped her coffee, then tore off a tiny

bite of donut and gave it to Henry. The thought of camping reminded her of her days as an intern in hot, mosquito-infested tents working on archaeological digs, listening to her tent mate snoring.

"How much?" she asked, leery.

"Well, when Janice and I talked about it she mentioned $1000.00 a month. That includes the lot rental, security, power, and all the campground amenities. KOA normally gets $75.00 a night but the owners are Janice's friends so they cut her a long-term deal."

"Could I look at it first? The most I could commit to is three months. I've got an offer for a teaching position back in Charlotte in the fall."

"Why don't I just give you the key now? I'll call the campground manager and tell him you're coming. If you like it, you can give me a holler and I'll let our satellite office down there know you're coming in to sign a lease and what we agreed on. You'll pass it going in. Ask for Cissy. If you don't like it, just return the key to her. What's your cell phone number?"

And that was it. Within moments Andrea was out the door, head spinning, key in hand, wondering if she had gone crazy.

A few miles down Hwy 12 she passed Coquina Beach, then the lighthouse on into the Pea Island National Park, surrounded by nothing but dunes, water, blue sky and dark green scrub cedars. Traffic was minimal, the yellow lines of the narrow two-lane road straight out in front of her, heat waves dancing in the noon sun. When she drove over the sweep of curving bridge arching gracefully over the Oregon Inlet the views were so stunning she almost shouted out loud.

The sheer panorama of it all—miles of water and waves, herons, shifting sand, salt air and sun— the mixture was intoxicating.

Twenty-five miles later she rolled into Rodanthe, smiling when she passed the house immortalized by the sappy romantic Nicholas Sparks movie that she and her mother had watched on a VCR back when she was in high school. Back then she'd thought it hopelessly corny, and had laughed at her mom for crying through the whole thing.

Grief was an unknown for her back then. Now she understood the pull of the movie and the house, so fragile, perching precariously in the surf as if it was going to collapse at the slightest gust of wind that puffed, any minute now. Such a metaphor for loss of any kind. She slowed the car and coasted through the beach town taking deep breaths. When would these sudden unexpected waves of sorrow stop hitting her from behind?

Only eight miles further and she pulled into the KOA, stopping in at the office to clear her visit with the attendant. He pointed the Airstream out to her, telling her that Loretta had called and asked him to hook it up to electricity and water for her and turn on the air-conditioning. To her delight the shiny aluminum Airstream was parked right next to the beach. It was a bit small, but from a distance it looked pristine.

The first thing she noticed when she opened the car door was the pounding of the surf, like music to her ears. The next thing was how hot it was, so hot that waves of heat shimmered off the concrete pads, undulating in the air. When she stepped out of the car warmth bathed her like honey, baking her bones.

She tied Henry by his leash to the side of the camper and took a deep breath, hoping that the inside looked as good as the outside, encouraged when the key turned in the lock, smooth as if it had been buttered.

Her first reaction was to laugh out loud. Chintzy retro, in a color scheme of aqua and pink—a pink chenille bedspread, aqua rug, matching teapot, toaster, and dishes—right straight out of a 1950's sitcom.

At least the bed seemed comfortable and the space was well laid out. There was a fully-equipped kitchen, a comfortable shower and toilet, and a dining table large enough for her laptop. There was even a large air-conditioning unit and a flat-screen television. What more could a girl ask?

Still chuckling, she checked the air conditioner, the stove, then took out her phone and called Loretta. She left her a voice message saying that she would take the place for three months and sign the lease at the Buxton office.

That done, she cranked the air-conditioner even higher, pulled back the covers of the chenille bedspread, set Henry on the bed and pulled him up against her.

"Welcome to your new home boy. Now, let's take a quick nap."

❧

Two hours later she woke up, more refreshed than she'd been in weeks. The air-conditioner still purred like a kitten, thank goodness. Her watch read four p.m.

Whoa! Most of the day was gone already. "Go for a walk boy? We've got our own private beach!"

The beach was everything she had hoped it would be, almost deserted, tide way out, and miles of endless blue-green water. By the time they reached the trailer she was famished. She put Henry in his crate, grabbed her handbag and car keys, and set out to explore.

The Food Lion seemed to be the only store in town, more like a general store than a grocery, catering to the tourists no doubt. She loaded her cart with a baked chicken, salad makings, a bottle of wine, condiments, a dozen eggs, apples, and a bag of dark chocolate with almonds. Good French bread and coffee, and her shopping was finished.

But then at the last minute she added cheese, crackers, and a bar of lavender soap. On the way to the register she spotted a bin full of cheap flip flops, then another display of sun lotion, adding one of each to her growing pile. A couple of magazines, a Lincoln Child archaeology mystery, a t-shirt with *Kinnakeet* written on it for half price, a bag of high-end dog food for Henry, and a gallon of distilled water. Yep, she was good to go! Henry seemed to think so too it seemed, as he barely looked up at her when she walked in the door.

There were no decisions to make, no bills to pay, no worries about what anyone was thinking. Heck, no one even knew where she was, except for the rental agency employees. She had all the time in the world to decide what to do with her life, say goodbye to her parents, her career, the old Andrea Warren. The only thing she needed to do right now was eat something and relax.

Her dinner, complete with a glass of chilled white wine, was the best she'd had in ages too, bar none. She consumed half of the chicken down to the bone, a huge salad (she'd forgotten dressing), and a hunk of bread, slathered with butter. She'd lost weight in the last few months. She could afford to gain a few pounds.

Lifting aside the print curtain, she watched the sun going down on the water. When the last light faded, she switched on a wall lamp overhead, curled up on the bed, and looked around her. Read? Watch television?

Come on, Andrea. Stop avoiding it.

That voice in her head was getting mighty uppity. The least it could do was give her time to get comfortable. She rummaged in her knapsack for her mom's nightshirt again, reminding herself that tomorrow she'd have to go shopping for a bathing suit and some more clothes. Maybe there was a thrift store somewhere close by.

Yeah, tomorrow she would have to get out early, before it got hot. She also needed outdoor supplies. A lawn chair and umbrella maybe.

Curling up on the bed, she checked her phone. No messages from Scott, thank God. A few emails from friends in Williamsburg. An invitation to a baby shower. A newsletter. Nothing urgent. Finally settled, she braced herself. She'd run out of excuses.

She started in on the letters, the oldest first, stacked back to back in the shoebox. Most were just cards, signed in a spidery handwriting, "Aunt Polly," and every now and then something like, "I'll bet that little girl of yours is growing up fast." All the things an elderly aunt would have said, without being too personal.

Then there was a slight change, more insistent, pleading.

> *I am not sure you received my last card. I*
> *would so deeply appreciate hearing from you.*
> *Love, Polly.*

The tone in succeeding letters became more urgent and even a bit ominous.

> *I know you have never wanted to talk about*
> *this in person, but there are things I have to tell*
> *you. Won't you please get in touch with me?*

And then finally, the last in a legal sized business envelope that was still sealed shut, folded in thirds in the bottom. Wiggling her index finger inside the flap she tore it open, pulling out a two-page letter, dated March 22, 1995. It was folded in thirds as well and when she opened it, saw that it was written in the same arthritic handwriting as the cards, but by someone discernibly older and with a shakier hand.

> *Dear Celeste:*
> *I hope you received my cards through the*
> *years. Since you haven't responded in any way,*
> *I have no way of knowing. But I am taking the*
> *risk to reach out to you one more time though*
> *I never wanted to put these things in writing.*
> *I didn't think it was safe. Even so, I cannot go*

to my grave without having told you what I
believe to be the truth. I only wish I had found
the courage to tell you before now.

First let me say that I know for a fact that
no matter how your marriage ended, Andrew
loved both you and that baby of his with all his
heart. I do not understand why he didn't fight
for you harder. But I swear to you it wasn't
because he didn't love you.

When I told him how heartsick I was that
you'd gone back to Salisbury with his baby, all
he told me is that it was for your protection,
and in time everyone would understand. So, I
took him at his word and didn't make a fuss
about it. I figured he had a plan of some kind.
He was a sensible boy.

Then a few days later he was dead. The
shock of losing him that way almost killed
me. No one could believe it, especially not his
friends. We were all torn up, as I know you
must have been too.

But something wasn't right about what we
were told. I knew that right away. What I want
to tell you now, what I should have told you
back then, is that I have never believed Andy
killed himself. The boy I knew would have
never done that, never in a million years.

But something was going on, and it won't
good. He won't acting right, like he was scared
of something, of what I don't know.

It got me even more scared when that deputy,
Talton, came poking his nose in everything. If
Andy had killed himself, why were they asking
so many questions? Then Steve kept asking me

if Andrew found those coffins. Of course, I told him that as far as I know those coffins, if they ever existed, are still in the ground. That is the God's honest truth.

Then Talton started putting pressure on me and Willie, acting like we were hiding something. Willie acted scared. Hooch stayed drunk all the time. I had my hands full.

I decided to keep my mouth shut. If Andy really was murdered, it might put us all in harm's way.

But it pains me to think that you and that sweet child of yours are going through life thinking that boy did not love you. You were nothing but a blessing to all of us. I truly believe if he let you go, it was for a very good reason. I think it was like he said—I think he sent you away to protect you, but from what I don't know.

Well, it is too late now. The doctors have told me I have Alzheimer's. That is why I am writing this letter. From what I'm told it won't be long before I don't remember anything at all. I thought I'd better tell you while I still could.

I would so love to see little Andrea one last time. I'll bet she is turning into a fine young lady by now. My sister Jane would have been so proud of her granddaughter, just as she was proud of Andrew.

I hope Andrea comes to realize one day that she comes from a long line of strong women you know, women with blood from both worlds. My prayer is that she will learn the truth about her heritage, what a good man her Daddy truly

was, and how much he loved both of you.
   Sincerely, Polly Vestal

Andrea sat on the bed, frozen, trying to absorb the words. Then she read it again, dissecting every sentence.

 Her father murdered?

Surely this was the ravings of a crazy old woman, desperate to make excuses for a young man she loved like her own son.

Then she remembered. *The journal*. There had to be clues there. Shivering, she picked it up, unzipped it, and opened it on her lap.

If she hadn't known any different, she would have thought she was looking at her own writing, the similarity unnerving. She flipped through all the pages, white loose leaf paper with lines, what looked to be about fifty pages in all, some class notes, references taken from textbooks and other secondary sources, but seemingly unrelated.

 Then about halfway through she hit pay dirt. A dated entry: September 7, 1985, a few weeks before his death. Then this brief notation:

Juniper wood consistent with earlier descriptions of riven coffins. Facilitated by extremely dry weather, exposing an area previously under water. Perimeter of study area approximately 10 x 10, five foot in depth, indications of disturbed silt and debris layering randomly occurring approximately every eight to ten years, possible terrain shifting due to excessive rain or storm events. Below the water table. Unclear but appears to be a cemetery of some sort. Need to broaden the search to 100-yard area.
   Findings to date:

Fragments of juniper wood (5 pieces in various
lengths) with evidence of hand carving
Three blue trade beads
A dozen or more potsherds scattered in area
over time (most from Woodland era pre-dat-
ing time of interest) indicating possible Indian
camp, dating inconclusive

Then a small, rough sketch of a map but no X
marks the spot. No identifying information of
where he made the find. Only Milltail Cr. written
on a curvy line intersecting the plot map, and then
this short, cryptic sentence: Going off the map
now.

In hiking lingo that meant going into the wilderness on unmarked trails. But how did that apply
here? Was "going off the map," his way of saying
that it was too dangerous to write anything down?
Or had he died before he had the chance to write
more?

Confused, she continued thumbing, noticing a
gap, as if pages were missing. Otherwise there was
nothing more, certainly nothing that indicated
he'd found anything important. She was about to
close it when she noticed something in the interior back pocket. She pulled out two small color
photos taken by an old Kodak Instamatic. They
stuck slightly to the leather, probably from all those
years in the heat of the attic.

The subject of one picture appeared to be some
wide chunks of old wood sticking out of the
ground, pointed at the end, and just barely discernible. Carved on top of the widest board was some
sort of writing and, above it, a symbol of some kind.

She put that picture down and picked up the other, a close-up of the first one. Though the boards were obviously badly damaged, she knew what she was looking at now—a Latin cross, with the channels around it cut deeply, burned out around the edges to make it appear raised. And underneath it four Roman capital letters: INRI, a symbol known by scholars all over the world: Jesus Nazarenus, Rex Judaeorum:

Jesus of Nazareth, King of the Jews.

Her heart hammered in her chest. The Roman cross was known to have been favored during the reign of Queen Elizabeth I, a universal symbol for the words written on the cross of Jesus at the time of his crucifixion and easily understood back in that era by the ordinary man or woman, even those who couldn't read. She shivered. Were these the coffins? It surely seemed so.

But what if this was all part of an elaborate hoax? It wouldn't be the first time an archaeologist had succumbed to the lure of notoriety. The controversy over the supposed Dare Stones was a perfect example. These could be pictures of dugout canoes made to look as if they were of Indian origin, artificially weathered, then deliberately broken up and buried, then dug up again.

But what if they were real?

Then she remembered the Beechland book. She dashed out of the camper, retrieved it from the Jeep and scurried back in again. Henry, curled up on the bed, only cocked his head, his gaze worried, alert.

Trying not to get too excited she flipped through the pages, until there, on page 118, the story about the coffins.

Supposedly a dragline operator back in 1950 had been dragging out a ditch for the West Virginia Tree Company, in what was known back then to be old Indian burial grounds down near Milltail Creek. The company was hoping to plant trees on the land if the swamps could be drained. Without thinking, the operator sliced into a mound, only to dislodge what appeared to be several wooden coffins, breaking them apart in the process. He watched in horror as dust and fragments of something like bone drained into the swampy water.

Upset that he had disturbed what appeared to be a gravesite, he stopped his operation, got out, and went in closer to investigate. The coffins seemed to be carved, or "riven," from juniper wood, a particularly solid wood that resists deterioration even if submerged in water for hundreds of years. He claimed they appeared to be Indian canoes cut in half and joined together with wooden pegs, a headrest carved out at one end. Some say he also insisted that there was a strange cross and letters carved on the top, others only an embellishment to the story through the years. No one seemed to know for sure.

Miles from civilization, the dredge operator made the decision to dig a large hole on high ground close by, placing what remained of the coffins in it. Then he left to report to his supervisors. But hindered by the lack of efficient travel to that area, no telephone, and no sense of great urgency, it would be weeks before they arrived at the site. By then there had been several big storms and lots of rain. Vines and weeds covered the area. No trace of the coffins anywhere. The swamp had reclaimed the dead.

She stopped reading, took a ragged breath. *This was huge.* If her father had found them, what would he have done with them? Who would he have told?

She read on. There was a mention of the ECU archaeologist, Dr. Phelps, discrepancies in reports given by the supervisor and inaccuracies in field notes. The result was that the coffins had never been found since then and no one with any authority or credentials seemed interested enough to dig. Shortly after the land became part of the National Wildlife Refuge, digging forbidden for good.

She flipped the pictures over. *Nothing.* Not even a date.

She started calculating in her head. Her father had died at the age of twenty-six. He grew up in East Lake, not far from the old Beechland territory, deeper inland where few people dared venture, a protected wildlife refuge now. He was getting a graduate degree in archaeology, which meant he was probably studying under this Dr. Phelps.

Of course, even she knew Phelps. He was a legend, an expert in the Woodland Indians of coastal North Carolina. She had read everything he had ever written.

No doubt her father would have fished and hunted those swamps, known them like the back of his hand. These stories took place in his backyard, may even have inspired his decision to become an archaeologist. If anyone could have found them, it would have been him.

She pushed everything aside, leaned her head

back on the pillow, switched off the light, her mind playing over all the possibilities, sifting through the facts.

She was being stalked by a man whose father had connections to Andrew Warren and Steve Strayhorn.

But that could be a coincidence. He was an attorney. It was a small world down here.

Besides, Aunt Polly had implied that her father's friends had been upset by his death. Had she been referring to Steve and Anna Lee? Either they were very good actors, or they hadn't seen his death coming.

And if her father had been murdered by those who wanted to get their hands on the coffins, surely the news would have surfaced by now.

Unless someone didn't want those coffins to be found.

Anger began to bubble, acid in her gut. Her father had been a young man, a good man who loved his family. A promising archaeologist.

If he was murdered, that changed everything.

🜂

Virginia
1591

They sit on the beach alone, mother and child, in the same spot they sit every day, perched high and sheltered from the wind between two dunes, with clear views in all directions. In front of them stretches the endless blue-green Atlantic, white waves cascading rhythmically against the sandy shore. Behind them lies the wintry gold maritime marsh and bog, its backdrop a glittering body of saltwater their friends, the Croatan – or at least what are left of them – call the Pamlico.

It is cold on the beach, but there is no wind, thanks be to God. Fingers numb, exhausted with the effort of gathering wood, she feeds the weak flames of a small watchfire with bits of dry driftwood, trying to stay awake. She tires easily these days. She is with child again.

The thought frightens her witless.

But not Virginia. Nothing frightens this happy child. Cloaked in remnants of her mother's tattered woolen cloak she plays, carefully measuring sand with her favorite conch shell. She pours and sifts into a broken piece of gourd, pretending to bake corncakes on a slab of driftwood, too wet and doughty to burn.

This is where they will stay all day until the sun dips on the horizon. Then one of the men will relieve her mother and they will go back to the palisade. The watch fire will burn all night, if it doesn't rain.

At first the "watching game" was fun. But now Virginia grows weary, whining as only a small child can, like a persistent mosquito. Eyes trained on the horizon, Eleanor tries to ignore her daughter's bids for attention, then finally pulls her into her arms.

Help me look for the ship, Ginny! Help me look for your grandfather!

But even Virginia can tell from the pinched gray look on her face and her red-rimmed eyes that this is a game that has worn thin for them both. For in truth Virginia knows nothing of ships or grandfathers, those words meaningless except for the pain that flares in her mother's eyes when she talks of them, the angry words that batter at her father.

What are we going to do Ananias? We must do something. We are starving!

But Virginia doesn't understand their worries. Her belly is full. She is the princess of Hatteras Island; everyone loves her. This is the only life she has ever known, this sand, these waves, the wind and the sun. She has no concept of the home her mother laments, the place she calls Cornwall. A wall of corn, how strange.

Her father says the world is her oyster. That makes her laugh too. Oysters are so ugly.

She loves her world, delights in the familiar touch of the brown hands that weave baskets, grows corn, nurses her mother when she suffers her terrible headaches. She is a child of the forest, the ocean, the sky. This is her home and it always will be no matter what her mother claims.

But now she wilts back into her mother's arms, sad. The sun is setting, going to its home in Papgusso below the horizon, and still he has not come, her secret friend. She has been waiting all day, and to a small child that is an eternity. She frets, sticks her bottom lip out, turns her face into her mother's bony chest. What if he has forgotten her?

But there, just as baby tears begin to sting her eyes, her tiny ears quicken to the trill of a bird, the sound she has been waiting for all day, a signal!

Careful now she wiggles up out of her mother's lap, pretends to wander aimlessly down the beach, shorebirds scattering in her wake. She stops and examines a shell, one eye on her mother, the other watching the thatch of sea oats on the dune just ahead.

She knows he is there.

The first time he played this game with her she was only a toddler. She and her mother had been sitting on a wool blanket on the beach, eating a picnic. Back then food was not so scarce and her mother's face not quite so lined and harried.

She wandered away down the beach, laughing and clapping as white birds whirled around her, dove and spun. She turned and there he was, crouched down in the sea oats, hiding in the dunes.

She was startled, but no more than if she'd seen a rabbit or a deer. Brown-skinned men with tattoos, naked except for a loin cloth, were common in her world, a comforting presence. They were the ones who fed her bits of food, carved toys for her, made sure she didn't wander.

But this one was different somehow, taller, his face a study in hard edges and scars, hairless chest devoid of the usual clinking beads or copper that would give his presence away to any but her. A small bird skeleton and feathers dangle from his

hank of jet black hair. She might have been frightened if it hadn't been for his smile—a smile so
dazzling that it rivaled the sun.

And it was meant only for her.

She sees that smile now, and the dark glittering
orbs gazing out at her from behind the dunes, tenderness masking calculation.

Delighted, she forgets to pretend and runs toward
him. But his sudden scowl stops her, confuses her.
She does not see what he sees, that her mother is
craning her neck from her outpost, eyes dimmed
by hunger and weariness, calling out to her daughter.

Virginia! Don't go so far, you hear?

She stops in her tracks, gazes back at her mother,
plops down in the sand, pretending to be looking
at something. She knows that if her mother rises
and comes after her, her friend will disappear, vanishing into the landscape as if he had never been
there at all, the only evidence the gifts he leaves
behind—a pretty shell, a feather, a flower.

Her mother lies back down. Now her friend
smiles and nods at her encouragingly, pointing
toward an abandoned nest in the crook of a piece
of driftwood, pretty rocks piled in it like eggs. He
raises a single finger to his lips to quiet her, then
like smoke vanishes into thin air.

She wants to cry and beg him to come back. If
only he would take her with him! But she knows
he is watching her, even if she does not always see
him. That is a comfort to her.

Happy now, wild and free, she runs back to her
mother, rocky treasures tucked into her apron
pocket, heart singing a song.

Later, when the fog surrounds their little cabin, when the cold seeps through the cracks, and a thin ice begins to form over the water in their gourd bucket, she will sing herself to sleep. She will snuggle down into her corn shuck mattress, rocks clutched in a pudgy little fist, tucked under her chin. Only then will she fall into a deep sleep and dream the innocent dreams of a child. In them she laughs and giggles, skips and dances, sings the songs of the people her mother calls savages, runs and plays with her friend. She is an Indian maiden and he is her prince, her weroance.

Of course, her mother knows none of this. Instead, Eleanor watches the expressions on her daughter's face as she is sleeping, fearing her child's demons—what if she has been cursed with the second sight too?

For that wretched killing fog, that terrible fog has followed her all the way across the sea, has found her even here. Even now it hides in the woods and the swamps, waiting to claim her and those she loves, like it claimed her first baby. She can hear it in the rattle in the chest of her husband, see it in the pinched, hungry faces of the colonists. Their eyes follow her everywhere she goes, blaming her and Ananias for their predicament, she the daughter of John White, the man who brought them here, only to abandon them. Where is her father now?

Likely in a watery grave. Or did the fog find him too?

Her hands trembling, she places a cross over Virginia's tiny bed, praying for protection as a gray mist settles and swirls around their tiny cabin, praying for the sighting of a ship before they must leave to go into the mainland on the morrow, praying for the safety of her daughter.

But most of all she prays that the woods of Beechland will hide them from their arch enemy, Wanchese, king of the dreaded Secotan, who has dared to send her a secret message:

> *I will slaughter each one of you, pick you off*
> *one by one when you least expect it.*
> *The crows will peck out your eyes and wild*
> *dogs will feast on your flesh.*
> *I will spare you only if you give me your*
> *daughter.*

PART II

CHAPTER NINE

ANDREA RAN, FEET POUNDING ACROSS
the miles of empty beach stretching out in
front of her, heart in her throat. An early morning salty fog shrouded the dunes, crusting her lips
and hair. Gulls wheeled and dove, like the thoughts
wheeling and diving in her head.

Her father was murdered, she was sure of it.

But who could she trust? She didn't have enough
evidence to present to authorities. Until she figured
out some things, spilling her guts to just anyone
could be dangerous, even after all these years.

She thought about calling Doc. He would tell
her what to do.

But not yet. She needed to find out more about
her father. She would reach out to Doc when the
time came, hopefully sooner than later.

By the time her Fitbit registered a mile she had
made up her mind. She would start by going to
Columbia to ask questions, reconstruct her father's
life as best she could.

Not that she had any illusions that she could
solve a case as cold as this on her own, but at least
she could learn more about the kind of person he
had been and how he had lived. That was why she

had come down here in the first place.

Five miles later she was back in the Airstream ready for the day at six a.m. Remembering at the last minute to scan the pictures and the last letter into her phone, she hid originals in a pocket in her knapsack, tucked inside the journal. The ashes could stay in her Jeep. Everything else she would leave behind.

The hard part was leaving Henry in Manteo at the vet's office. His parting look of worry and betrayal sent arrows straight to her heart. It was all she could do not to change her mind, grab him out of the vet tech's arms, and go straight home.

She filled up with gas in Mann's Harbor, and with the free cup of coffee that came with the purchase and headed back west on Hwy 64. But by the time she reached the mainland she tossed the bitter contents out the window. Her stomach rumbled with hunger, but she was too tense to eat anything.

At least the weather was perfect. The miles to Columbia sped by this time, each landmark familiar now, as if she had lived here for years. The "black water" canals that flanked each side of the two-lane highway teemed with wildlife, wood ducks, and various reptilian creatures—croaking frogs, at least one water snake winding through the canal, and turtles sunning on logs. White lilies floating on the water shone like stars in the night sky.

But the closer she came to East Lake, the harder it was to fight the fear. With each passing landmark, she relived the day before. There was the spot where she'd had the flat tire. There was the beach at Old Ferry Landing, now the scene of a possible murder. She shuddered as she passed over the bridge, all the peace she'd garnered on her last trip here now gone.

By the time she reached the edges of town she was jittery as a feral cat, eyes darting up and down side streets, sure that any minute she'd see Scott's white truck. She parked behind the library on a side street in the most inconspicuous place she could find, careful to stay out of the line of sight of Main Street and the Inn where she had stayed across the street.

At least the library felt safe. When she opened the green metal door and stepped inside the cool, dim interior, the familiar mustiness of old books, dry ink, and years of lemon oil polish soothed her frayed nerves. She'd spent so much of her life hiding in places just like this, poring over old Archaeological Reviews and research papers, dreaming of the day when she would be published too, a young Harrison Ford in the making. She wondered if her father had sat in this library, dreaming the same dreams when he was a child. The thought sent chills down her arms. She'd lost count of the times she'd awakened the night before; stared at the photographs yet again.

Walking toward the front desk, she spotted a petite dark-haired woman sitting on a bar stool behind the desk, tapping on a keyboard, staring at a white screen. Andrea approached her and spoke, her voice respectfully low.

"Hi. I hope you can help me?"

Brown eyes topped by fierce black eyebrows gazed back at her, shining brightly behind dark Harry Potter frames. She looked so much like an inquisitive little sparrow that Andrea almost laughed."Yes?" she chirped.

"I'm visiting the area to do a bit of family research. Do you have an archive of the local newspapers going back to 1980? I need to find an obituary but I don't have a date of death."

"No problem. Follow me," she instructed, waving Andrea toward a bank of computers against a far wall, her Birkenstocks thumping purposely against the worn commercial carpet, coin earrings swaying in time. When they reached the computers, the woman turned toward her.

"Here you go…just log in as a Tyrell County guest and you should be good to go," she said, striding off again.

But a half hour later she was still hunting. If her Aunt Polly had died since the postmark on her last letter it sure hadn't made the newspapers. Frustrated, she headed back to the front desk.

"I can't find a thing. Maybe she moved away. Did you ever hear of a woman around here by the name of Polly Vestal? I don't know if that was her maiden name or married. She would be very elderly."

The librarian pursed her mouth then shook her head. "You might want to do a county census search," she advised.

"I tried that. She was listed in a census back in 2000, but nothing since. Her letters had a Columbia postmark but it was a post office box, not a street address." She hated how whiny she sounded, but she hadn't expected to hit a dead end so soon.

"Well, I'm sorry honey. Folks around here can be secretive. They don't like the government too much. Are you sure she died?" Then, tapping her pencil against her cheek, "If you leave me your number I'll be glad to call you should I think of something else."

Andrea jotted down her contact information on a Post It note, handed it over, and said good-bye. Then she stopped, remembering something. Maybe her father's death had been covered in the newspapers. She turned back around.

"Ma'am, I need to go back to those newspaper archives again. My father was a local from over in East Lake. He supposedly committed suicide over on the banks at Old Ferry Landing back in the eighties. Do you think that there is a possibility it was covered in the news?"

The woman's eyes softened. "Ah, honey, that's terrible. I'm sure it must have been, though likely it would have been covered in the Manteo newspaper since that's in Dare County. I'll take you to that archive." And as she led Andrea back to a micro-fiche she added, "By the way, I know how you must feel. I had a brother to do that a long time ago. Always there in the back of my mind," she whispered, offering Andrea a seat at the machine.

Andrea only nodded. What else could she say?

This time her search only took a minute. Not that the short article told her anything she didn't already know. With one exception. Right there about halfway down— *Talton*—the name of the officer who had found her father's body, and the one that had harassed Aunt Polly and Willie, had to be.

Excited now, she logged out of the archive and into a browser, but when she searched for the name in the area nothing came up. Thanking the librarian again, she grabbed her knapsack and headed out the back door toward the county sheriff's office, located in a small red brick building next to the county courthouse a few blocks away. She had passed it driving in. Maybe they would know this Talton. She took off on foot, cutting through the back streets.

The office was tiny, like the town, looking much like it had at the turn of the century when it was built. Inside, it was like stepping into the sheriff's office in Mayberry. She wouldn't have been surprised to see Andy Griffith behind the desk, leaning back in his chair and grinning.

Instead she was greeted by a rather hefty, matronly woman appearing to be in her mid-fifties or early sixties, hair teased into a perfect jet-black helmet. Cigarette fumes wafting across the large gunmetal gray desk circled her head. It was all Andrea could do not to cough and choke trying to introduce herself.

"I'm Andrea. I hope someone can help me. I need some information about a death that happened back in the eighties, over at Old Ferry Landing at East Lake."

"Well, I'll do my best," the woman offered, raising her eyebrows. "I'm Mildred, by the way."

"My father's name was Andrew Warren," Something about the woman put her nerves on edge.

Mildred narrowed her eyes and cocked her head.

"Honey, are you sure you want to go through with this? Might be better to just let the dead rest in peace," she stated, dropping her eyes to the papers on her desk, ball point pen poised in the air.

"All I want to know is the truth."

Mildred gazed at her, eyes hooded. "Well, ask away."

"I found a newspaper article naming the deputy who discovered his body, Fred Talton. I think he was a Dare County officer. Did you know him?" She tensed, waiting for a snappy comeback.

"Yeah, I ran into him from time to time. I can call over there and ask for you, if you'd like. I'm sure someone will remember something." Before Andrea could respond Mildred had dialed the number and was speaking to someone.

"Retired and moved down to Florida, huh? Fort Myers area you think." She went quiet for a moment, then chuckled. "Well, don't that beat all? I'd be jealous too." She paused, listened a moment, then her mouth drooped. "Sorry to hear that. Hey, thanks for your help. See you at the conference next week in Raleigh, okay? You too. Bye now."

Mildred put down the phone and stared at it for a moment. When she lifted her gaze upward toward Andrea, her face was a mask, her voice blunt.

"Found him face down in the canal behind his trailer a couple of weeks back. Daughter-in-law claims he was being treated for prostate cancer. Son says he had struggled with depression off and on all his life." She looked down again, shuffled papers.

Andrea was stunned. "Did the person you were talking to mention her name?"

"Nope, and if I were you I'd let her alone," Mildred replied. "Folks around here don't like outsiders prying into their business, especially when they are grieving."

Andrea bristled. "Well, this *is* my business. And

I'm grieving too, by the way. My mother died three weeks ago. That's what started this whole thing."

Mildred stared at her, eyes hooded like an old bird. "Sorry for your loss. But I don't see that gives you the right to meddle in other folk's business."

This wasn't going well. She was an archaeologist, for Pete's sake, not a detective. Sucking in her breath, she gave it one last shot.

"Okay. Maybe you can help me with something that *is* my business. I'm looking for an old aunt of mine. Polly Vestal."

Mildred barked a laugh, wagged her head. "Miss Polly? Everybody knew her, knew your Daddy too. Got an old trailer up the river here. I knew the minute you came in here who you was. You look a lot like him you know."

Andrea tensed. Mildred got a faraway look in her eye.

"He was a quiet thing. But Polly Vestal? Now she was a character. Came in here at least once a week to complain about something or the other. Yeah, she was a regular all right. She hated tourists, hunters, and moonshiners, though not in exactly that order. Some people thought she was crazy as a loon, but Polly was sharp as a tack. If people thought she was crazy it was only because she wanted it that way. Not me. I kind of got a kick out of her," she said, chuckling. She threw down her pen and gazed at Andrea inquisitively. "I've not seen her since she got put in that nursing home over in Creswell. She okay?"

Her question seemed innocent enough, but there was something in the set of her face that made Andrea's skin crawl.

"I have no idea. I never met her. All I remember is getting a few Christmas cards from her, but they stopped coming when I was in high school."

"And what do you want to know about your Daddy?"

"Anything you can tell me. All I know is that he and my Mom were separated because he was never home much. She said he kept coming back here to East Lake on the weekends, working on an archaeological dig. You know how these things go…" she said, unwilling to say more.

Mildred rolled her eyes a bit, waved her hand like she was shooing off an annoying fly.

"Well, that's interesting, but no, I don't recall him talking about his work. Had no idea what he was studying in college. Of course, the locals around here are always finding lots of Indian stuff. I'm part Indian myself. My people and the Warrens were distant kin I think, not that we'd claim each other." She busied herself sorting papers.

So that was it. No telling who was related in a small town like this, what grudges people held.

"Is there anything else?" Andrea asked.

Mildred shrugged; threw her hands up in the air.

"Listen, I'm not trying to be a hard ass. It's just that I've learned not to talk too much in my position, okay? Only stirs up trouble." She stopped, put her elbows on her desk, red nails clicking when they formed a temple in the air.

"His Daddy would go on a bender every now and then, took it out on his family. We sent a deputy out there a few times, called Social Services." Mildred stared at her, distaste oozing in her voice.

Andrea didn't flinch. She wouldn't give the

woman the satisfaction.

"From what I heard, Jane Warren was a saint, and a hard worker too, I'll give her that much. But she should've never married that man. When your grandmother Jane died, Andy went to live with Polly, Jane's sister. Back then Polly lived way out, up near Gum Neck. If it weren't for her and a few of his buddies from high school, I don't know what would have happened to him. He was a scrawny thing, but nice looking. After he went off to college I'd see him every now and then in town, always muddy and in a hurry."

Muddy and in a hurry. Her mother had always used that phrase to describe her childhood.

"I'd heard he got married and had a baby, then split up. Gossip around here flies, if you know what I mean." Andrea could only nod, tongue-tied.

"Honestly, I felt real sad when I heard he died. None of us knew the boy was in that bad of a way. Then not long after that his Daddy died too. You'd think those old coots would know better than to drink that poison they make." She shook her head back and forth.

Andrea bit her tongue, her response cool, but polite.

"Well, thanks. Interesting, but you didn't tell me anything I hadn't already figured out. Listen, can you tell me where Polly lived before she went into the nursing home?

"She had a trailer up on the Alligator River. It's not worth much I don't think. I'm sure it's on record in the county courthouse, maybe a deed or something. But if I were you I'd check out that nursing home." She opened her bottom desk drawer and dug out her pocketbook. Clearly the interview was over.

"Thanks, I'll do that. But I need to ask one last thing. Do you know a Willie Batts? I was told he was her friend."

Her eyes narrowed. "Honey, you don't want to be getting up with the likes of Willie Batts. He's an old alcoholic who latched onto Polly years ago. We all told her to steer clear of him, but she felt sorry for him, helped get him sober, even bought him an old boat. Claims he's descended from the famous explorer, Nathaniel Batts, but that's probably just the liquor talking. Everyone around here is related to somebody famous, especially when they're drunk."

"Is he still around? I'd like to at least talk to him."

"Well, yeah, you'll probably find him down on the town docks. That's where he stays between rounds. He goes out crabbing in the early morning, then back out fishing in the afternoon. He comes and goes." By then she was nudging Andrea toward the door. "Listen, I've got a lunch date. Good luck now. Sorry I couldn't help you more." And before she could respond Andrea was left on the sidewalk, her head spinning. Mildred got into her vehicle and drove off.

Andrea stood there, rattled. Spying a concrete bench under a mimosa tree off to the side of the parking lot she sat down, began sorting things out, lightheaded from needing food and the stress of the ugliness of the picture she had in her head—a thin, dark man with fists raised, a haggard-looking woman crying in the background, the terrified eyes of a defenseless child.

It didn't help when the courthouse clock began chiming the noon hour, its sonorous tolling reminding her of a funeral, the funeral her father had never had. Misty-eyed, she imagined him sitting on this same bench as a boy. Had he been afraid to go home?

But what good was it doing to stir all of this up now? It had nothing to do with his death. She might as well go on back to Manteo, file a petition to reopen the case, and let Dare County law enforcement handle everything.

Still, she felt this compulsion to visit Polly, if only to see for herself what the woman looked like. The least she could do was let her know she hadn't been forgotten, say her goodbyes.

But first she needed food. As she considered her options a gray unmarked SUV pulled into the dirt parking lot. Curious, she watched a man emerge, surprised at how tall he was, how blonde. Even from this distance she could see that he had the rugged good looks of a woodsman, but the polish and dress of an educated man. A bit older than her perhaps, maybe in his late thirties. The holstered gun hanging from his belt let her know right away he was an officer of the law in plain clothes.

She wasn't too concerned until he started walking toward her across the grassy lawn. She clutched the knapsack, felt her heart quicken, but he smiled and extended his hand.

"Hey, I'm Derek. Mildred called me. Said you might need rescuing," he offered, his smile wide. Without waiting for an invitation, he plopped himself down beside her like he'd known her all her life, elbows propped on the back of the bench.

"So, are you doing hard time on this bench for a reason?"

The line was so cheesy she laughed out loud, his boyish mannerisms so unaffected she stifled the urge to reach out and pat him on his head. Instead she shook his hand.

"I'm Andrea, Derek. Nice to meet you. I was simply contemplating where to eat lunch in such a small town. And yes, this town needs some comfortable benches."

"Easier to hose pigeon poop off the concrete than wood. What is it with courthouses and pigeons anyway?"

"I don't know. Maybe it's the peanut gallery?" grinning at him to soften the words.

"Aha! Now, that's good. I'll have to remember that one."

Then his smile faded.

"Looks like something's weighing heavy on your mind. Can I help?"

She bristled. "So, Mildred couldn't wait to run her mouth?"

"Mildred never did have much of a bedside manner." He glanced at her sideways and winked.

She looked away, trying to decide if she was angry.

"Well, I'm a big girl, I can take it. Be easier once I get some lunch in me. Anything good around here?"

He grinned. "Well, imagine that, Andrea. We both need to eat. And that little café right across the street cooks the best burgers around. Walk with me and I'll regale you with all my charms, like how I catch crooks, help damsels in distress, and generally save the world."

She bristled. Had he thought she was hinting?

"It is kind of you to offer but I think I will pass. Enjoy that burger." She stood up to go.

He touched her arm. "Listen. We both need food. We'll go Dutch, dine in public. Service is fast. I won't even ask for your telephone number afterwards, I promise."

She hesitated. He seemed to be a nice enough guy. But then, she'd thought the same thing about Scott. It helped that he made her laugh. It wouldn't be a bad idea to be seen hanging out with law enforcement, especially if Scott was still in stalker mode. What could it hurt?

"Well, if you insist," she countered, smiling.

As they crossed the street making small talk, she kept her eyes open. No white Dodge truck and better yet, no sign of Scott. As Derek promised, the service was quick, the smell of French fries and onions intoxicating.

"Hey, there's a picnic table out on the deck overlooking the water. Will that work?" Within moments they were seated at the rough wooden table, tearing the wrapping off their food.

"These onion rings are awesome."

Derek nodded. "I pretty much eat there every day when I'm in town. Not that I'm here that often. I know every greasy spoon between here and Raleigh. Trust me, this one beats them all." To illustrate he picked up his burger, examined it appreciatively, and chomped down.

"How long have you been in law enforcement?"

"Hmm... let's see... it will be three years in August - three long years."

"Really? I thought you'd be passionate about upholding the law. You seem like the type. Are you a Deputy?"

"Yes, and I *am* passionate about the law, just not in this capacity. I have an MBA from the Fuquay School of Business at Carolina, 2009. I had some grand idea that I'd start my own company or something. If you remember that was the year that everything collapsed. No one was hiring and it was a bad time for startups so I enlisted in the Marine Corps as an officer. That got me two terms in Iraq and Afghanistan in Special Forces, training new recruits. After my last one I decided it was time to hang up my uniform, took this job so I could be close to home. How about you?"

"Well, I studied archaeology. Now I'm taking a break to learn more about my family before I head back to Charlotte and look for a job. Family here?" she asked, hoping to divert him.

"Nope, don't fit that profile either. Married for a short while out of college, but the military ruined that. We parted friends, no children. She's remarried, happily this time I think." He looked up at her, grinned. "He's rich, that helps. I was never ambitious enough for her."

He licked ketchup off his fingers. "So, I came back here to nurse my wounds and keep an eye on my Mom. My Dad passed away awhile back. Oh, and I have a dog. And a couple of cousins." Then, "Hey, they should hire you on the newspaper here. You'd make a great investigative reporter."

Andrea winced at the jab. "Sorry. I guess I'm on edge with strangers. My Mom died recently, then some guy down here started stalking me." Avoiding his eyes, she reached for an onion ring but dropped it again, no longer hungry.

"Good Lord, girl. No wonder. What happened? To your Mom, I mean."

"Heart attack. No history of heart problems, none that I knew of anyway."

"Tough. Sorry to hear that."

"Thanks." Then, "I hope it's okay, but I need to ask you a question." "Sure, fire away. I'll do my best."

Andrea shoved the remains of her lunch away, leaned across the table.

"The guy I mentioned, the stalker? Short version of the story is that he sat down next to me in a restaurant in Nags Head when I was here, about three weeks ago. We chatted. I had a flat tire out on Hwy 64. He came along behind me, stopped, and fixed it. Seemed like a very nice guy, so we had dinner, down at the Rusty Bucket. Then I had to leave town that night to rush to the hospital. I forgot to let him know. Besides, I figured I'd never see him again." She paused, caught her breath, resumed. "Anyway, and this is the hard part, when he called a week later and I told him what had happened, he acted like he didn't know a thing. Then he got all nice, invited me to stay in his guest cottage while I sorted through everything that had happened. At first I declined then I thought about it. I needed to take care of some business down here. So, I took him up on his offer…."

Derek gazed at her, his face impassive.

"I know, I know. It was stupid of me. But remember, I was in shock."

She sighed. He must think she was an idiot.

"How did he act?"

"At first it was okay. No alarms bells. In fact, he was a perfect gentleman. He cooked dinner for me and we talked."

"But that wasn't enough, was it?" he offered, face grim.

"No, he didn't hit on me if that's what you think. But as dinner progressed he seemed on edge, worried about something. I was tired, began thinking I'd made a mistake, especially when I told him I'd seen someone in the upstairs window as I walked to the house. He blew it off as a broken window. It kind of irritated me. I know what I saw. I decided to cut the evening short, go to bed early. But the next day he took off to some mysterious meeting up in Norfolk, told me if I needed anything to make myself at home. I was alone there and spooked. So I left, headed to the beach for a while."

"When did you start to get suspicious?"

"Not right away. If you want to know the truth though, I was kind of relieved he left. It gave me some time to go through some things I'd inherited from my mother. I needed privacy to do it on my own terms."

"That's understandable."

"Yeah, it was fine until I went up to the big house to find something to pry open a trunk the things were stored in. He'd said to make myself at home so I didn't think too much about it. But this is where it gets crazy. While I was up there I found my mother's telephone number written down on a scrap of paper, a landline that was unpublished. It freaked me out. I started poking around, saw his laptop, and the browser was open. After all, if he'd wanted to hide anything, I figured he would have shut the thing down."

Derek sat up, frowning. "Find anything?"

"Yes. And it frightened me. He had pictures of me taken from a distance at my mother's funeral. And pictures of her house from all different angles. The thing is, I'd never told him exactly where she lived. And he'd done all kinds of searches on my career, links to all kinds of information about my life."

His eyebrows lifted. "No wonder you freaked out."

"It gets worse. I poked around in an old desk and found an address book that belonged to his father. Get this, I found my father's name, and some others close to him. Of course, this could all be a coincidence, but it just seemed strange to me. Too strange."

His eyes widened. "That must have scared the hell out of you."

"Yes, it did. But this is the part I don't get. Why would he leave his computer open like that and risk me finding out?"

He shrugged. "Some stalkers like to play cat and mouse, you know. Adds more spice to the game." He sighed, "Listen, how can I help?"

"Any chance you could run a background check and see if he has a history of this sort of thing? It creeps me out knowing he might still be following me."

"Well, I'll have to warn you, guys like this can be pretty evasive. What's his name?" He wiped his hands on his pants, then pulled his phone out of his pocket.

"Scott McWilliams. He lives on the Montrose Planation outside of Edenton. Supposedly he teaches at the College of the Albemarle. His wife died in the World Trade Center on 9/11. At least that was the story he told me."

"Let me work on it. If anything turns up, I'll let you know. What's your cell number?" He took a pen out of his shirt pocket, wrote her name on a clean napkin, slid them both across the table.

She hesitated. But how could he help her if he didn't know how to contact her?

She scribbled her number next to her name, then slid the napkin and pen back. "Thanks Derek. It helps knowing someone has my back."

"No problem. If McWilliams gives you any more trouble, give me a buzz." He slid his business card across the table, then his pen back in his shirt pocket, tucking the napkin away. "This won't be the first time I've had to throw cold water on a dog in heat. A smart, good-looking woman like you shows up in a small town like this and the pea brains around here take a nosedive, if you know what I mean."

"Yeah, I do," she replied, chuckling.

Still smiling she stood, brushing crumbs. "Thanks again. I'll wait to hear from you." Waving goodbye, she took off walking back down to the street toward her car. When she turned to wave again he was already on the phone.

Well that was something anyway. But what to do next?

Willie Batts. If she was quick she might catch him before he went back out on the water.

But then, maybe it would be better to visit Aunt

Polly before she approached Willie. At least she could rule out paranoia. If the old woman started going on about government spies, that would change everything.

Within minutes she was on the road headed toward the nursing home. As she passed the creek, she spied a hawk flying directly over the bridge in front of her car, a small snake dangling from its beak. *Aha!* The hunter slaying evil. She smiled.

Now that had to be a good omen.

☙

"Excuse me; I'm here to visit a woman by the name of Polly Vestal."

"Why yes ma'am. Miss Polly's in room 305. Right down that hall."

Well, that was easy enough.

Walking down the hall she couldn't help but cringe at the moans, the pitiful eyes and clutching hands, and worse, the faint smell of urine that permeated the air. She finally reached Room 305. Aunt Polly sat slumped over in a wheelchair, staring at a television screen blaring on the other side of the room.

Her great aunt. How sad and strange that she'd never met her before now.

Despite the woman's age, right away she spotted their strong resemblance, mainly in the cut of the chin, the shape of her head. Thin white hair stuck out in odd angles around a puddle of wrinkles and sags, her toothless mouth a crater. She wore a bib over a shapeless housedress, and bedroom shoes. She didn't acknowledge Andrea's presence, only stared at a game show as if in a trance.

Bending down in front of her, she whispered "Aunt Polly." Nothing.

Not knowing what else to do, Andrea walked over to the television and turned the volume down, standing in front of the screen to block her aunt's view.

Polly scowled and huffed, then looked away, mute like the screen.

Andrea tried again, more cheerful and upbeat. "Aunt Polly, remember me? You used to send me Christmas cards. You knew me when I was a baby."

A blink and a scowl.

Frustrated, her voice a notch louder, more insistent. "Do you remember Andy? Andy lived with you. You took care of him after Jane died."

Polly's eyes widened, mouth turning down in a mournful howl. "Jane? Is that you? Jane? Jane?" She seemed frantic, swinging her head back and forth, looking around the room.

"No, I'm Andrea, Andy Warren's daughter. Andy died, remember?" She reached out, patted her arm.

As abruptly as she had gotten upset, she calmed. She nodded sadly, head wagging up and down now. "Andy…" she whispered, rheumy eyes searching the room. Then without warning she reached out, grabbed Andrea by the wrist, and stared deep into her eyes, her own green eyes piercing and sharp.

"Did you get my letters?" the old woman demanded, her voice firm and clear.

The transformation was so abrupt Andrea stammered. "Yes, Aunt Polly, I found them in the trunk," then in a rush, "My mama, Celeste, she died. I'm sorry but she never read them. She didn't tell me about you." Her eyes filled. "I'm so sorry. We didn't know!"

Polly's stare went blank, then fierce. "Hide them, you hear? And don't talk to Talton," she hissed.

"You don't have to worry about Talton anymore Aunt Polly. He's dead."

She drew back, snatched her hand away, and began moaning, "Anna Lee? Where's Anna Lee?" Then she turned on Andrea, suddenly hostile. "Who are you! You're hurting me! Stop! Get away from me!" she shouted, fear and confusion disfiguring her contorted face. Andrea ran out of the room looking for help, almost running into a young, plump strawberry blonde nursing assistant standing just outside of the door.

"I'm so sorry. I didn't mean to hurt her! I was only hoping she would remember me."

"Oh, don't worry honey, she does this all the time," the girl crooned in a distinctive flat coastal brogue, patting Andrea on the shoulder. "Lord, she's one stubborn lady. Probably why she's lived so long." She smiled, patted her again. "Let me go check on her okay?" she added, heading into Polly's room.

Andrea stood in the hall and waited. Within minutes the nurse reemerged. "She's fine. Already dozing off. But I'm curious. You said you were a niece, right?"

"Yes, she's my great aunt, or at least I'm pretty sure she is. Our family was estranged and we all thought she was dead. Now, I'm afraid it may be too late."

"I'm sorry shug. It's hard with Alzheimer's. Did she know who you were?"

"I'm not sure but I think so. I just hate I upset

her so badly."

"Oh, it ain't you, honey. She has good days and bad. Sad to watch her go downhill so fast. Give us a call if you decide to come back again. We'll make sure to have her up and dressed. You can take her out in the garden." She smiled and leaned in conspiratorially. "Bring some cookies. She loves cookies."

"Thanks, I will." Then, as an afterthought, "Honestly, I don't know how you do this every day."

"Oh, you get used to it. My aunt and uncle own the place so I practically grew up here. You enjoy your day, okay? We'll take care of Miss Polly." She smiled again, then turned and padded off down the hall, rubber tennis shoes squeaking on the tile.

Andrea stood there a moment. Something about the girl was familiar, but she couldn't put a finger on it. Well, at least she had been helpful.

Outside, she made a beeline for her car, head pounding. After the dim hell of the nursing home, the sunshine felt good on her shoulders. Polly's words rang out in her head.

Don't talk to Talton.

It wasn't much to go on, but at least it was a beginning. She dialed 411, asking for Fort Myers. But there was no listing for anyone by the name of Talton.

She needed to check in with her Aunt Connie. If she didn't her aunt would no doubt call her and barrage her with a hundred questions, but she would deal with that tonight when she got back home. The digital clock on her phone read 3:00 p.m. She still had time to find Willie Batts.

She headed back toward Columbia.

CHAPTER TEN

THE HARD PART WAS FINDING the docks, tucked back in at the end of a dirt road. It was exactly the kind of place she knew she should probably avoid, for now anyway. But once the narrow lane opened to the water, the place wasn't as scary as she thought it would be. Lonely, but peaceful, pines rustling in the breeze, needles soft under her feet. Sunlight dappled the water.

No wonder Willie practically lived down here. It was the perfect place for a troubled life

to start over. No state park though, getting a good whiff of drying out fish scales and motor oil.

She spotted him right away. He was sitting in an old camouflage flat-bottomed boat tied up down at the end of the dock, right where Mildred said he would be. He might be a rough character, but he looked like a typical old fisherman to her, skin wrinkled from years in the sun and water, hair grizzly under a dirty old ball cap, lower half of his faded plaid shirt stained from grease and motor oil. He was bent over, fiddling around in his tackle box, blue smoke from a cigarette dangling from his lips, curling lazy swirls upward around his head.

"Excuse me. I'm looking for Willie Batts," she

called out as she walked toward him down the pier.

He stiffened, not looking up even though by then she was practically standing over him. She decided he was hard of hearing, when he looked up at her, squinted, then mumbled, "Yes ma'am. That would be me," as if the answer should be obvious. Then he looked back down again, picking at a lure. She noticed that his hands, liver-spotted, shook.

"Well, I'm Andrea Warren, Polly Vestal's great niece."

He wouldn't look at her or answer; dropped the lure back into the tackle box and snorted.

She tried again. "I'm sorry, maybe you didn't hear me," but before she could finish he grabbed the butt of the cigarette between two fingers, swung around to stare at her, lips curled in a snarl.

"I know who you are. You Andy Warren's kid, ain't you?" His tone was cold, with barely concealed contempt.

"Yes sir, I am," she whispered, caught off guard. But just like that, the fire in him died down. "Well, it took you long enough. Too long if you ask me. Polly done lost her mind." He spat into the water, stuck the butt back into his mouth.

"It's not my fault," she retorted. "I was only a child. I promise you if I had known I would have been here long before now." She shivered. She needed a sweater.

He cocked his head up at her, squinted in the sun. "Well, your Ma could have come. No excuses for that. Polly needed her." His voice cracked with emotion.

Andrea let out a sigh, tried to keep her voice

steady.

"I know, but she had her reasons. I think she was afraid of what she'd find out." Hearing the words out loud she felt a gush of grief for her mother swelling, threatening to spill over into tears again.

Damn. Would she ever be able to say her mother's name without gushing like a baby?

"Well, I hope she got along alright," he finally mumbled.

"She died of a heart attack a couple of weeks ago," she murmured, just barely loud enough to hear.

His head ducked. "Sorry to hear that."

Andrea stepped in closer, dropping to her knees. "So, you knew my father?"

He stiffened, temper flaring again. "Hell yeah, I knew him. It was me taught your Daddy how to tie lures." He tossed the remains of the cigarette out into the water; lit another. He turned away so she couldn't quite see his face, gnarled grease caked fingers holding the butt deep, palm against his mouth. He stared out over the water, angry.

He's not angry, he's nervous.

Or maybe he just needed a drink. She let him take a few puffs. When she spoke, she picked her words with care.

"I went to see Polly this morning, but she became upset so I left." She paused, looked around. "I need to know some things."

He sucked on his cigarette, considering her words. Then, more calmly, "I quit going awhile back. Visitors don't seem to do her any good."

She let his words hang in the air for a moment. They listened to the birds chirping. A small fish jumped up beside the boat, plopping back down in the water again. Finally, Andrea spoke.

"My mother never read the letters Polly sent."

Willie cut his eyes at her, grunting.

"She kept them, but she never opened them. I didn't even know I had an Aunt Polly, much less that she had suspicions about my father's death. I guess my Mom figured if she didn't look at things too hard it would be like none of it had ever happened. She gave me very few details. She had no pictures. She was devastated, you know. Right before she died she told me that the letters were up in the attic in his old college trunk, along with his field journal and an urn containing his ashes."

He snorted, rolling his eyes. Ignoring his outburst, she continued.

"There was a manila envelope in the batch. It contained a long letter from Polly." She paused to let the words sink in, then: "Do you know what I'm talking about?"

He went very still, like an animal caught in a trap, then began shaking his head back and forth in denial.

"Are you shaking your head because you don't know anything? Or because you don't want to talk about it?"

He froze, then jerked back around, his face a study in righteous indignation.

"Missy, if I was you I'd go on back to wherever you come from. Let the dead rest in peace," he growled.

"So. You do know something. I figured you did."

"Don't go puttin' words in my mouth," he snarled. He tossed the cigarette, scrambled to the end of the boat, starting up the motor.

"Don't leave! I didn't mean to offend you. But, you don't understand. I've got to have some answers. If you don't tell me no one will!" She burst into tears.

His face flushed. She thought he was going to curse at her. Instead he stood up and offered her his hand.

"Aw hell, quit your cryin' and git in the boat. If you want me to talk, you are going to have to take a ride with me," he ordered. When she hesitated, he spat, "And I ain't gonna hurt you, okay? This towns got big ears." Then more civilly, "Besides, you need to see where your Daddy come from."

Without thinking, she blindly reached toward his hand, clambering down into the boat. *Dear Lord, please don't let this be the biggest mistake of my life,* she prayed to herself.

They rode in silence, Andrea's heart in her throat, nerves jangling. But the combination of water, wind, trees, and sky worked their magic, like a tonic. Even if Willie had talked crap to her, for some reason she felt safe with him. God knows he was too old to manhandle her, and the reverence in his voice when he spoke of Polly made it clear that he wasn't the kind of man who made a habit of hurting women.

And, even if he did have a strange way of show-ing it, he seemed to care. All Andrea knew was that in this moment in time it was right to be in the boat with him, as if her whole life had been point-ing to this moment. Had she dreamed about this before? It sure felt so.

Maybe Willie felt that way too. She noticed he

was calmer now, and the look on his face almost pleasant. She wondered if he had been around when she lived here, but for some reason was afraid to ask.

They rode for what seemed like miles, then slowed. She watched as Willie maneuvered the boat up into a shallow creek. Within moments they were under a thick green canopy arching overhead as far as the eye could see, shadows deep and cool, water here black as a moonless night. Every now and then she heard something rustling in the bushes as they passed. Frogs plopped into the water. A red fox trotted along the bank, away from her kits. Crows cawed overhead. Time seemed suspended here, the world of traffic and cell phones miles and miles away.

She thought about her studies. She remembered how John Lawson, the explorer, wrote that the trees were so tall a man could ride under their branches without even bowing his head; how the forest teemed with wildlife, herbs, and natural lakes.

But life had been so brutally difficult back then. Young women like her rarely lived past their childbearing years. She wondered what had happened to her grandmothers, all the generations that came before her. Did they look upon this scenery as their home? Were they glad to be here? Or did they bear their children in pain and suffering; die horrible deaths? Wish they'd never seen America?

She shivered, forcing her mind back to the present. She watched the old man as he steered them along the creek, deftly avoiding logs and low branches. A couple of times he pointed out an otter, or a copperhead snoozing on a rock, but other than that they saw nothing and no one. Finally, after a mile or so, they emerged into a wider more open part of the creek, surrounded by high land. He killed the motor and let them drift.

"You fish?" He asked, rummaging in his tackle box.

"No, but be my guest."

He smiled slightly, lit another cigarette; remained still. Then squinting, cigarette dangling from two fingers, he pointed outward at their surroundings.

"This is Milltail Creek, you know. The place where your Daddy was looking for them coffins."

She nodded, holding her breath.

Satisfied, he flicked his ashes. The water seemed to be mellowing him.

"You know, I come here a lot. Your Daddy loved it back up in here too. Big ole Indian village used to be here, back in the day. Still find all kinds of arrowheads and pottery and stuff if you know where to look." He had to stop to cough. She could hear the rattle in his chest, his eyes watered and turned red. It took a few minutes before he could speak again. When he resumed, his voice sounded rusty as a rake scraping concrete.

"This is where those old timers harvested sassafras. Those colonists from over in England everybody makes such a fuss about." He shifted in his seat. "You know that's who you came from don't you?" his gaze probing, shrewd.

She shook her head, not knowing know how to respond. When he grinned at her she noticed that his teeth were brown from the nicotine.

"It's the truth. Folks don't believe it cause won't nothing ever written down. But Polly knew. So did Jane. They was their people. Back in the 1800's they used to be a little community and farms back up in these swamps. Beechland it was called. But they all died off or moved away. An epidemic got most of them, but some claim it was the devil got them because they didn't have no church, no Bibles. They lived like the ancient ones, back in old England you know, them same ones that built Stonehenge." He stopped, coughed a bit more before continuing.

"If you go back up in there far enough you can find the evidence, if you know what to look for. Flower beds, old sunken graves, some pastureland where they kept cows. It's all protected land now, part of a national forest. Can't dig here without a permit, not even worms. Course that never stopped the locals. This was your Daddy's playground, his and Steve's."

"Steve?" she whispered.

He took a drag on his cigarette, then let it out slow. "Steven Hunter Strayhorn the Third," he answered, drawling out the words, tone dripping sarcasm. "We called him Scoot. Andrew's best friend, at least back then. They grew up together in East Lake. Daddies were in the moonshine business together, except one was dumb enough to drink it. Old man Strayhorn wouldn't touch the stuff. All he was after was the money. Hauled that stuff up to New York to the speakeasies and made a fortune selling East Lake moonshine. Wet gold was what they called it back then." He spat, bitterness creeping into the lines on his face. When he spoke, his eyes were cold.

"Scoot's daddy was smart. He parlayed the profits into land; made another fortune in the stock market once the Depression was over. Married a rich woman. Had children. Scoot was his youngest and he was a handful. Always getting into trouble. Sent him off to a fancy military academy up in Virginia to clean the swamp out of him. Up until then them two boys was inseparable. After that everything changed." Propping his right leg up on the seat in front of her, he laid his left palm upward, cupping his right elbow. Smoke curled lazily across the creek.

"What happened?" she ventured to ask, mesmerized.

He turned toward her, eyes hooded. "Same things that always mess up men. Money and sex." He took a drag, then thumped the butt angrily into the creek. "And liquor." His voice dropped a notch, sad.

"There was a girl, name of Anna Lee. She's the one they call the Bear Lady now. Pretty as could be back then, like a fairy walking through the woods. Scoot and Andy was both crazy about her. They was like them Three Musketeers, you know, at least when they was younger. But then Scoot left and after that the girl took off to New York without even saying goodbye. Became a model, or least that's what I heard. Word got around that old man Strayhorn despised Andy and Anna Lee. He wouldn't let Scoot come home, but after the girl left, he'd come home near 'bout every weekend, even during college. Then he got kicked out for cheating. Then he came home for good, started working in his Daddy's business, learning the ropes. I'll give it to him, the boy was smart, but he was lazy. He never would have made it without his Daddy's money." He snorted in disgust, stared off into the trees.

Andrea held her breath, waiting.

"That's when Scoot got the bighead, starting ordering Andy around, kept using him as a gofer. Andy took it in stride. Even then they was both up in them woods all the time, looking for them coffins."

"I take it by the pictures he took they found them," she murmured, testing him. Willie shot a sharp glance at her, rubbed his face with his hand as if he were tired.

"Polly thought your Daddy found them, wouldn't let Scoot in on the secret."

Andrea's heart dropped. "Polly's letters didn't say so."

His gaze swiveled away, voice strained. "She was afraid to tell anybody." He turned back toward her, pointed at her, his forefinger shaky. "You gotta understand. That boy hung the moon. But something was going down those last few weeks. Andy was acting strange, like something was bothering him, seemed mad at the world, even his friends. Polly was afraid Andy was up to no good. He sent you and your Mama away. Then, just like that he was dead." He paused to catch his breath, choking on his raspy words. "It about killed her."

Andrea paused, let him sit in peace a minute, then, "What about the pictures?"

He waved as if shooing a fly. "I don't know nothing about no pictures. But Andy was hiding something, what I don't know. Might be what got him killed."

"Do you think Anna Lee had anything to do with it?"

His tone was derisive. "Nah. She's a tree-hugger, that one. Wouldn't hurt a fly. She and Andy were a couple in high school but her Daddy put a stop to that too. Sent her away to New York, got her that modeling job. But when old man Whitlow died she inherited a bunch of money. Came home, bought some land. Everyone knew she had her cap set for your Daddy, could see that plain as day. But by then your mama and daddy was married and you were on the way. They was happy as clams. Anna Lee was too late."

Andrea stared off into the woods. Anna Lee really had been her mother's rival.

"If my parents were so happy, why did my mother leave?" she asked, bitter.

"I don't know. All I know is the three of them started looking for them coffins and things changed."

Andrea shifted on her seat. "What was Scoot doing all this time?"

"Still working with his Daddy. Making money like crazy. He had big plans. Going to buy up East Lake and turn it into the next Busch Gardens. Already had a name for it. The Lost Colony Gardens."

"What did my father think about that?"

"Hated the idea. Didn't care about the money or getting famous. All your Daddy wanted was to prove the stories once and for all. He kept saying it was important to his family. Once he enrolled in graduate school, it was like he couldn't stay away, no matter the toll it was taking on his marriage.

Course he was doing carpentry work too, to pay the bills. I guess everything took its toll. Then your Mama up and left." He shook his head like he didn't understand.

"Then he died and everything stopped cold," Andrea added, stating the obvious.

"That's about right," he answered softly.

"How did Anna Lee take it?"

"You know, I never saw her much after that. Folks said she was acting strange. She up and bought a thousand acres for that bear sanctuary of all things. That's why they call her the Bear Lady. Lives like a hermit now. Prefers the bears to people. Even trains them in survival skills, lets them sleep in her bead." He shook his head again. "Don't even have electricity. I take her my catch every now and then. Bears love fish." He spat, flicking yet another butt in the water.

Andrea couldn't breathe, her chest hurt. "What do *you* think happened?" she managed to whisper. He looked at her, his stare penetrating. "Well, don't you dare ever say I said this, but Polly was right. It sure as hell won't suicide."

"Did she ever say who she thought did it or why?"

His mouth twisted. "No ma'am, she didn't. We never talked about it. Not that I blame her. I was a mess back then too. Stayed drunk most of the time. She was afraid I'd shoot off my mouth. But she cleaned me up, bought me this old piece of a boat. Then she got the Old Timer's sickness. That's what finally sobered me up," he added, eyes reddening. "I took care of her long as I could," he added, stumbling on his words. Then "Shit!" he spat out under his breath.

Andrea looked away down the creek. Water bugs darted across the glassy surface of the water, still now and peaceful. Dragonflies dipped and swirled. Branches of oak, sassafras, birch and elm created an arching tunnel stretching into the distance, disappearing around the bend. The tops of the beech trees whispered in the afternoon breeze. Birds trilled *follow me, follow me*.

Everything around her dimmed and receded, and as gentle as flowing silk she slipped out of her own skin into the skin of another. She was alone now, paddling in her canoe. She wore a deerskin apron, a necklace of shells, blue beads, and a small pouch of herbs dangling in the cleft between her naked breasts, hair bound by leather strips, bones, combs made from the skeletons of fish, bear grease shiny on her bare skin.

The half of Andrea still in the present watched from a distance, entranced by the grace of the girl's movement, red tattoos on once pale skin, tanned and leathery now from too many years in the sun. Not white, not Indian, but blood from both worlds.

But wait! *Over there.* The girl saw something. Saw them before she heard them, the flash of white slender limbs. One was tall, dark-headed, the other stockier, blonde. Gradually she caught faint sounds—reckless challenges, playful taunts, the easy familiarity of two young boys at home in the woods.

Andrea knew right away that the taller one was her father, even if the other girl, the one in the canoe, saw only strange young men, dressed in strange clothes.

As she watched the taller one stopped, put out his arm, silencing the other. She could have sworn he saw her too, looked directly at her, locking into her gaze as if their spirits were connecting across the centuries. Then he smiled at her, tenderly it seemed, and put a single finger to his lips, cautioning her.

But who did he see? Did he see her, or that girl in the canoe?

Out of nowhere the name, *Virginia,* popped in her head. Then, just like that, she was back in her own skin.

She sat, unable to move, disoriented, the sense of loss and emptiness so profound it winded her. If she could just have stayed in that canoe for a while, talked to the boy that would become her father!

But it was more than that—much more. For an all too brief oasis in time she had truly been a different person, wild and unfettered, at one with the creek and the woods. There was no grief, no sadness, no overwhelming sense of failure, a freedom so palpable she could taste it on her lips.

Then she just like that she had been sucked back into her own self, once again carrying all the baggage of her present life, alone in the world with no one to love. It was all she could do not to burst into tears.

Flustered, Willie turned to adjust the angle of the motor, pretending to find something interesting in his tackle box, whether out of respect for her privacy or embarrassment, she couldn't tell. Either way, it was awkward. How would she ever be able to explain what had just happened?

She couldn't. No one would ever understand. It

was best to pretend it hadn't happened, even to herself.

"So. You're a direct descendant of Nathaniel Batts, huh?" she blurted. "He was quite the Indian trader I've read…." She barked a laugh that sounded false, even to her.

Willie turned toward her and shrugged, raising his eyebrows. He pulled at an ear, his expression unreadable. But, to Andrea's relief, he didn't comment about what he'd seen.

"Well, that's what I been told. Not sure that's a compliment though," he retorted. Cupping his hands, he lit another cigarette, then threw the lit match in the water. Andrea watched it sizzle and die out. He lifted his ball cap, wiping his brow with the back of his arm, then slapped the cap back down on his head again in a move so practiced and swift he must have done it a thousand times. Then he turned to her, face inscrutable.

"You seen somethin' didn't you?" he stated, like it was the most natural question in the world.

His question caught her off-guard. She looked down, then away, embarrassed.

"Listen. Polly saw things too," he reassured her, his demeanor calm, like he was talking about the weather. He picked up his rod, began fiddling with the line. "Dreamed things that came true."

Andrea held her breath, afraid of what he would say next.

"At first it bothered me, made me worried for her. Then it pissed me off, especially when she wouldn't talk about it. After that I just left her alone, figuring it won't none of my business." He glanced over at her. His next words were more deliberate.

"And it still ain't."

Andrea blinked. *What was he saying?*

He cast the line out, let it settle. Then, "She always said the women in the family had them visions strong. Polly thought it was a gift. Your Grandma Jane did too. And Andy never said, but he had that air about him."

She was tongue-tied, struck dumb.

Then his voice dropped a notch. "I been debatin' whether to tell you or not. But I figure you got a right to know. Every child has a right to know where they come from. If they don't know where they come from, how they know where they's going?"

Those words again. Wide-eyed, she nodded.

"Hooch Warren won't really your Granddaddy. Andy knew it, but as long as Hooch was alive there was no actin' on it. Your real Granddaddy lived up in Buxton, died shortly after he and Jane met. Everyone always said Jane was the love of his life. Problem is that once he died, his family wouldn't claim her." He paused; spit into the water. "Didn't want to share the money is what I think, and back in those days she couldn't prove the baby was his anyway. Jane was broke and scared. Her own family pretty much disowned her, such as they was, all except for Polly. Hooch married her on the condition she wouldn't tell anybody. She agreed, but she wouldn't let him sign the birth certificate. It didn't help none when your Andy popped out looking just like his real Daddy. Then the rotgut went to Hooch's head and he started taking it out on the boy. Polly hated Hooch for that." He sighed, looked haggard for a moment.

"So that is why the asshole drank himself to death?" she asked, voice bitter.

His eyes slid away. "Honey, drunks don't need no excuse. I should know."

"Who was my real grandfather?" she whispered.

"Jesse Elks. Elks is an old Hatteras Indian name you know. That's where your Daddy got the Indian from. He worked up at the old Chicamacomico Life-Saving Station. Died saving a boat load of fisherman during a storm."

Suddenly she felt drained. It was all too much to take in. The sun was behind the trees, shadows had lengthened. A whole new family somewhere, a family who'd denied her father. How had his family lived with themselves knowing they'd turned their back on their grandchild?

But at least her real grandfather had been a good man, a hero. Better than a drunk who'd made liquor for a living. Thank God, she didn't have those genes.

She decided to ask one more question. "Do you have any idea where my father might have been digging when he died? I have some of his field notes, but they end abruptly, and some pages seem to be missing."

Willie gazed up at the sky, scratched his neck. His top lip curled in disgust. "No. Don't care either. Better off left in the ground is what I say. If you ask me they is cursed."

She decided to try a different approach. "Do you remember a man by the name of Talton?"

He sat up abruptly and turned his back to her, jerking on the starter rope until the motor rumbled. All the color had drained from his face. When he answered, his voice was terse.

"Nope, can't say that I do," he mumbled, turning up the motor a notch until it was so loud there was no way they could carry on a conversation. He began maneuvering the boat back up the creek, in a hurry this time.

He was lying of course. She could see right through him, watching as he wove the boat through the narrows until they emerged back out on the Alligator River, gunning the motor up to high speed when they reached the open water of the sound. She focused on the scenery, thinking about what had happened back there, her mind a blur. Within minutes they were back at the docks. Helping him tie up, she ventured one more question.

"Willie, I forgot to ask, is the older Strayhorn still alive?"

He huffed, annoyed. "Robert Strayhorn, King of the World, died about ten years ago. Scoot took over the business. He has a grown son about your age who works with him. He's still up in Norfolk, though I suspect he's retired now. I have no idea how he is."

"What kind of business?"

"Builds marinas mostly, up and down the coast from Florida to Cape Cod."

Then he turned to stare at her, his look cold now, and something else.

Frightened?

"Listen, I'm not as dumb as people think. I know what happened up in Williamsburg. Polly kept track. She was proud of you. It's a shame you never knew her because you two is just alike. And

I warned her like I'm warning you." He coughed, spat into the dark water, grimacing. "Don't expect there's a hope in hell you'll back off."

"I hear you." But her mind was racing.

He stood up to his full height, wobbling a bit from the movement of the boat, his hand shading his eyes from the late afternoon sun. She noticed he seemed pale and a bit unsteady on his feet. When he spoke, he pointed at her with a gnarled finger and hissed.

"I'm telling you. Don't go poking at a nest of rattlesnakes, you hear? And if you don't have the sense to listen to me, don't say I didn't warn you, you got that?" He turned his back on her, his shoulders slumped. "Now get on out of here." His voice was muffled, gruff with emotion.

In that one small moment, something about him moved her deeply. She could only imagine the pain he'd gone through in his life, the secrets hidden underneath that crusty exterior. How terribly old he looked, and sad. A scared lonely old alcoholic who'd lost his best friend. She almost jumped back down in the boat to give him a hug, then thought better of it. He wasn't the type. Besides, she'd better get a move on if she didn't want to find her way out of here in the darkness. Maybe she would get the chance tomorrow.

She said her goodbyes, thanking him. She chuckled to herself when he swiveled his head around to look at her and winked, that endless cigarette dangling out of his mouth.

The old coot. He had a heart after all. Yeah, she'd give him that hug tomorrow, even if he didn't particularly want it.

Walking back to the Jeep she thought about everything he had told her, the window he had opened into the past. And what about that surreal vision? Had she really seen Virginia Dare and her father as a boy?

Of course not. She'd seen him because she had wanted to see him. All those stories about a gift of some kind were only superstitious fantasy, something he'd probably made up to ease the awkwardness of the moment.

Then there was that bit about Anna Whitlow. That added a whole new dimension to her parent's troubles. Had her father been involved in a sordid love triangle? Her mother seemed to think so.

Or had Steven Strayhorn been jealous of her father because of those coffins?

Maybe it was both.

Well, there was only one way to find out and that was to visit the woman, as unappealing as the prospect sounded. And what would she say to her? Confront her about the breakup of her family?

Yeah, right.

Well, she'd have to find out for herself. She'd figure out what to say once she was face to face with the woman. She climbed into the Jeep, then googled the National Park Service for Dare County, asking Siri the number for the office, pleased when a woman ranger answered. Andrea talked fast, making it up as she went.

"Yes, hello. I'm a free-lance writer. I'm here on vacation this week and was hoping to get an interview with the Bear Lady for a piece on eccentric outdoorsmen in our state. Can you tell me how to get in touch with her?"

"Well, ma'am, you'll have to take your chances. Eccentric is an understatement. No phone, electricity, or running water. If she's not at home she's out walking in the woods somewhere. She doesn't leave her property very often."

"Do you think she will talk to me?"

"Can't say. Sometimes she welcomes company, other times she runs them off."

"Well, can you tell me how to get there?"

"Sure. Just look for the state Bear Crossing sign on Highway 64 then turn right on River Road apiece. You'll know you're there when you see the footbridge crossing the canal. It's on the left. Park your car on the side of the road and follow the path about a quarter of a mile. If you see any bears keep your distance and don't feed them, okay, no matter what Anna Lee says."

"Don't worry; I have no interest in the bears. Thanks for the information." Ending the call, she threw the phone on the passenger seat beside her, resigning herself to the task ahead.

It was time to face her mother's rival.

❦

River Road was easy enough to find, but the footbridge was another matter, overgrown with brush weed and willow, as was the path going to the cabin. She had to skirt briars, small cedars and sassafras saplings, ground moist and spongy under her feet. The path was shaded by immense tall pines that blocked out most of the light that filtered in from overhead. Every so often she heard a rustle in the underbrush, but no bears so far, thank God.

The cabin turned out to be nothing more than a

shanty on stilts, unpainted, a couple of cinder block steps going up to the front screened door. She was surprised to see that all the windows and doors were open. Standing on the top step she peered into the dimness. From what she could see the furnishings were sparse—a rickety-looking wooden table, a couple of scarred old chairs, a recliner by the fireplace—and in the room behind it a single bed, faded comforter thrown haphazardly over it. No sink, refrigerator, television, or anything appearing to need power or water, as the ranger had predicted.

"Ms. Whitlow?" she called. No sound except a lone crow cawing overhead. She scanned the woods around her but saw nothing. She called out again, but there was still no answer.

She tested the screen door. It opened with a screech. One step and she was inside, her eyes adjusting to the dimness, not stopping to consider she might be trespassing. She made out a bookshelf in the corner over a small desk, right away noticing a grainy black and white photograph in a tarnished silver frame. Tiptoeing, she walked over and picked it up, peering at it closely. Her heart skipped.

Three happy young people, two boys flanking a beautiful young girl dressed in a long empire-waist granny dress with long, blonde hair, arms draped around each other in solidarity. Comrades in arms.

Scoot, Anna Lee, and her father.

Here were the three would-be Musketeers, off on their grand adventures, no thought to what tomorrow would bring, so carefree.

And so totally ignorant of the legacy of pain they would leave.

Suddenly the tiny cabin felt airless, dark, like a tomb.

Get out of here, Andrea. The voice was firm but calm, unequivocal.

She placed the frame back on the desk and walked quickly to the screen door. Her foot was halfway down in mid-air when she froze.

There, on the bottom step a snake, thick as a man's upper arm, diamond-paned, fangs bared in its beady-eyed triangular head. She screamed, jumping back as it struck air, twisted back down, then smoothly wrapped himself back into a coil, head raised, gold eyes malevolent, forked tongue flicking the air. She froze, heart crashing against her rib cage. To her relief, it finally lost interest, slithering off into the weeds under the house.

Andrea bolted down the path, through the woods, across the footbridge to the Jeep. Breathless, she jerked open the door and hopped inside, slamming it shut so hard her teeth rattled. She closed her eyes, lowered her forehead to the steering wheel face down, gasping for air.

Damn, that was close.

It wasn't as if she'd never seen a snake before. Archaeologists were taught to expect most anything. She even owned her own pair of snake boots. But this encounter was different somehow. She could have died out here.

Maybe it was best she didn't meet with the woman. Not yet anyway.

Exhaustion washed over her. She was done, too tired even to drive back to Manteo. At least Scott seemed to be leaving her alone. She'd get a room at a motel out on the interstate and get an early start tomorrow. She'd go back and see Willie after a good night's rest, try to get him to tell her more about Anna Lee.

She sure as heck wasn't going to come back here if she could help it.

CHAPTER ELEVEN

BUT TOMORROW NEVER CAME, NOT for Willie anyway.

DARE COUNTY FISHERMAN
DROWNED IN COLUMBIA CREEK

She remembered picking up takeout, getting a room at the local Hampton Inn, trying to watch the news as she ate her food. But too tired to focus, she switched it off again, put her phone on mute to take a short nap. She slept straight through until mid-morning.

Groggy, she'd heard a thump, a newspaper hitting the door. She tossed it flat on the bed, not particularly interested. But its headlines caught her attention.

Now she sat on the side of the bed staring out of the window, eyes red, tracking the beads of warm rain that funneled down the plate glass of the window, shivering.

She groaned. *What if this is my fault?*

Think Andrea, she coached herself, trying to remember every word of their conversation.

Don't say I didn't warn you, you got that? She could see his lips mouthing the words, silent now, stiff, and cold, lying on a metal table in the morgue.

His crooked finger pointed at her. She grabbed a pillow, burying her face.

Think, Andrea!

Willie had been old and obviously in ill health, and a fiendish smoker. He was an alcoholic with tremors, living on borrowed time. It had nothing to do with her.

Thank God no one had seen her at the docks yesterday; she was sure of it. As far as she could tell, the place had been empty all afternoon.

Then again, Mildred had known she was looking for him.

Oh God. She had to tell someone. To keep quiet would make her look guilty.

But wouldn't stepping forward now stir up things for no reason? No foul play had been reported. If it was, she could call Derek, tell him what happened. He would understand.

Of course, Willie had been frightened of Talton.

But it couldn't be Talton; the man was dead. *Or was he?*

She grabbed her phone off the bedside table.

"Hey Siri."

"Yes, Andrea"

"Call Dare County Sheriff's Department in Manteo, North Carolina."

"Okay, got it. I've found Dare County Sheriff's Department in Manteo, North Carolina. Is that correct?"

"Yes."

Siri rang the number. Within seconds a man answered.

"Hello, I hope you can help me. I heard that Fred Talton passed away and I'd like to do something for the family. Can you tell me where I might reach them?"

"Sorry ma'am, but we can't give out that information." The voice was clipped, cool.

"I understand. But can you at least tell me what city he lived in. I heard Fort Myers, is that correct?"

"I wouldn't know ma'am. I didn't know the gentleman in question."

"Well, thanks anyway," she sighed. She was about to say goodbye when she had an idea. It was a long shot, but she could at least try.

"Hey, if you happen to speak to his family would you ask them to call me? I'd like to send them a donation. You know, for old time's sake. He did a favor for me one time. I'd at least like to show my gratitude to his family. My name is Andrea, Andrea Warren."

She waited as he jotted down the number, told her he couldn't promise anything, and ended the call.

She collapsed in a side chair. At least she had done something, even if it was wrong.

Maybe she should go back and see Aunt Polly, see if she was having a good day. Hopefully no one would tell her that Willie was dead. She picked up the phone, found the number for the nursing home on Google and clicked the call through.

"Shady Grove Nursing Center. May I help you?" the girl said, in a familiar twang.

"Yes, I'm Andrea Warren. I visited Polly Vestal yesterday. Do you think she's well enough for me to visit her again today?"

The girl hesitated, mumbled something to someone nearby, then came back on the line. "I'm sorry

Miss Warren, but your aunt had a stroke last night. We rushed her to the emergency room. She's in a coma. I'm afraid it doesn't look too good."

Andrea hung onto the phone without saying anything, fighting the urge to scream.

"Which hospital?"

"I'm not allowed to say, honey. You're not verified as next of kin."

"That's crap" she replied, her voice cold, wishing she could cram the phone down someone's throat. Instead she hung up without answering, threw it across the room, then sat down on the bed, pulling the bedspread around her shoulders.

Talton, Willie, and now Aunt Polly. What was happening here?

In the quiet, the phone rang where it had landed. Scrambling, she crawled on all fours to fish it out from under the chair, answering it without looking at the number.

"Andrea?" It was a man's voice. Her heart began hammering.

"Yes?"

"Derek here. Are you okay?"

"Sure," she answered, trying to sound nonchalant. "Great to hear from you. What's up?"

"Just wanted to let you know I ran McWilliams's record. The guy is squeaky clean. He was probably just infatuated. If you haven't heard from him by now I wouldn't worry too much. And technically, he's not broken any laws. Sorry about that."

Well, that was at least something.

"Thanks. You don't know how much I appreciate your help."

"Same here Andrea. Call me if you have any

more problems. You were right to put an alert out. Some girls wait too long."

Andrea breathed. He'd said nothing about Willie.

"Will do. If you're ever in Charlotte for a meeting, give me a call. I'll treat you to dinner for your effort."

He chuckled. "I might just do that. Take care."

"Bye now." And she hung up the phone.

It was time to go home and lay low. She could hire a good criminal investigator. She had the money now. Let the authorities handle this.

She moaned, curled up in a fetal position. *Who was she kidding?* No one in Charlotte would be interested in this case. It was too far away. She wouldn't feel safe there anyway.

And Aunt Polly, what would happen to her? Would she and Willie go into a pauper's grave unremembered, as if they never mattered?

Not if she could help it. Anger was beginning to surface. Three people connected to her father in a short span of time. Was it coincidence? It couldn't be.

Trying not to panic she stuffed her few belongings into her knapsack, checking on the pictures and the letters again, so deep in her thoughts that when the phone rang again she jumped. She glanced at the number, but didn't recognize it.

"Hello."

"Is this the woman who called about Fred Talton?" The voice on the end sounded young, maybe a teenager. Alert now, Andrea sat down, gathered her wits.

"Yes." She answered, trying not to sound too desperate.

"You said you'd pay, right?"

"Yes. What can you tell me?"

"You pay first then I'll talk. I need rent money fast. Five hundred or I don't tell you a thing."

"How do I know you aren't just trying to con me?"

"Listen lady. You called looking for us, not the other way around. Buck's out of work and we got a new baby. This mess with his Daddy has been hard on us. I'll tell you what I know, but you got to pay up first. But I will tell you something. Fred Talton won't depressed and he won't dyin' of cancer either."

The room started going hazy again.

"How do you want me to send the money?" she whispered.

"Wire it to me through your bank. I'll text you my information. Once the transaction goes through, call me back." The girl hung up.

Andrea sent the money order. But when she tried to call the girl no one answered. On the third try she threw the phone on the bed, disgusted.

She'd just given away five hundred dollars to a stranger!

But, just when she'd given up, it rang again.

"Sorry, I had to nurse the baby. He was screaming. I got the money, now what do you want to know?"

Thank God.

"The newspaper said your father-in-law found my father's body on Old Ferry Landing back in the eighties. His name was Andrew Warren. Did he ever talk about that?"

"Lady, that was a long time ago. Fred found lots

of bodies. People committed suicide all up and down the beach."

Andrea sucked in her breath. "I never mentioned suicide."

Silence on the other end.

"Tell me what you know, or I'll call the bank right now," Andrea responded, her voice cold.

The girl mumbled something under her breath, then started talking, low. "Fred's cancer was gone. The day before he died he bragged about how he was going to be buying a new charter boat any day now. He even promised Buck a new truck. He was blowing through money like it was nothing, acting like he was a big shot. Buck thinks he had someone by the short hairs and was pulling hard, if you know what I mean."

"Do you have any idea who it was?"

"No, but lately he'd been advising Buck to get him a job in law enforcement. *Work smart, not hard,* he said. One night when he was drinking he got to bragging. Hinted that he helped some rich man out down there cover up a murder, made it look like a suicide, and how he was going to take that information to the bank."

"What makes you think he was talking about my father?" Andrea asked, leery.

"Well, for starters he said it was over something that got found down in the swamps. I ain't stupid. I looked you up online. I know you are an archaeologist."

"Did he say who did it?" Andrea asked.

Her answer was quick. "No, and neither of us asked. We both learned a long time ago that it was safer that way. Stayed away from him as much as possible. We only moved in with him 'cause we had to." She paused, sighed in frustration. "Listen, I got to go, and don't call here anymore, okay? Buck don't know about this and I ain't tellin' him. He's a proud man. I've told you all I know."

"I understand. But if you find out anything else will you leave me a message?"

"We don't need no more trouble around here," she stated, her meaning clear.

"Thanks for your help. I hope things get better for you. Hey, I don't know your name…"

But the line was already dead.

She laid the phone down on the nightstand, then closed her eyes. Her chest hurt, her arms ached. Now the haze was forming behind her lids. The room began to spin, going dark, as she fought not to panic. Slowly she lowered herself onto the bed. Was she having a heart attack? It sure felt like it.

God, help me please!

She shut her mouth, sucking in air in long slow draughts, holding it until she had to release, then huffing it out in small breaths, almost like she was in labor. Like her therapist had taught her, back when she had panic attacks in high school.

Shaky, drained, she crawled into bed, hiding under the dark of the covers. What was she going to do? She had to do something. If she gave up now, she'd never be able to live with herself.

Then, as if the very thought summoned up her gift, a whole scene materialized in her head, like a scene from a grade B movie. Willie defiant, sneering in the face of certain death, feisty until the end. Tossed into Columbia Creek, like yesterday's fish guts.

Refuse, garbage; nothing.

Then a kaleidoscope of color twirling and spinning. A scene change. A room in the nursing home, the pill given to Polly at supper, the needle slipping into her vein. A few spasms and the old woman was comatose.

But it was more than a simple vision this time. This time she didn't just see their deaths, she felt the evil in the pit of her stomach. These weren't the actions of a cold-blooded killer methodically getting rid of the evidence. These were vicious acts meant, not only to warn her, but to hurt her.

Why? What had she ever done?

There would be no justice either, not for poor old folks already at death's door, considered a drain on the taxes of more upstanding citizens in the county. Good riddance is what most would likely say. Lonely, bitter tears began to slide down her face.

Then her gut began to boil, spilling over into her heart, filling it with a bitter gall. She pummeled the bed with her fists, outraged.

By God, this was her family. Andrew, her mother, Polly, and Willie. They had sacrificed everything for her!

But why? What was she not getting?

She sat up in bed, threw back the covers, and looked around the room, chest tight again with anxiety. She glanced at the bedside table.

The phone.

She clicked open her GPS settings, froze.

Impossible. She vividly remembered turning off location services before she left Williamsburg trying to conserve data. But there it was, turned on again, tracking her every move.

Someone had accessed her phone, either remotely or when she wasn't looking.

But when?

The restaurant. She had left it there for hours. Had she told Scott? *Yes, she had.* He could have called the waitress. She would have done it for him, anything he asked.

But hadn't she read about an app that could remotely access and install a tracking device with a phone number? She'd given her number to lots of people already.

Suddenly the device felt like a snake in her hand. Trembling, she clicked off tracking and changed her passwords. That was all she could do for now.

Wracking her brain, she scanned the details of the last few weeks in her mind. And the more she thought about it, the more things didn't add up. There had been nothing on Scott's computer connecting him to her father—no pictures of coffins or any other apparent interest in local archaeology—in fact, he'd barely asked her any questions about her father at all.

But maybe she had simply overlooked the evidence. He *had* shown a lot of interest in that trunk. Too much, it now seemed.

The thought made her blood run cold.

Think Andrea! You're a scientist, remember?

She forced herself to slow her breathing, corral her racing thoughts so she could examine the puzzle from different angles. She was a trained archaeologist, used to solving riddles.

Grabbing a notepad from the side table, she began jotting down facts, forcing herself to sift through the evidence, dig through the muddy layers of her life.

First and foremost: Polly had said that her father had died trying to protect his family. But if so, from what? And if the killer was trying to send a message to her, what was he saying?

You are getting too close.

It made sense. Everything would have been fine had she gone on home to Charlotte. But no, she had come here asking questions. But why didn't the enemy just kill her and be done with it?

They think you know where those coffins are.

That had to be it. Then another thought surfaced, an inconsistency that she hadn't thought about until now. Willie said he knew what had happened in Virginia. But who told him? Polly was already in the nursing home by then, and she doubted the man had internet access.

Scott? Talton? Strayhorn? But why would they involve an old drunk?

Now that she thought about it, Willie had acted strange. And he seemed not to be surprised when she showed up. Had he been told she was in Columbia?

Her mind was racing. Now everyone was a suspect.

It had to be Scott McWilliams. He was the one person at the center of everything, going all the way back to their fathers. The big boon for Scott was when she walked into that restaurant unannounced. He must have felt like the heavens opened and dropped the goods right at his front door.

How could she have been so stupid?

But why did he leave her at the Montrose like that; what happened?

Norfolk.

She felt her throat tighten. Steve Strayhorn lived in Norfolk. Scott had rushed off to meet with him, report to the one person in all this who had the money, the resources, the motive to kill her father and cover it up. Scott was only his henchman, someone hired to do the dirty work.

Steven Strayhorn was her enemy, she was sure of it.

Willie had sure seemed scared of him. Had warning her cost him his life?

Her mind spun in circles. So many pieces to the puzzle and none of them quite fit. She got up out of bed and walked over to the mirror. A sallow, sunken face looked back at her. Her lips were cracked and pale.

But as she stared, the room began to recede, telescoped out. She was no longer in the present, but somewhere in the distant past. *Her past.* She could smell the smoke, hear the laughter, the chants, the singing. She was standing at a pole in the center of a circle dressed in a loincloth, laden with pearls, blue beads, shell ornaments, feathers in her long red hair.

Her heartbeat quickened, joining the soft patter of drumbeats thrumming at the base of her spine. The beats, more insistent with each passing moment, rose inside her, pulsing through her groin until she thought she would faint. The air was as pungent and sweet as summer rain. The music rose and fell in a cadence, chants and shouts as young warriors circled, dancing and spinning, arms raised to the sky. A cacophony of sound, color, and joy – oh the joy! She thought her heart would burst.

And then suddenly, everything stopped. In the absolute quiet a warrior stepped forward, eyes fierce and possessive, muscles knotted, crisscrossing the length of his lanky body. The same warrior who played games with her as a child. Tattoos covered his arms and ankles, smears of red and black paint glowing on his cheeks and upper body. Shells, beads, small skulls, and feathers dangled from the shank of hair falling from his brow and the leather thong hanging around his neck. He is so beautiful and so fierce, all at the same time.

He is her Wanchese.

And she will be his *Metaquesunnauk*, Queen of the Secotan.

The room spun, turned dark. Andrea collapsed to the floor.

☾

She awoke to the sound of banging on the door of her room.

"All right, all right. I'm coming!" she muttered, staggering up onto her feet. When she finally managed to get to the door and unlock it, the manager stood in the hall, staring at her, his eyes cold.

"You okay?" he blurted, eyeing the room behind her.

"Yes, I'm fine, thanks." She pushed the hair out of her eyes, straightened her t-shirt, embarrassed. Why was he looking at her that way? Then suddenly it hit her:

"Oh my gosh, no! I'm not high okay. Just overslept a bit, that's all. I promise."

"Well, checkout was at noon. I almost called the cops. Maid service needs to get in here if you're leaving," he stated, his voice gruff.

"Yes. Sorry. I'll pay for the extra day, no problem. Just put it on my credit card, okay?"

He smirked at her, then turned and walked off in a huff.

She eased the door shut, then made her way blindly back to the bed. Every muscle in her body ached, like a ton of bricks had been dropped on her head.

She glanced at her phone. Froze. *Six frickin hours!* It couldn't be.

She remembered talking to that woman down in Florida. Being so angry she couldn't think straight, but the rest was a blur. What had happened to her?

One thing she did know was that, without leaving the room, she had gone somewhere, done something, and that what had happened to her was important.

She stared at herself in the mirror. She picked up a strand of hair, let it fall. Then gradually it started coming back to her, slowly at first, in fragments.

A deerskin apron. An Indian village. Dancing and singing. A ceremony of some kind.

The Ceremony of the Green Corn. Her wedding day.

But not hers, not really. It was the wedding of Virginia and Wanchese.

Virginia.

The name reverberated in her head, like an echo in a vast canyon. And with the name came a realization that she could deny no more.

Willie had been right. She wasn't going crazy,

because her gifts were real. If anything, she was thinking more clearly now than she'd ever thought in her life. These voices in her head, these visions and dreams, they weren't her imagination, or the product of wishful thinking. These were the voices of her ancestors calling out to her, guiding her, showing her she had a power that had been handed down to her through the ages, a gift from her divine Creator.

The power of blood from both worlds.

INSCRIPTION ON THE FIRST DARE STONE,
CLAIMED TO HAVE BEEN FOUND ON THE
SHORES OF THE CHOWAN RIVER NEAR
EDENTON, NORTH CAROLINA,
NOW IN THE POSSESSION OF
BRENAU UNIVERSITY IN
BRENAU, GEORGIA.

*Ananias Dare & Virginia Dare went hence into
Heaven 1591
Any Englishmen, show John White, Governor of
Virginia.
Father, soon after you went to England, we came here
Only misery & a war torn year
About half are dead for two years or more from
sickness, we are four & twenty
Savage with a message of a ship was brought to us
In a small space of time they became afraid of revenge
(by British) and all ran away
We believe it was not you
Soon after the savages, fearing angry spirits.
Suddenly murdered all, save seven
My child, Ananias too, were slain with much misery
Buried all four miles east of this river on a small hill
Names are written there on a rock. Put this there also
Savage show this unto you & hither we promise you
will give great and plenty presents
Elenor White Dare*

God have mercy on their souls.

PART III

CHAPTER TWELVE

S HE CHECKED OUT EARLY THE next morning and headed straight back to Rodanthe, thankful that the extra night in the motel had given her the time she needed to come up with a workable plan.

Once there she was relieved to see nothing appeared to be out of place in the Airstream. The guy at the office seemed unconcerned. She bought a local newspaper, relieved to see there was nothing new about Willie's death.

So far, so good.

After throwing the food she'd bought in a trash bag, she carefully wrapped the urn in a blanket and hid it in the boot of the Jeep. Then, making sure she'd left nothing important behind, locked the trailer back up again. A quick stop by the realtor to pay the rent for the rest of the summer and she was done, glad when no one questioned her for leaving so soon.

Within the hour she purchased a prepaid cell phone, tossing the old one in the trash bag fully charged, then threw the bag into a bin along the side of the road. That ought to distract her stalkers, for a few days anyway, she figured, and headed on to her next stop: a hair salon.

"You gotta be kidding me. Your hair is gorgeous!" said a younger version of David Bowie, marching her to a chair in a booth in the back of the salon.

"I know, but I want to commemorate a life transition," she explained, her smile enigmatic. Then as an afterthought added, "Coming out, you know."

"Oh, I get it now," he drawled. Then, as if he was confiding a well-kept secret, he leaned over and whispered in her ear. "You'll look mah-ve-lous dahling, I promise."

He sat her down, whisked out an apron and tied it behind her neck, stroking her hair like it was a kitten. "How short do you want it?" he asked her, all business now.

"Short and blonde like yours," pointing at his head.

"You got it girlfriend." He picked her hair up in one mass, lifted it off her neck. "Want to donate this beauty to Wigs for Kids. It's a nonprofit that gives the wigs to kids with cancer."

"Of course, take it all off, okay?"

The words barely out of her mouth, he swooped it back into a tight ponytail, wrapped it tightly with a thick rubber band. Then, before she had a chance to change her mind, he picked up large shears, lopped it off, then crammed the hank in a plastic bag and stuck it under the counter, all in one quick stroke.

She sat staring at herself, stunned, feeling like a body part had just been amputated. There in that bag hidden away under the counter was the girl she used to be, the woman gazing back at her in the mirror was a stranger.

Seeing the look of shock on her face, he spun her chair around, cranked her down a few notches and laid her back for the shampoo, talking and asking questions in rapid fire succession. Once she was towel dried, he began trimming in earnest. He reminded her of Edward Scissorhands. Hair went flying.

She learned everything about him and then some—his life, his boyfriend, struggles with his parents, and the latest scandal among his regulars. Who'd been caught with whom, who'd regretted it, who got the mansion back in Raleigh or the beach house in Nags Head.

She felt like a shorn lamb. But he still wouldn't let her look, ignoring her anxiety. Instead, he proceeded right into the coloring process, not spinning her chair back around until she had been blown out and styled. Then *finally,* he untied her apron, brushed off her neck, and spun her around.

Her mouth dropped open. Who *was* that creature in front of her? A blonde no doubt. But that face, all angles, with a gamine, elfin quality she'd never seen before. And those dark orbs glowing in her face. Even she had to admit those eyes were captivating, otherworldly almost, twice as big as they had seemed before.

She turned her head from side to side. Who was she kidding? She was gorgeous! She laughed out loud.

The stylist leaned in, his face next to hers. "That ought to make a statement," he announced, winking. Elated, she doled out $200.00 in cash, praised his handiwork, and skipped out the door.

Outside in the sun now, her neck and arms were

tender, like a baby's. The sensation of renewal and change was so powerful she wanted to shout out loud and run. Her stride was deeper, her legs seemed longer, and she felt light, like a world of weight had been taken off her shoulders. And from the smiles of passersby, and catcalls from a gang of adolescent boys, the world seemed to agree.

This was a coming out of sorts, though not in the way the stylist had interpreted. Somewhere deep inside she had known that to be more confident she truly had needed to shed that old look, divest herself of that self-critical hall monitor in her head. This wasn't a disguise or a cheaply made movie she was about to star in; this was her life. She wasn't going to hide from her enemies anymore, *hell no*. She was going to expose them to the world.

But not yet. After all, her transformation wasn't complete. Her reflection in plate glass windows screamed for a wardrobe overhaul. Within moments she was down at the Outer Banks Mall inside an outdoor gear outlet trying on new clothes. She finally settled on two sets of sturdy khaki cargo shorts, two white sleeveless tees, and a pair of summer hiking boots and socks. On the way out she picked up a pair of black Rainbow flip-flops, at the last minute throwing in a short red knit t-shirt dress. She loved the color and feel so much she decided to pay for it, put it on, and wear it out. Within moments she was out the door, her old jeans and t-shirt in the bag.

She still had time for one more thing, perhaps the most important. She pressed the button and spoke: "Siri, find a tattoo parlor."

Just a little one, on the inside of her right arm

above the wrist. And she knew what she wanted: *a tiny soaring hawk*. A symbol of her "gift," as Willie had called it.

The artist she chose claimed to have learned his techniques abroad, and had the highest rating for cleanliness on the beach. Body art was his calling. She drove up to his store, walked right in, and within an hour he was done.

"I could do another one, a little red heart to go with that dress," he suggested.

"Hmmm, maybe in a few weeks. If I show up here again, you'll know I lived." He chuckled, but didn't ask her to elaborate.

Wow, was all she could think, turning her wrist back and forth, making the hawk look like it was flying. He really had done a wonderful job.

Of course, now she noticed how tired and dirty the old Jeep looked. It screamed broke college student. She asked Siri to find a car rental agency, encouraged when a franchise she recognized popped up nearby in Kitty Hawk, and even more pleased when they agreed to let her park the Jeep out back for a month while she rented a sparkling late-model white SUV, although she was careful not to mention the ashes. "I'll be back, Dad," she promised before she got behind the wheel of the new car.

She sat for a moment, staring at her new look in the vanity mirror. Then she shoved it back into place, took a long, deep breath and summoned up her newfound courage. She turned left onto Ocean Highway toward Hwy 168 North and pointed the car toward Norfolk.

CHAPTER THIRTEEN

A S SHE DROVE SHE TRIED not to think about what lay ahead, turning up the radio loud. She thought about the voices she was hearing, the wild dreams in her head. Before long she was flying up the Chesapeake Expressway and onto I-464/264, crossing the James River Bridge, rolling up Princess Anne Blvd into the famed Historical District of old Norfolk.

The street names were certainly evocative - Manteo, Powhatan, and Elizabeth - ironic given the circumstances. The streets themselves were wide, flanked by massive old pin oaks. The houses all had brass plaques, the occasional Land Rover sitting in the driveway. The house she'd lived in growing up in Myer's Park would be the maid's quarters here.

She found Strayhorn's address easily enough. Set back from the street by a stone's throw, the brown brick mansion, plantation shutters drawn, it looked more like a fortress than a home, at least to her. A semi-circle of concrete driveway dominated the front lawn up to the entrance, flanked on each side by blooming white crepe myrtles and manicured green sod. The entire lawn was bordered on three sides by black wrought iron railings set into a waist-high brick fence.

She parked across a side street diagonally to the house, got out of the car, hesitating for a moment before crossing the wide street, then marched right up to the massive dark green front door. Sucking in a deep breath, she punched the brass doorbell, listening as its muffled chime echoed somewhere deep in the recesses of the house. While she waited for someone to answer, she peeked through the wavy panes of leaded glass that flanked the door, glimpsing a dimly lit foyer, a soaring staircase, pale Persian rugs on wide heart pine flooring, expensive art in gilded frames.

No movement, no sound except for the loud tick of a grandfather clock in the entryway across from the door. She was about to turn away when she heard the tap of footsteps, then the click of the lock as the heavy door opened.

May I help you?" asked the woman, in a soft country brogue, her dark face solemn.

"Yes, I'm looking for Steven Strayhorn. He was a friend of my father's. I was passing through town, thought I'd look him up. I'm sorry that I didn't call first."

She frowned, cocking her head. "Ma'am, I'm not sure this is a good time. Mr. Strayhorn is very ill."

"Could I simply say hello? I promise I won't stay but a moment. This may be my last chance."

The nurse sighed, black eyes soft with uncertainty. "Well, I can't promise anything, but I'll see if he is agreeable. What did you say your name was again?"

"Andrea Warren. I'm sure he'll remember once he hears the name."

"Well then, come on inside, you can wait here in the foyer." She opened the door wider, ushering Andrea in, then padded away on her rubber soles. The grandfather clock ticked the moments away. She waited, heart knocking in her chest. Somewhere a door closed.

It seemed an eternity, but the nurse finally returned, motioning for her to follow. Nerves strung tight as a bow, she followed her through the formal dining room into a butler's pantry, then down a tiled walkway and out into a plant-filled atrium. And there he was.

Steve Strayhorn, her father's old friend.

The mastermind of a plot against her? Hardly.

The man, or what was left of him, sat slumped in a wheelchair. Pale, skeletal, bald, liver-spotted skin like crepe paper. A few more weeks and he would be dead.

Weak-kneed from shock, Andrea squatted down to eye level in front of him, staring into his eyes. He peered back at her, eyes moist with unshed tears, mouth slack under the tubes pumping oxygen up his nose.

"Mr. Strayhorn, I'm Andy's daughter. Andrew Warren. Remember?" she whispered.

He jerked a bit in recognition, then tried to clear his throat. When he finally spoke, drool dripped from a corner of his mouth.

"We grew up together," he managed to mutter. He blinked once, so heavily drugged he could barely sit up.

She stood, backed away a bit. "I was afraid you might not agree to see me."

Eyes flicked away, gazing off into the distance. "It

was hard to lose him," he whispered. Then, as if the exchange had taken all of his energy, he closed his eyes and moaned.

The nurse stepped forward, troubled. "Mr. Strayhorn, I think it's time for your medication. You can't get overtired, you hear?"

Before the woman could stop her, Andrea stepped in, leaned down, and put her mouth to his ear.

"I'm sorry to bother you while you are so ill, but I need answers from you. Please help me."

He drew back, peered up at her. She took the plunge.

"Was my father murdered because of those coffins?"

He stared at her, mouthing like a gaping fish.

"That will be quite enough!"

The voice came from a man about her age standing at the entrance, his expression cold and furious. As he stepped in, the nurse stepped forward, wheeled the old man out of the room so fast that she didn't have time to say anything else to him. Instead, Andrea was left standing alone in the center of the room.

Great. She hadn't counted on having to deal with the son.

"You can leave now. If you don't, I'll call the police."

She swung to face him. "I take it you overheard then," she stated, nerves taut.

"Yes. Not that I'm surprised. Vultures usually do circle the dying."

She flushed. "So...you think I came here for money? You think I'd stoop that low?

He gazed at her, his eyes slits. "You're a Warren

aren't you. Like father, like daughter."

She wanted to claw his eyes out. "I don't want money. I want answers. My father was murdered." she hissed.

He rolled his eyes in disgust. "Listen, we all know how Andrew Warren died. His suicide has haunted my family for years. My father blamed himself, thought he should have been able to stop it somehow. He lost his best friend, for God's sake. Do you have any idea what it did to him seeing you after all these years? He's dying and here you show up on our doorstep, like a ghost trying to haunt him"

"Did it ever occur to you that it was guilt that haunted him all these years, not sadness?" she shot back, watching as his face went pale, his fists clenched.

"And did he tell you how he was the one who was rabid to find those coffins? About all his big plans to turn that whole area into a tourist attraction? He certainly had the motive."

He stiffened, glared at her with rage. She pressed on.

"The man who told me all this drowned this week you know, Willie Batts. But then again, perhaps you know something about that too. And, by chance do you know a Scott McWilliams?"

Finally, he exploded. "This is ridiculous. I'm warning you, if you don't leave right now I'm calling the law."

"By the law do you mean Talton? He's dead too, you know," she goaded.

He held up his cell phone, index finger suspended over the keypad, jaw clenched.

"Don't worry, I wasn't even here," she bantered,

palms lifted in mock surrender. "I'll see myself out." But at the door she turned around and faced him again, lifted her chin.

"You know, I truly do hope your father is as innocent as you seem to think he is. It would be terrible for him to die with blood on his hands. But even if he is a murderer, you had a father most of your life. Mine died when I was four. And for the record, he may not have pulled the trigger, but I think he may know who did." She paused, raised an eyebrow at him, staring at him as if she could see into his soul.

"And I think you do too."

Then she turned her back on him and strode out the door.

❧

Of course she had been bluffing. Strayhorn had seen right through her too, ordering her out as if she was the criminal. All she had done was tip her hand, and for what? Nothing good would come out of this visit she was sure of it.

What had she expected? For the old man to confess, fall on his knees and beg forgiveness? And if he had, what would she have done? Turn in a dead man?

She felt like a fool.

But the longer she sat there, the clearer her mind became. Maybe the meeting hadn't been such a disaster after all. At least she had summoned up the courage to face her enemies. And if the son was behind all the deaths, at least he would know she wasn't as naïve as he thought she was. Maybe he would call off the dogs, for now anyway. She bet anything they were calling Scot McWilliams right now to warn him to lay low.

Then she had an idea. *Doc.* Doc would know what to do.

Thirty minutes later she found herself knocking on the door of his townhouse.

"Andrea my dear! It's so wonderful to see you," he intoned, looking just as he had the last time she had seen him, her last day in Williamsburg. He held both of her hands. "My goodness, you look amazing! Not that you weren't always beautiful, but heavens! What a change!" He said, winking at her and laughing as he ushered her inside. "And I see you're still wearing the necklace I gave you. How sweet!"

Andrea chuckled and shook her head. "Doc, you old flirt. I'm surprised when you answered when I called. Shouldn't you be on a cruise sipping mimosas down in the Caribbean or something?"

"Oh, I have far too much to do here. To tell the truth it feels good to just stay home and rest these tired old bones for a change. I'm so glad you called!"

Shuffling down the hall, he motioned her to follow, regaling her with a list of his latest speaking gigs and a conference he was planning to attend. She was not surprised to see that his living quarters looked just like his office once had; books piled everywhere, dusty cases of artifacts, stacks of the *Washington Post* and *New York Times*, the resting place for various small plates and empty tea cups. As they stepped into the dark pine-paneled den he switched on a floor lamp next to his recliner, and after shooing an overfed Siamese cat off the end of the couch, motioned for her to sit down.

"Would you like a cup of Earl Grey? And I've got some wonderful Scottish shortbread cookies I brought back from the airport in London."

"No, I stopped and got a cup of coffee on the way in. But do you have time to get a bite of lunch? I didn't think to ask when I called."

"Andy, normally I would jump at the chance to be seen with such a charming young woman, but unfortunately I have a doctor's appointment at two. Checking up on the old ticker, you know." He lowered his considerable girth into the recliner, leaning back in his chair. Lacing his hands on the back of his head, he asked, "How about you? I thought you were in Charlotte."

"Charlotte's fine, if you aren't looking for a job in archaeology. Right now, I don't know where I'm going to be living. My Mom died shortly after I saw you, so I decided to get out of town, take a vacation, learn more about my father. Long story short, a lot has happened since her funeral." She looked down, studying the worn carpet beneath her sandals.

His reaction was swift. "Andrea, I'm so sorry. How terrible." The concern in his voice made her throat thicken. She struggled to speak.

"Thanks, but that's not the reason I came. I need to ask you some questions, get some advice."

"Go on." His tone was soft, his expression puzzled.

"There was a trunk in the attic she'd never told me about. It contained a few of my father's personal effects, you know, the usual—clothes, books, wallet, that sort of thing. But there were letters from an old aunt I never knew about, and his field notes." She took a deep breath. She had deliberately left out the part about the ashes. Her father's ashes weren't anyone's business but hers.

"You remember he committed suicide when I was young," she added.

"My dear child, of course I do. You became an archaeologist to follow in his footsteps. We talked about it from time to time. I know he would have been so proud of you."

She hesitated briefly, then blurted. "Well, I've found evidence that he may have been murdered."

"Oh my goodness! Are the police involved?"

"No, not yet. I have no real proof. All I have is an old letter my aunt wrote to my mother. My mother never opened it. I didn't even know my father had family that was still living. She was in a nursing home with Alzheimer's, but yesterday I was told she is now in the hospital in a coma.

"That's a shame. That's a terrible disease."

"Yes, it is, but when she wrote those letters she was still well. She'd been trying to talk to my mother for years. But you know how my mother was. The subject was taboo."

"And what makes you think your aunt wasn't already unwell. It's a progressive disease you know."

"Because some things about the suicide aren't adding up. She thinks he was in trouble because of some coffins he found."

He sighed, the look on his face troubled.

"Andrea, I don't know what to say. Are you sure your mother didn't know anything?"

"No, she put everything in the trunk in the attic and closed the door to the past. She was so angry at him, not just for the separation, but because of the way he chose to die. It makes me so sad that she never knew the truth. That would have changed everything Doc." She paused, batted back tears. "Listen, I'm not asking you to help me solve a murder, if that's what you're worried about. I simply need your advice about something I found in the trunk." She reached into her knapsack and handed the pictures to him. He picked up a magnifying glass he kept on the side table by his chair, raised them closer to the light, examining them closely. She could see the color rising in his neck. He looked up at her.

"Are these the only originals that you have?"

"Yes, but I made copies."

"What do you think they are?"

"I know you are going to think I'm crazy, but they may be coffins found in the swamps of Dare County by a dragline operator in 1950. He was by himself, didn't know what to do, so he reburied them. But they were never found again. I think my father may have stumbled on them."

"Yes, I'm familiar with that story. But the archaeological community has always assumed they were more recent than the colonial period."

"Well, a local historian is so convinced he wrote his master's thesis about it. He had inside knowledge because he was an employee of the company who hired the dragline operator. Even though he's in his eighties he seems very sharp. Not a weirdo or anything. He knew the man, interviewed him, as well as the other two men helping with the search. He swears they are still there, not far from Milltail Creek, where my father and his friends spent a lot of time."

"But these could have been taken anywhere in the world, Andrea. They're worthless out of context."

"I know, but I haven't told you all of it. I have my father's field notes. They were in the trunk. He describes finding them, but then the narrative stops. And a few pages seem to be missing."

Doc pursed his mouth. "Interesting," he murmured, tapping his fingers on his cheek, deep in thought. "Can you show them to me?"

She reached down to her knapsack, handed the Day Planner to him, pointing out the pages she had bookmarked. She watched him read. When he was done, he shrugged as if he was confused, put them down, and with raised eyebrows studied the pictures again. "I admit they appear to be early colonial coffins, the carving on the wood dates them easily enough. Do you mind if I keep the pictures and study them? I'll blow them up in the lab, try to get a sharper image. I'll call you with my findings. In the meantime, I'll keep them safe, I promise."

She hesitated, waffling. She hated to let them out of her sight, but of course he needed to study them. The originals were blurry. The copies on her phone were worthless. With no access to a lab now, Doc was her only hope.

"Not a problem. I'm glad you can help me."

When he spoke again, his voice was gentle. "I know all this must be very hard on you dear, being an orphan now with no brothers or sisters. I'll do anything I can to help you. But promise me you won't get your hopes up. I suspect these are fakes."

She bristled. "Well, if they are, my father didn't make them. And besides, other things have happened." She stopped, hesitant to say more, but it was too late.

He leaned forward, touched her arm. "What things, Andrea? I can't help you if you don't tell me."

"I'm being stalked. It's too long of a story, but trust me, I know. I just don't know why. But there is more. Yesterday morning, after I talked to a local fisherman in Columbia, he drowned in the creek. He knew my father quite well and more importantly, who might want him dead. And then I learned Polly had fallen into a coma. She was healthy when I visited her the day before."

He sagged back in the chair, frowning. He looked tired, old.

"Andrea, both these people were elderly. Couldn't their deaths simply be a coincidence? I don't mean to make you feel bad but perhaps your visit after all these years was too much for them."

Andrea nodded, throat tight. "I know. I thought about that. I feel horrible. But then something else happened that changed my mind. Right after I heard about their deaths I decided to look for the man who found my father's body on the river. Just so happens he died two weeks ago too, about the same time my mother did. The story out there is that he had cancer and was depressed, so he killed himself when no one was home. But I talked to a family member. She said his cancer was gone, and that he bragged about having covered up a murder a long time ago when he was drinking. She thought he was blackmailing someone. Said it was over something found in the Dare County swamps." She leaned back, winded, a headache beginning to thud behind her eyes.

He sighed, shaking his head in annoyance. "Andrea all this is circumstantial. You have no proof that this man's death, if it was murder, had anything to do with your father. May I remind you that you are a scientist. You know the dangers of assuming too much. And honestly, it all sounds a bit farfetched to me. If your father did find the coffins again, don't you think they would have surfaced by now? Who would keep such an enormous find a secret?"

"I wish I knew. Maybe he hid them and someone thinks he's told me where they are. That's my theory anyway."

"Maybe. But there are more reasonable explanations, you know. Remember Occam's Razor…"

"I know, I know… among competing hypotheses, the simplest one with the fewest assumptions should be selected. How many times did you repeat that to us in class," she recited, finishing his sentence for him.

His reply was gentle. "You are making a lot of wild connections, my dear, with little or no proof."

She glanced away, across the room. No way she could tell him about her visions. She'd be a laughing stock. Finally, she looked back at him. When she answered him her voice was firm and unyielding.

"Don't ask me how I know, but I just do, okay? Call it what you want, but something is telling me I'm right and that I should be worried. Doesn't that count for something? People are dying. Isn't that proof enough?"

He frowned, shrugging. The cat jumped up on his lap. "Well then, let's assume you are right and your father was murdered. That doesn't necessarily mean that it was because of the coffins. Maybe he made some locals mad, or perhaps it's the land itself that was more important. You said that the dragline operator was in there because a large company was planning on developing it. What if they destroyed them? You, of all people, should know what developers and landowners can do if they feel threatened."

Her neck stiffened. "You're talking about Williamsburg now, aren't you?"

"Of course. I'm protective of you, Andrea. If you're dealing with the rich and powerful here, then it could only end badly, like it did last time. I know it hurts to think that your father died the way he did, but stirring up things without having enough evidence won't bring him back from the dead. I suspect the coffins, real or not, are long gone by now. It's been over thirty years."

Her heart sank. She lowered her eyes and stared into her hands. "No one seems to care."

"Andrea, I do care and, trust me, I understand your frustration. But I worry about you."

Suddenly she saw herself through his eyes, how she must look to him—like an overly reactive, distraught young woman claiming to be a victim yet again. And she had fed right into that picture, hadn't she? She with her cloak and dagger stories. And why should he believe her? She had been his prize pupil and, in the end, she'd made a fool of him. She slumped backwards.

"Sorry if I wasted your time," she murmured.

He reached over, patted her on the arm. "Andrea, you have never wasted my time. It was a delight to see you. I only wish it had been under different circumstances." He sighed, leaned in even closer, his voice soft.

"Lie low for a few years, let things blow over. If I were you I'd look at finishing your education. I'd be glad to write a letter of recommendation to a doctoral program, maybe up in Massachusetts. They loved you up there. I could probably get a few others on board. Leave ghost hunting to reality television. Focus on the science, my child." He leaned back slightly, then heaved himself up off his chair. Shuffling to his feet, he offered her a hand. "Now, I'm done preaching. Sorry, but I really must get on to that appointment. I'll walk you to the door."

Her head was pounding. Ignoring his hand, she stood, feeling more alone than ever. "I'm sorry Doc but I'm not going to run this time. I was powerless to do anything about the ossuary but crawl away with my tail tucked between my legs, but this time is different. I can't let this go, not this time. Too much is at stake. Don't bother to see me out, okay?" Trembling, she strode to the door, slammed it behind her, and ran to her car.

She sat behind the wheel, fuming. He had treated her like a child.

It couldn't have been locals. Andrew Warren had been raised by a man who was one of them. And if Doc's theory was correct, and it was more about the land, then who was around that would know?

There was only one person and that was the

author of that book about those coffins. She picked up her phone and dialed 411.

CHAPTER FOURTEEN

SURE, HE'D TALK WITH HER. The only catch was she would have to interview him at a local Quaker historic site nearby where he was volunteering as a docent for the day. "We'll talk while I give you a tour," he suggested, clearly eager for her to show an interest.

"Sign me up." She'd gladly spend an hour hearing about some old Quakers if Mr. McMullan would answer her questions.

The historic site near Hertford was only an hour or so from Doc's place, just a couple of miles off Hwy 17. Right away she was drawn to the tiny gem of a house perched on a rise overlooking the Perquimans River. The gravel road up the slight incline was at least a quarter of a mile long and straight as an arrow, flanked by flowering cotton plants stretching up the rows on each side. Even from that distance she could tell it was late seventeenth century. The Flemish bond brickwork, gambrel slate roof, traditional Elizabethan diamond-paned leaded windows rivaled those found in Yorktown. She was surprised she'd never heard of it before now.

She pulled into the parking lot of the Visitor's

Center. A tall, white-haired elder statesman stood on the veranda waiting for her. He reached out and warmly shook her hand.

"Welcome to the Newbold-White House," he intoned, obviously in full tour guide mode.

"Why thank you, kind sir, "she responded in like manner, for the next half hour following him around as he walked her up the hill, regaling her with the history of the place.

Not that she knew that much about the Quakers. Her knowledge of the Albemarle focused more on the Indians once here, predating any white settlers by at least 20,000 years.

"Who settled this place?" she asked.

"A man by the name of Joseph Scott. It was called The Vineyards back then. At one time it encompassed almost a thousand acres, between he and his son. We believe he came here around 1683."

She stopped and looked around. "I noticed there was a Thomas Scott on the ship's roster of the Roanoke colonists. Any chance he was a descendant of Joseph?"

"Well, that's an interesting question. I don't think any of us have ever connected those dots. One of our board members has been doing some research on the subject but she hasn't found anything definitive so far." By then they were inside, looking out the mullioned windows toward the river.

"How far away are we from Beechland?" she asked.

"Only about an hour by water. We own a reproduction of a periauger likely used back then so we can reenact those voyages. It would have been easy for the colonists to navigate these waters, if that is what you are thinking. The Indians here were friendly enough. But lately we've been concentrating over in the Rocky Hock area of Edenton and Salmon Creek. There have been some promising finds there."

"So I've heard," she murmured, staring out the window at the river again. She spotted a large antique sailing vessel coming up from the direction of the Albemarle Sound. It looked like the one she'd seen a few weeks ago when she had been standing on the Alligator River Bridge. That must have been it.

"Is that a periauger?" she asked.

"Why yes, it is. The crew took it out today on a demonstration. It was made down in the Wooden Boat Museum in Beaufort. It's our pride and joy. You ought to go out on it sometime. We offer tours on special occasions."

"I'd love to, but not sure how long I'll be in the area. Do you have a brochure?"

"Why don't we go back up to the office and I'll give you one."

As they walked back down the hill he shared a few details about himself, his impressive work history as a research scientist at RTI in the Raleigh-Durham area, how he had recently completed a book on the history of "Blacklands" farming, and how upon his retirement he had gotten involved in the Lost Colony research. That, and the opportunity to teach, sent him back to graduate school at the age of eighty to get a master's degree in history.

Andrea shook her head in disbelief. "I'm amazed. It takes a lot of determination to do what you've done at any age. You must be pretty sure of finding things if you spend so much time looking."

He chuckled. "Well, look long enough and you tend to find things. Although, sometimes it's not what you wanted," he bantered. By then they were in the office. He offered her the wing chair as he sat down behind the desk.

"But you still haven't found those coffins?" she asked, gently steering the conversation again.

"No, we haven't found the coffins, not yet."

"Do you believe they are still there?"

"Yes, I do." Then, a bit flustered, "Miss Warren—Andy—can I ask you why those coffins are so important to you?"

She turned her head and gazed out the window across a field. If her visit with Doc and Steven Strayhorn had taught her anything, it might be wise to tell this man as little as possible.

"I'm an archaeologist, albeit unemployed right now. My father, Andrew Warren, spent a lot of time looking for those coffins before he died in 1985. Before that he was an archaeology student at East Carolina, studying under Dr. Phelps. Grew up in East Lake, knew the Beechland area like the back of his hand. I am told finding those coffins became his obsession."

His mouth dropped open, speechless. She kept going.

"Evidently the school didn't know what he was doing. His searches were conducted on his own time, mainly on the weekends."

"This is the first I've heard of your father. And I thought I knew everything about the subject." His gave a sigh, pursing his lips. "So, what is it you think I can help you with?"

"I want to clarify some details, particularly about the area where the coffins were found. Who owned the land in 1985? And if my father did find those coffins before he died, what would the owners have stood to lose?"

"Do you think he found them?"

"I don't know," she lied.

He turned to gaze out of the window, then, narrowing his eyes, turned back toward her. "At the time the riven coffins were first found, in 1950, the Dare mainland was owned by the West Virginia Paper Company, later known as Westvaco. That company was purchased by Malcolm McLean, who created a company called Prulean, with the Prudential Life Insurance Company. They were going to drain the swamps and turn it into farmland. But their venture failed to receive a "dragline and fill" permit from the Corps of Engineers, so Prulean had to give up. Since it was no longer viable for farmland, they granted it to the Nature Conservancy. But The Nature Conservancy couldn't manage such a large gift. They turned around and gave it to the Department of the Interior for the U.S. Fish and Wildlife Service to create the Alligator River Wildlife Refuge. So, to answer your question, Prulean owned the land."

"So, what impact would a major find like that have had on the value of the land?"

"Malcolm would have been thrilled. It would have raised the value as a potential historic site and offset the millions originally invested. Your father would have been given a medal and paid handsomely for saving the ship. Of course, you do know that once it was out of the hands of private investors, any digging would have been illegal, don't you? But you said your father passed away before then, correct? That's a shame."

She nodded. *Another dead end.*

He paused and stared out the window, expression sad. "You know, my dream for the last ten years is that someone—anyone—would find those coffins." He turned to her and winked. "Be careful, looking for them can become an obsession, you know." His smile was rueful.

She cocked her head. "I know. It's frustrating. But honestly, I'm more interested in my father's role in all of it than looking for them myself. At least I don't have to take on a major corporation with big money. On the other hand, now I'm back at square one." Discouragement began to rise, tightening her chest. But she had one last question.

"You're not far from Edenton. Did you know the McWilliams family?"

His eyes lit up. "Sure did. As far as I know they were fine people, particularly Bill. We served on several committees together. He was a very capable attorney. He died way too young. A terrible loss for his family and his community."

"So, did he ever express any interest in the history of the coffins?"

"Not at all. Bill was never much of a history buff. In fact, he thought it was all a huge waste of time."

His phone buzzed in his shirt pocket. He reached in; glancing at it. "That's my wife Norma calling. We are scheduled to be somewhere by five. I better close up here and get going. So, are you going to write about your findings?"

"I'm technically an archaeologist, if that is what

you're asking, but I have no plans to publish my findings. This is strictly a personal project."

"Well shucks. I thought you were going to make me rich and famous," he bantered, shrugging his shoulders, chuckling at his own joke.

"You've been very kind. As I said, I'd appreciate it if you wouldn't say anything to anyone yet. I promise I will let you know if any additional information surfaces. I'm not quite sure what to do next, not yet anyway."

"Oh, mum's the word. Keep in mind, however, that it's not a good time to go down in the swamps looking for anything. If you do, be sure to put on your snake boots and take a gun," he advised, raising his eyebrows.

"Weren't Quakers pacifists?" she teased, grinning back at him.

"Well, I'm a Whiskipalian, so that lets me off the hook. But the last time I checked snakes don't discriminate between denominations," he joked.

Smiling, she said her goodbyes, waving as she walked to the car. At least he'd been helpful and didn't treat her like a child.

But if corporate intrigue had been ruled out, where did that leave her now?

As she turned onto the highway, she looked back at the house. The afternoon sunlight gleamed like a beacon as it bounced off the majestic diamond-paned windows, shooting off rays of light like a star. The Quakers called themselves Children of the Light.

I sure could use some of that light now, she thought, pointing the car east toward Edenton.

&

She ended up at the town park in Edenton over-looking Edenton Bay, the late afternoon June sun warm on her face, thoughts clouded. What if every-thing was simply a product of her overwrought mind. Dreams, visions, amateurish attempts at detective work. Who had she been kidding? Doc was right. She had made too many assumptions, and look where they had gotten her.

She surveyed her surroundings, suddenly weary to the bone. Ancient cypress trees and Spanish moss, civil war cannon lined up in a row, a parade of grand three and four story historic houses com-plete with deep verandas, cupolas and trailing ivy. A scene right out of a movie.

Is that what she was doing? Starring in her own movie, writing a script to fit the few facts that she knew? And what did she really know for sure?

Nothing.

She should file a report on her way out of town and be done with it.

And his killer will get away with it....

Shut up, already! Geez, she was sick of that voice already. Angry now, she got up off the bench and walked over to the handrail and stared down into the water. Her own reflection stared back at her, wavy.

Then another face took the place of her own. A warrior, face painted red and black, eyes like obsid-ian. His image undulated in the water, staring at her. He touched his finger to his lips, then faded away.

Lord, now she really was letting her imagination

get the best of her.

Then she heard a voice from behind her. "What's the story, morning glory?"

"Derek! What are you doing here?" she exclaimed, relieved. Maybe a real live person would keep her from conjuring up ghosts.

"Well, I just got out of a training in the county courthouse down the street. I plan to reward myself for living through all that boredom by having dinner at Waterman's." He pulled back, looked her over. "By the way, love the look. But I almost didn't recognize you. What brought that on?"

She turned, stared down again, relieved to see nothing but her own reflection. "Trying to morph into a new life, I suppose. But evidently it didn't work." She gave him a quick, wan smile and added, "I think it's time to go get my dog."

He frowned. "How about dinner first?"

"Thanks Derek, but I'm beat. I need to get on back home, wherever that is."

"Hey, no pressure. Maybe some other time." He paused; leaned on the rail.

"You aren't here to confront McWilliams are you?" he asked, glancing sideways at her.

Her mouth twisted. He'd read her mind. "Honestly, I thought about it. But I don't think that would be wise."

He let out a sigh of relief. "That's good. You need to stay away from him." He rubbed the back of his neck with one hand. "Headed home to Charlotte?"

"Probably. I can put in a security system and change the locks. I may take a vacation, go check out doctoral programs up north."

He patted her on the back. "Well, be safe. I gotta

run, okay? Give me a call if you need me."

"I will. Thanks for trying to help."

She watched him as he walked away. Maybe she *should* have accepted his invitation to dinner. But she doubted she'd be good company. She was too tired and too much going on in her head to make small talk. Not after the kind of day she'd had.

She gazed off across the bay, an idea forming. She wasn't afraid of Scott anymore, and if she had her bearings right the Montrose was just a few miles from here. It would be easy enough to ride by the house. If his truck was gone all she had to do was get the nail off the hook on the back porch, open the guest house, get the trunk, and be gone in fifteen minutes. At least she'd have something to show for her day. If he was home she'd keep on driving. If he showed up unexpectedly, well Derek was close by.

She looked at her phone. It was almost five p.m. She'd better get a move on.

CHAPTER FIFTEEN

NO WHITE TRUCK, NO LIGHTS on any-where. The grass needed cutting. It looked as if he'd taken off and gone somewhere for a few weeks.

She hoped he'd gone to hell.

The guest house was unlocked, thank goodness, looking exactly like it had the day she'd left. A plastic cup she used still sat on the kitchen counter. But a quick check of its rooms made it clear the trunk was gone.

Damn. He must have taken it up to the big house.

She ran up the hill toward the kitchen, glancing up at the second-floor window, just in case. No curtain moved, thank goodness. As she expected the door going into the kitchen was unlocked too.

Inside, the kitchen hadn't been touched. How long was that—almost a week? Even the dirty dishes from their dinner were still in the sink, dried and moldy looking. *Ugh.* That was strange. Scott seemed to be the meticulous type.

But maybe that had all been an act, like everything else. For all she knew he could be a total slob. She glanced around the kitchen. The laptop was gone, of course.

A sweep of the downstairs revealed nothing – not even in the closets. Taking the steps two at a time, she made it to the upstairs landing, unsettled to find herself face-to-face with the portrait of Mary Montrose McWilliams, dark eyes staring right at her, following her as she walked down the landing toward the bedrooms.

Carolina's mother. *It had to be.* Limpid brown eyes, dark hair in a bun, white ruffle around the neck—the pale face under its domed glass frame made the hairs stand up on her arms.

Be careful.

The voice was only in her imagination, of course. Even so, it unnerved her. Heart quickening, she ran from room to room opening each bedroom door, six altogether, each in various phases of reconstruction. Except for one, which was locked. She rattled the door knob in frustration, then looked around the landing.

There! A pair of old-fashioned scissors lying on the old oak bureau in the hall under the portrait, but the blades looked too thick to do her any good.

Then—a moan—coming from inside the locked room. She could have sworn the sound was human. Had Scott kidnapped someone and tied them up in there? The thought made her nauseous. She was about to pull out her phone and call Derek, when she heard the screen door slam.

Crap!

She peeked out the window, exhaled sharply in relief.

"Derek, I'm up here!" she called out.

Silence.

Louder. "Derek, I'm on the second floor! Get up

here. I think there's someone locked up in a bed-room!"

Be careful.

That whisper again, louder now, swirling around her head.

He stood at the base of the stairs looking up at her, blue eyes shining. "I thought I warned you to stay away from here. What are you doing?"

She could tell he was angry at her, but there was something else in his expression, more than just anger. Cunning?

"You know, you're probably right. I shouldn't have come," she answered, trying to sound non-chalant. Then that whisper again:

Be careful.

The portrait stared at her. "Be right there." She grabbed the scissors and slid them into the waist of her pants, then made a pretense of casually skip-ping down the stairs, brushing past Derek without stopping.

 But instead of letting her pass, he grabbed her wrist, his fingers covering her hawk tattoo, still fresh. "Don't do something stupid, Andrea," he warned her. "You could get us both in trouble."

"What are you doing, you idiot! That hurts." She twisted away. "Let me go!"

But he only tightened his grip, staring at her.

And in that moment—a flash really—she saw a scene unfolding.

Derek and Willie arguing, then a fist up against the side of Willie's head. Willie plunging into the water.

Rage gripped her body, made her go rigid.

"Get your hands off me," she hissed.

He pulled her roughly into the study, threw her

down into the leather chair. He loomed over her, smug and disdainful.

"You're just as stupid as your father," he snarled.

She lunged at him, tried to kick him between the legs. He shoved her back down into the chair, simultaneously pulling out his gun, clicking off the safety.

"Who killed my father?" she growled, chest heaving.

He cocked his head, face impassive. "You, Andrea. You killed your father."

"Is that so? Me, a child? Right." Her voice dripped sarcasm.

Be careful.

"He was doomed the minute you were conceived."

"Cut the crap," she spat.

Ignoring her he sidled over to the window, pushing aside the heavy velvet drape. Something about the way the curtain moved triggered a memory.

Derek. He was the one watching her from upstairs the night she was here. He and Scott were working together! Her heart sank as he turned, walked back over to her, and sat down on the ottoman facing her. The look of hatred in his eyes made her shudder.

"It was difficult, but I learned to tolerate your existence. Everything would have been fine if you'd just gone on home to Charlotte, you know. But you had to get nosy, didn't you? Had to start asking questions?" He rolled his eyes and shook his head as if he was talking to a disobedient child.

"So, you're working for Scott?" she whispered.

He bristled. "That moron. You've got to be kidding me." He reached in his shirt pocket with his left hand, punching in a number with his thumb.

"Bring him down," he ordered, pocketing the phone, looking at her with something almost like pity. A door opened upstairs. She heard feet shuffling down the hall. As she waited, the grandfather clock ticked loudly in the hall.

Scott appeared, inching his way down the step. But not the Scott she remembered, the stalker. This Scott was almost unrecognizable, face horribly bruised and bloody, arms tied at the wrists behind his back as he limped down the stairs. His head hung, eyes down. And behind him, a hand holding a gun into his back. Scuffed loafers, shapeless pants, maroon sweater.

Doc.

She wanted to vomit.

The old man said nothing to her as he emerged into the room, simply raised his eyebrows and flashed a rueful half-smile. His self-satisfied, arrogant expression spoke volumes.

"How could you?" she whispered, broken.

He sighed heavily, as if weary of the world. "How could I not? I've been waiting for this for years." Then he cocked his head to the side and smirked. "It won't be the first time an archaeologist has been bribed, you know."

"Williamsburg? You engineered that?"

"Of course, Andrea. And it worked didn't it, at least for a while. You handed those pictures over so fast I couldn't believe my good fortune."

Despair washed over her. "How long?" she whispered.

"Oh, a long time, Andrea. A very long time. Did

you honestly think you got that scholarship on your own?"

She closed her eyes. "Why?"

He sighed, as if the effort of explaining was beneath him.

"I met Andrew when he was a graduate student. He was considering transferring into our program. Steve Strayhorn has been an old friend of mine for years. I even went exploring with them every now and then. In fact, it was Willie who used to take us out, and Willie who eventually introduced me to Derek here. Made sure he had a good supply of cheap whiskey, kept the wheels greased, you know, but I don't think he ever really figured out anything. He was too drunk most of the time."

"So, what changed then?" She could barely get the words out.

"You showed up. Of course, I knew you eventually would. And I was right, wasn't I?" His tone was soft, oily. "We couldn't believe our good fortune when your mother died and left you the trunk. Her timing was perfect."

Her head was beginning to spin. "But there was nothing in the trunk. I showed you everything."

"Well of course not. We know you have the key."

She glared at him. Her fingers itched to reach for the scissors. Instead, she sucked in a deep breath.

"I don't know what you are talking about. Did you kill my father?"

"Oh, I may be many things, but I'm not a murderer." He turned to Derek, like he was the ringmaster in a circus. "Why don't you tell her? It's your story after all."

Derek smirked. "I'd be delighted." Then he

turned to Andrea, "You see, you deprived me of a family, Andrea." He paused, waving the gun in the direction of the old man. "And Doc here, well, your father deprived old Doc here his rightful due."

"What do you mean?" she whispered, acid burning in her throat.

"Don't be so dense, Andy. Can't you see the family resemblance? Andrew Warren was my father first. He betrayed me and my mother when he conceived you!"

The reality of what he was saying was dawning on her.

His singsong voice continued. The gun waved in her face. "Now you're getting it sweetie. You're my little sister. You stole my father from me."

"Why didn't your mother tell him?" she cried. "Because she couldn't, not at the time anyway. Grandpa Whitlow sent her to New York to get an abortion, swore he'd disown her if she told anyone. But she gave birth to me without telling him and put me in an orphanage. She planned to come back and get me when she could."

Andrea stared at him. *This madman was her brother.*

Derek tone softened; almost became childlike. He let the gun dangle between his knees.

"She didn't know that the orphanage was a bad place."

"Did she kill him?" she whispered.

His jaw jutted out, his head wagging back and forth in denial. "No. My mother is a wonderful woman. It was an accident."

"What do you mean *an accident?*"

"She was angry because he wouldn't believe her. They argued. She pushed him. He hit his head on an iron stake." He stuck out a jaw. "As far as I'm concerned, he got what he deserved."

She shook her head in disbelief. "Why didn't she call for help?"

"She did. She called Strayhorn. He told her he would take care of it." He grinned as if he was cracking a joke. "And he did."

"Strayhorn hired Talton to cover it up, make it look like a suicide?"

"That's about right," he responded, voice smooth and silken. A picture of the snake on Anna Lee's doorstep flashed into her head.

"Then your mother went over the edge, didn't she?" she whispered.

The switch in mood was abrupt. "Shut up, bitch. You don't know a thing about my mother. There's nothing wrong with her."

She froze. He stood up, kicking the ottoman away.

"I'm the oldest child. I'm the son. He should have believed her. She would never have lied to him. He owes me! Where is the damn key?"

She cut her eyes up at him. "I said I don't know anything about any key. All I found was the pictures."

"You're lying." Spittle flew in her face.

"Why would I lie? Either way you're going to kill me. Let the professor over there lead you to them. He thinks he knows everything." She glared at Doc.

Derek reached down, grabbed her by the arm so hard she cried out.

"Help me put them both in the truck," he ordered, twisting her arm behind her back. Doc nudged Scott's back with the gun.

"You heard him, son. Start walking."

Only then did Scott raise his head. Both eyes were almost swollen shut and glazed. He looked as if he had been drugged.

Within moments they were outside. As Doc watched from the top of the steps, Derek reached into the backseat of his truck, grabbed a nylon cord, wrapping her wrists together. Then he shoved them both in the backseat, side by side; slammed the door shut.

"Call me when it's over," Doc called out to Derek.

 Derek turned and looked at him, his eyes glassy, vacant. He cocked his head. "It's already over Pops," he stated, voice flat and cold. Andrea gasped, twisting around in her seat in time to see Derek lift the gun and shoot the man between the eyes. She heard the body tumble down the steps.

 Moaning, she burst into sobs.

Derek seemed totally unfazed, almost cheerful. He walked back to the body, nudged it with his foot, then opened the bed of the truck. He pulled out a canvas, rolled the corpse in it, then pulled it onto the bed, grunting and heaving. Then, brushing off his hands, he hopped into the driver's seat, slamming the door shut behind him. Gunning the motor, he let it idle, then swiveled his head around to them.

 "That's five dead, sis. All because of you. Want to go for six?" he joked, winking at her.

She shut her eyes, forcing the tears back, biting her lip until it bled. Snickering, Derek pulled out of the driveway toward the road. Beside her, Scott let his head fall on the back of the seat, his eyes closed.

At the end of the driveway he turned left, to the south. In a state of euphoria, he kept laughing at his own jokes, bragging about his exploits, thumping on the top of the steering wheel with the palms of his hands like he was playing bass to a rap song.

No matter how much she squirmed, the rope wouldn't budge, burning her wrists. The tattoo throbbed. He was taking them somewhere secluded, no doubt. In this part of the world, that could be anywhere.

Then, out of the corner of her eye, Scott moved ever so slightly, his head inching toward her shoulder. Repelled, she shifted away from him. But he only slid further toward her, his face down now, leaning forward at bit. She thought for a moment he had passed out. Then he turned his face toward her ever so slightly, motioned with his eyes. When she looked in the direction he wanted, she caught movement behind his back. It appeared he was trying to work his hands out of ropes, but she couldn't tell. There wasn't enough light.

Suddenly Derek growled, jerked up to peer at them in the rearview mirror. "What's going on back there?"

Scott froze.

"He passed out," she blurted, holding her breath. He kept glaring, but by then they had begun passing over the Albemarle Sound Bridge so he had to focus on driving, keep his eyes on the road. As they passed over the sound, she saw Derek's shoulders relaxing from behind, only letting her breath out when he turned up the radio a bit and began whistling a tune.

She gazed out over the water, eyes bloodshot, head pounding. The sun was setting, a wide panorama of pinks, gold, magenta, and violet, its beauty almost painful. She wondered if it was the last sunset she would ever see. Beside her she could feel Scott's hands working his ropes.

But how could she ever trust him? He was the one who had gotten her into this mess.

It didn't help that Derek was too quiet now, brooding. But at least he'd turned the music up loud, to a local country station, that would help mask any sounds they might make. Still, she didn't dare move. He was too on edge. She couldn't even feel her hands anymore. Her arms and shoulders were on fire.

Then, under cover of darkness, she could feel Scott shifting again. Ever so slowly he was moving his left hand from behind his back and sliding it down behind hers. Her gush of relief was so intense she had to clamp her mouth shut to keep from crying out.

She alternated between clearing her throat and sighing—anything to cover the sounds Scott might make as his left fingers worked to untie the rope that bound her. In the light of the dashboard she could see sweat beading his brow.

But what would they do if they managed to escape? For all she knew he was plotting to free himself and leave her behind, or worse, take her as a hostage, use her like Doc had. She still had no idea the extent of his involvement.

Hope flared a bit when Derek turned down River Road toward Anna Lee's cabin. But instead of stopping at the footbridge he kept driving for another half mile or so, turning right onto what seemed to be an abandoned logging road. Her heart began thudding, she broke out into a cold sweat, all hope of escape dwindling away. In a panic, she began twisting her wrists. The air was stifling. She couldn't breathe.

Agitated, Derek slammed his palm against the radio, cursing at the DJ. *Stop playing the same songs idiot!* Muttering, he lowered his window, dangling his arm out. Driving with one hand on the steering wheel, his eyes scanned the woods like something primal, nervous, cursing angrily when a big white barn owl swooped from the left across the path in front of them, then upward into the woods on their right, eyes glowing as he passed.

She shivered. A symbol of wisdom or impending death?

The ruts became deeper, the switch weed higher, headlights bouncing wildly as the truck swayed and lurched in the primitive road. A few deer bounded off, startled, but a doe and her spotted fawn seemed trapped in the headlights, huddling together as they passed, as terrified as she.

They were emerging into a clearing of some kind. The truck slowed to a stop. Derek shut down the engine.

In the quiet she heard bullfrogs croak, then plop into the water with a splash. Cicadas trilled in the woods. Stars pulsated in the dark sky. They were miles from any town. By the time anyone found them, they would be nothing but bones.

Feverishly, she began praying. *Please God!* Beside her Scott tensed to spring.

But just as he was about to make a move Derek leaned forward and slapped the windshield with the palm of his hand. "Damn mosquitoes," he muttered.

Scott collapsed back against the seat and moaned in despair. Unaware, Derek turned and looked back at them.

"You ready to take a little walk, Sis?"

Panic washed over her and her legs began trembling. The one opportunity Scott had to take Derek down and now the chance was blown. She couldn't help it; she burst into sobs.

"Stupid bitch," he muttered, then opened his door and hopped out, strolling casually over into the weeds on the side of the road. Whistling, he unzipped his pants and peed. Afterwards, he made a show of straightening his clothes, yawning and stretching, dragging out the moment. Finally, bored with his own show, he strolled over to her door and jerked it open, motioning for her to get out of the truck.

Scott lay in the backseat, pretending to be unconscious. Perhaps he really was, she couldn't tell. Dragging her up to the front of the truck, cursing when she tripped on a small root, Derek slung her up against the metal grille, her back against the hot metal. Then, satisfied she was where he wanted her, he trotted backward a few yards and took out his gun, pulled out the cartridge and quickly shoved it back in place, checking the magazine. Then, as if he was preparing for target practice, he pointed the barrel toward her, aimed at her between the crosshairs.

She froze. Closed her eyes.

But instead of shooting, he lowered the gun, began walking around in aimless circles. Ranting, he babbled on and on about how horrid the orphanage had been, abuse at the hands of vicious foster parents; what a hero he had been in Iraq and Afghanistan. Once, when he thought she wasn't paying close enough attention, he screamed at her, blaming her for everything bad that had ever happened to him. Then, for no apparent reason, he changed tactics, begging her to understand that he was the victim in all of this, not her. But as he tired he wound down, stopped to stare off into the woods as if he was deciding what to do next.

That is when she heard the chanting. At first far away, then gradually louder, it reverberated in her head. And with the voices came a vision, like a hologram of sorts, circling around her. The figures seemed formless, without shape. But as the chanting became louder and clearer, so did her ability to see them. She could see three arrows tattooed on their arms, the symbol used by Secotan warriors, firelight flickering on their tortured faces. The closer they came the louder their voices— blood-curdling yells, in agony for the beheading of their great *weroance*, Wingina. One warrior stood out of all the rest, beautiful and fierce, obsidian eyes glowing.

And as the chanting grew, history began to unfold before her eyes, like a banner across the night sky. She saw murders, massacres, and starvation. Christian martyrs being persecuted. Slavery, inquisitions, and beheadings. Innocent women being burned in the name of witchcraft, babies being dashed against the rocks by wicked kings, Quakers being branded, their ears cut off. Jews being gassed in ovens.

She wanted to scream out loud for their pain. This was the story of her ancestors, thousands of years of earthly fathers and mothers calling to her down through the ages, reaching out to her, calling her tell the truth about their stories and free them all for good!

Power in the blood that came from her Creator. Power in the blood from both worlds....

That blood surged through her now, giving her the strength to reach deep inside of her heart and soul.

Slowly she began using her fingers to search for the grille behind her. Locating one of the bars, she grabbed hold of it, using it as a brace to free her right hand. She could feel the skin peeling as she worked the cord. In agony, she bit her tongue.

Then, just like that, her hand pulled free.

Still, she didn't move. Instead, she called out to her brother, softly at first.

"Derek?"

He cocked his head, his lip curled. She spoke again, her words soft, insinuating.

"We don't need the key. Doc figured out where the coffins were when he saw the pictures this morning. That's why I left them with him. Doc and I planned to meet at the Montrose and go look for them, then you showed up and spoiled his plan."

Frowning, Derek stepped in closer. Right away she could see he was confused. Sensing her advantage, she pressed in.

"I swear it's true. I got to Edenton early so I waited on the waterfront. I lied to you because

I didn't want you to follow me. But you did. We should never have underestimated you." She held her breath, praying he would believe her.

"Why didn't he just kill me then?" he growled.

"Doc was a master manipulator, Derek. You know that. He planned to use you to do his dirty work first. Once we all were dead, he could claim he discovered the coffins. But you were smart. You stopped him first."

He glared at her, then turned away, his face in the shadows. She kept talking, hoping if she talked fast enough he wouldn't see the obvious holes in her story.

"I can show you where they are. But without an archaeologist to give them credibility the coffins have no value, not even on the black market. I can help you. Please…."

Derek crossed his arms, slowly turned back around. A nerve in his face twitched.

"You're my brother. I'll swear you killed Doc protecting me."

His head tilted. Shadows moved across his face. Her words were coming in a rush.

"Willie and Polly were old. It was just a matter of time anyway. I'm sorry you got a raw deal. Let me make it up to you."

She stopped, held her breath. There was nothing left to say.

At first his expression was unreadable, the only sound their breathing. He stared at her, his eyes icy blue pools. Then, suddenly, his demeanor darkened. He growled at her, like an animal. He strode up to her, glaring, grabbing her by the neck, pointing the gun at her forehead, his face inches from her, voice low and deadly.

"You think I give a shit about those coffins, you bitch? All I care about is getting rid of you," he bellowed, spit flying in her face.

Suddenly another vision flashed in her head.

A lone soldier on reconnaissance. Starving refugees, innocent women and children. Cries of agony and disbelief as one by one they fall to the ground.

Derek, the natural born killer.

She could see it all so clearly now, even down to how he would get away with their murders. He would arrange their bodies to make it look as if Doc had killed them and then himself. He would meticulously clean and place the unregistered gun in Doc's hand. Then he'd go back to the Montrose, wipe the place of all evidence, wash the blood from his truck, and go eat a steak somewhere, relishing every gory detail.

The script kept rolling, like a movie, though it only took a few seconds for her to see the entire story flash by. He would take Doc's car to the site where they died. Plant evidence and DNA in the backseat. He would have phone records, of course, and conversations he recorded, evidence of his background check on Scott. He would be hailed as a hero, and even recruited to help with the investigation. With all the overwhelming evidence, the case would be closed.

Bile rose in her throat. Slowly her hand crept upward under her shirt, fingers latching onto the hidden scissors in her waist band. Then howling in blood-curdling wrath, she plunged the blades between his ribs. He screamed once and clutched at himself, staggering backward, blood pouring from between his fingers.

But like a wounded animal, her attack only fueled his rage. Before she could move he grabbed her wrist, twisting her arm until the scissors fell, then whirled her around, pointing the gun at the back of her head. Andrea breathed a final prayer, trembling so hard she could barely stand.

But then, a movement off to the side, in the shadows of the truck. Scott! He lunged at Derek, toppling him to the ground. Derek caught him in a headlock, ramming his head viciously against the right headlight so hard it shattered, slicing his forehead open. Scott collapsed to the ground, blinded, eyes covered in blood.

Andrea bolted, running down the opposite side of the truck toward the woods, Derek close behind. She tripped and stumbled. He grabbed her up by the waist with his free arm, clutching his side, dragging her back to the front of the truck next to Scott, who lay in the dust moaning. Triumphant, he danced backwards away from them, gun trained at their heads, holding his side with the palm of his free hand.

"Get up you bastard. Next to her," Derek growled, waving the gun at Scott.

Slowly Scott crawled to his feet and pulled her to him. She buried her face in his chest; he laid his head on hers. Shuddering once, he put his mouth to her ear.

"I'm sorry," he whispered. She nodded, hugging him tighter, choking back a sob.

Derek pranced around the circle of light like a prizefighter, laughing at them maniacally. Then, breathing heavily, he bent over, hands on his knees, chuckling as if it had all been so much fun. Finally, he pulled himself back up to full height, jerking his head to crack his neck, shaking the dust off his shoulders, then planted his feet in the sand—cocky, belligerent, self-satisfied.

"Won't need to go to the gym for a few days, that's for sure." Then, as easily as it had come, the humor drained from his face. Weary of the sport, he surveyed his surroundings, pursing his lips. His head swiveled back at her, nailing her in his line of vision.

"Do you think I'm an idiot, Andrea? I didn't need Doc and I sure as hell don't need you. So, I'll give you thirty seconds to tell me where the key is to that safe deposit box." Then, in a singsong voice: "If not, I'll shoot each of you slowly, starting with the limbs, at close range. Now let's see, which one will go first?"

She heard Scott's heart pounding, smelled his fear. He whispered *please forgive me* again. Then he tensed, held up his hands in surrender and stepped away.

"Let her go. I have it. I stole it from her when she stayed in the guest house."

She swung around, staring at him in disbelief. He wouldn't look at her.

Derek smirked. "That's not how it's going down, buddy. Tell me the truth or I shoot her in the head."

Then, like a dream, an apparition materializing, a woman stepped out of the woods. At first Andrea thought it was another vision. But then the woman walked toward Derek, her hand outstretched, her face calm. White shirt shining in the night, long model's legs in boots and jeans, strikingly beautiful, even after all these years.

Anna Lee Whitlow. The woman who killed her father.

"That's enough, son. Give me the gun," she ordered, kind but firm.

Derek's face drained of all color.

"Mama?"

She stood still, smiling at him, eyes filled with understanding. At first he appeared confused, then torment spread across his face. He turned red; his mouth tightened. His eyes shot fire.

"You did this to me! You did this to me!" He screamed at her, waving the gun around. She sighed and rolled her eyes as if he were a small child, one that was becoming tiresome.

"Son, I asked you to put the gun down," she stated, annoyed, stern.

His head wagged from side to side like a horde of bees were swarming around him, fury mounting. "This is your fault, you bitch! I'm warning you. Don't come any closer!"

Backing up, he moved to the opposite edge of the light, putting distance between them, jabbing the gun in her direction. "You're crazy! I should have killed you a long time ago! I'm tired of covering for you!" he screamed.

Except for a few moths floating in the light, nothing moved. All Andrea could hear was Derek's ragged breathing, like an enraged bull. She watched as mother and son locked eyes.

Anna Lee frowned. Then a look of profound sadness came over her face. Slowly, as if in a trance, she raised her fingers to her lips, shattering the silence with one ear-splitting whistle, then a guttural cry that rang out in the night air.

"Wingina!"

They all stared, frozen as a massive black bear lumbered out of the brush from behind Derek. He whirled to face the beast, raising his gun in panic. Andrea screamed. Scott grabbed her by the hand, pulling her behind him as they ran to crouch behind the truck door.

Derek's first shot went wide. The second landed square in the beast's belly, but not before it pounced, long-curved claws swiping at Derek's throat, slicing it open. His head jerked back, blood spurted, knees buckled. The bear moved in, tearing at his shoulders with his fangs. Derek choked in agony then collapsed backwards on the ground, his gun tumbling out into the circle of light, landing with a thud.

Scott ran out from behind the truck, grabbing the gun up out of the sand, and still crouched, swung up and pointed toward the animal, shot, but missed. The beast turned, rising on its hind legs, it's roar echoing throughout the forest. Scott shot twice more, one shot after the other, hitting it in the right shoulder. Growling in pain, twisting, the bear dropped down on all fours, bounding toward him. Scott emptied the chamber, then ran down the side of the truck toward the tailgate, motioning frantically for Andrea to follow.

Hiding, they watched as the bleeding animal, blinded and confused, finally turned and lumbered back to straddle Derek, swaying back and forth over him, grunting in pain.

Anna Lee stood motionless, staring at the scene before her. When she issued her next command, her voice was oddly tender, eyes shining with unshed tears.

"Wingina, down," she whispered, her voice barely discernible.

At first the bear seemed not to hear her. He drooled, groaned in pain, lungs struggling for air. Blood matted his thick fur. Then, in slow motion, like a massive tree he toppled, falling on top of Derek. One twitch of his legs, then both man and animal went still.

Silence. Nothing moved. Dust swirled in the circle of light, drifting slowly to the ground. A dark bloody pool began forming, reflecting the light of a gibbous moon shining above them.

Anna Lee stood at the edge, eyes vacant. Andrea buried her face in her hands, too horrified to do anything but sob. Leaning against the tailgate for support, Scott moaned, put his arm around her, pulled her to him.

Speechless they watched as Anna Lee began walking toward the mound of fur and flesh. When she reached the bodies, she knelt beside them, blood staining her knees and hands. Stroking and patting them in turn, she murmured endearments. Finally, she leaned down to kiss them each on the side of the head.

"Goodbye sweet children," she whispered.

Then she turned to stare at Andrea, the look in her eyes no longer vacant but tortured and pleading. "Please forgive me," she begged, her voice so raspy and broken Andrea could barely hear her.

Then, without waiting for an answer, she reached into her back pocket and took out a small hand gun, pointed it at her chest, and pulled the trigger.

CHAPTER SIXTEEN

SHE STOOD IN THE SHOWER of her hospital room, the hot water cascading down over her, shivering, unable to move. Even the slightest decision seemed fraught with dire outcomes. Finally, she managed to turn the hot water off, letting the cold stinging needles pound her skin, scrubbing around and around in circles until she rubbed herself raw. Then she wrapped her arms around her body, rocking slowly back and forth.

Rocking, rocking, rocking. But nothing could wash away the nightmare still playing out in her head. Bloody dirt pooled at her feet, but it still clung to her heart and soul.

Worried, the nurse came to check. She had to pull her arms away, lead her out, and dry her off. She patted Andrea dry without talking, helping her into the standard-issue hospital gown, put her to bed, leaving her alone in the room.

Andrea could hear the whispering in the halls but couldn't make out what they were saying. It didn't matter anyway. She didn't care.

Too numb to cry, she stared down at her arms, turning them over and over, examining the rope burns crisscrossing her wrists, fingernails jagged and broken. Another nurse came in, a male this time, to hook her up to an IV. Fluids for the dehydration he said, caused by the shock and the lack of water and nothing to eat all day.

It was only then that the shivering set in hard, like she had a fever breaking, teeth chattering so violently she bit her tongue. The nurse called the doctor, piled on blankets from a warmer, someone gave her a shot in the arm. *"Sleep"* she heard a voice say through the fog enveloping her. Within moments Andrea felt the warm rush of the drugs working their magic, pulling her down into oblivion. Those last few seconds of consciousness she lay there in the dim light of the hospital room listening to the beep of the monitor, staring at the fluid dropping from the bag down into her body and thinking:

My brother.

❦

Three days in the bed and she'd had enough. With one too many strange looks from strangers, and so many unanswered questions of her own, she'd moved way beyond shock. Now she was angry. And it was all directed at one person.

Scott.

If Scott hadn't lured her back down none of this would have ever happened.

She'd been warned not to talk with him until the investigation was over. It might "muddy" the waters, according to Jack anyway, whoever he was, one of those too eager young detectives from the SBI who'd been assigned to keep an eye on her.

Well, screw Jack.

She got dressed, asked for Scott's room number at the nurse's station, then padded on bare feet down the hall. She was surprised to see his head bandaged and his arm in a cast. Before she could change her mind, she hurried in without greeting him, standing there clenching her fists.

He smiled at her and seemed about to speak, but she cut him off. "Don't you think you have some explaining to do?" she said, glaring at him.

"Well, hello Andrea. I'm fine. Thanks for asking." He looked away, jaw clenched. She had hurt him. *Good*.

He pulled himself up in the bed, adjusting his covers.

"Andrea, I know what you are thinking. No, I don't have the key to the safe deposit box. I was only trying to protect you." He lowered his eyes, picking at the blanket with his good hand.

She sucked in a breath, glaring.

"Derek was messing with my head, Andrea."

"What do you mean?" she muttered.

Scott sat up straighter, "It isn't what you think. He was in that restaurant the day I met you, over at a table in the corner. Bobbi was his girlfriend, off and on anyway. He was very jealous and possessive. Knocked her around a lot. He thought I was there to poach on his territory."

"So, it was your pecker that almost got us killed?" she drawled.

"No! We had a casual fling once, a huge mistake. She was just using me to make Derek jealous. I told him but he didn't believe me."

"I'm listening," she answered, crossing her arms over her chest.

"I knew nothing about any this until I was being held captive. He bragged that Doc had been watching you for months, hoping you'd show up down here. He recruited Derek months ago. That highway patrolman that stopped you? That wasn't just anybody. Doc wanted to make sure you really were going to Charlotte so Derek called in a favor, had you pulled. But it didn't stop there. Doc told Derek if you showed up down here looking for information about Andrew Warren he was to let him know right away. Bobbie overheard you and recognized the name. She told Derek. He tipped off the old man. She's being questioned about it now."

Her head was reeling. "Of all the restaurants I happened to go to, I picked the one where Derek hangs out? Give me a break. And please tell me you didn't puncture my tire," she whispered.

He slumped. "Of course not. I'd never do anything like that. Derek had girlfriends all over. Bobbi called him, so he came in to check you out. I could see him outside, hanging around your Jeep. I figured he was up to something, if nothing but to get back at me. That's why I paid my bill and left, to find out what he was doing. But by then he was already gone. I didn't say anything because I didn't want you to be frightened. But I swear, I didn't know he was dangerous."

She was feeling stupider by the minute.

"Why did he puncture my tire?"

"He never said. At the time I didn't think it was that serious. He pulled stunts like that all the time; hit up on girls that way. I followed you to East Lake so I could get to you first. I knew if he saw me he would pass on by. I didn't know it was more complicated than that." He took a deep breath, sighing in frustration, then rolled his head back on the bed, pleading with her. "I know I should have told you. But I thought I knew Derek. Hell, everyone thought they knew Derek. He was known for being spiteful, playing games, but he'd never acted like he was a lunatic. Don't you think I'd have warned you if I knew what would happen?"

"When did you know?" she demanded, ignoring his question.

"That was him on the phone while you were in the bookstore. He called me. He told me he was giving me a courtesy call to let me know that his department had opened a cold case on your father, Andrew Warren, that the suicide was now a confirmed murder. He made it sound official, hinted that you had stepped forward with information that would implicate my father. Things he said jogged my memory, like Dad getting really depressed, mentioning his shock at a young client's suicide. But I was only a kid at the time, so I wasn't sure."

"So why didn't you just ask me then?" she flared.

"Because I got scared, Andrea. Then, after you left so suddenly, he sent me the obituaries, the pictures he'd taken of your house and the funeral. He made it sound like you were crazy with grief, out for revenge. My mother and I had already been through so much. Can you imagine what it would have done to her if she learned her husband, a man she believed was above reproach, had been involved in a murder? And, if something happened to me, she'd never survive...."

"Was he?" she whispered.

"Andrea, I swear, my father wasn't that kind of man! Ask anyone in Edenton. And if by some bizarre stroke, he had been involved in any way, don't you think Derek would have made sure to have thrown that in our faces the night everything happened?"

She blinked, then nodded, uncertain now.

"You have to understand. I didn't know what to think. I remembered we'd kept all my Dad's client files locked up in a storage facility we own in town. Mom couldn't bear to deal with anything so I just put it all in there and left it. That night I opened it and found your father's file. But there was nothing out of the ordinary except the mention of a key to a safety deposit box he wanted your mother to have, a will, and what he planned for the trunk and his ashes. Nothing worth killing over, not that I could tell."

Her back stiffened. "A key? Where?"

His eyes clouded over. "I don't know. I couldn't look for it because I was locked up that night, remember?"

Andrea pulled herself up out of the chair and walked to the window. *A key?* She turned and faced him again.

"So, was that Derek I saw in the upstairs window?"

He closed his eyes, wincing. "He hid his truck down behind the barn. Said that all that he wanted was to listen in on our conversation. He was a detective, Andrea. It made sense. He was still trying to convince me you were crazy and that he needed to be there as a witness in case you lost it. He made it sound like he was trying to help me."

"So, you set me up?" she blurted, outraged.

"Andrea, he convinced me that if I spent more time with you, you'd play your hand. But I knew I'd gotten it wrong as soon as you got there that afternoon. Right away I could tell you weren't hiding anything, and you sure weren't unstable. Over dinner it became clear you knew nothing about my Dad either. I began to realize Derek had been conning me. I was horrified. I knew I had to get you back to the guest house. My plan was to confront him and ask him to leave."

"I thought you were upset with me. You know, for ending the evening early," she mumbled.

He gazed at her, eyes dull with pain. "I was upset, but not at you. When he came downstairs and I told him you'd ended the evening early, he started getting agitated, talking crazy. So, to get him off the property I told him I'd found the file and that I'd take him there so he could read it himself." He stopped and took a gulp of water from a glass on his lunch tray. Beads of sweat stood out on his brow.

"But after he read it he went ballistic, especially when I couldn't cough up the key. He went over the edge and pulled out his gun; interrogated me all night. That morning he ordered the breakfast delivered, to cover for me not being there. Then he made me call you, but when I tried to warn you he knocked the phone out of my hand. He threw me into the truck and took me back to the Montrose. He was going to kill both of us, I think."

"Why didn't he," she asked, numb.

"You were already gone. That really pissed him off. That's when he beat the hell out of me. Then he locked me up in the upstairs bedroom…."

"Why didn't you text me before you left the house that night?" she flared back at him, shaking.

"I couldn't. He was watching me like a hawk," he shot back.

"When did he start tracking me?" She glared at him.

"He slapped a device under the Jeep during your mother's funeral."

Her eyes widened. "The Jeep? I thought it was the phone. So why didn't he kill you and come after me right then?"

He sighed, his face draining of color. "Doc talked him out of it, Andrea. Convinced him to use me as a cover to get closer to you. You've got to understand, Doc was the mastermind calling the shots. He told Derek to give you a long leash and track every move you made. At first Derek was pissed off, but then it turned into a game for him. He would come back every night and tell me all of it in excruciating detail, blow by blow, even down to how good you looked with short hair."

"So, when did things change?" Her head was beginning to hurt.

"Derek swung out of control. He had already killed Talton, then he went after Willie. Then you flipped the script, switched cars and went to visit Strayhorn. Then you showed up at Doc's place. That blew everything out of the water."

She sighed, so weary she could lie down on the floor. "I don't understand. Why didn't Doc mention those coffins throughout the years I was a student?"

"I'm not sure but, from things I overheard, I think

he was afraid to tip his hand. He kept hoping you'd confess that you knew where they were, right up until the end. He was obsessed with getting the credit for finding them. Then you showed up with those pictures he didn't know what to think. By then he was in too deep. So, he went along with Derek's plan to take us out in the woods and rough us up. Obviously, he didn't know Derek had different plans. That's why Derek killed him, I suppose."

"So, why did he kill Talton?"

"Talton kept tabs on you through the years too, but for entirely different reasons. He was going to blackmail Strayhorn about the coverup. He came back to the area about a month ago, hired Willie to take him out fishing. He hadn't counted on Strayhorn being too sick to care one way or the other. One night he got drunk and told Willie parts of the story, just enough so Willie put two and two together. Willie made the mistake of going to Derek. He thought he was protecting you, for Polly's sake. The old man was clueless, Andrea."

She closed her eyes. Her heart hurt in her chest.

"Did Derek tell you he killed Willie?" she whispered.

"Yes," he replied, lowering his head. "He described it in vivid detail."

Tears filled her eyes, spilling over. About that time the nurse walked back in.

"Ma'am, the patient needs his rest."

She shrugged, began walking toward the door. When she reached it, she turned to face him, her expression cold.

"We aren't finished here yet," she warned, then vanished down the hall.

She sat on the bed in a dark motel room outside of Edenton. No one knew where she was except Jack. She didn't even have a cell phone.

She'd already talked to her Aunt Connie, who'd seen the story on the news. She had called the hospital in hysterics, but then claimed there was no way she could come all the way from Salisbury. In other words, the same old excuses Andrea had always heard since she was a child.

Not that she minded. Aunt Connie was a complication she didn't need right now anyway.

Hunkering down, she locked herself in her room, watching old movies, one after the other, using the food vouchers she'd been given to order take-out, or walking next door to a fast food restaurant. She slept on and off when she could. Mostly she lay awake, staring at the ceiling. Every word, every action, every terrifying moment was burned in her brain.

Remembering.

Three days later Jack paid a visit, advising her that, since her story checked she could return home to Charlotte, but if she traveled out of state she'd best check in with them first. At least he had carried the rental car back to Southern Shores for her. That was something. He delivered her Jeep to her, along with the urn, her knapsack, her father's journal and her cell phone, all confiscated from Derek's truck the night deputies arrived on the scene. As far as she could tell nothing seemed to have been touched. The pictures were still being held as evidence. They had been in Doc's shirt pocket when they found his body at the bottom of the steps. All she had to do was pick up Henry later in the day. After that she could leave the Outer Banks for good.

Thank God.

Jack gave her an update on Scott, not that she asked. All told he had a concussion for sure, two broken ribs, a ruptured spleen, and a partially dislocated shoulder, but he was being released today. Wasn't she glad?

She didn't say anything. Instead, she asked about the file. Where was it? Jack assured her they had taken all the snapshots of its contents they needed and left in the desk drawer where they'd found it, in the study of the Montrose.

Now alone again, she fumed. How could she leave town? Scott had a file, a file with her father's name on it, and that was technically her property. Not to mention the trunk. It might not be worth much, but it was hers. She sure as hell wasn't going to make the mistake of leaving anything behind again. So, before she could talk herself out of it, she punched in his number.

"I need to get my trunk and that file. Can you meet me somewhere?"

"Well, hello to you too, Andrea. Hope you are well."

"Cut the crap Scott. I want my things."

"Andy, I can't drive. My mother is picking me up."

"Oh," she said, not knowing what else to say. She'd forgotten that part.

"Andrea, I told Mom everything," he whispered.

She was silent for a moment, not quite knowing what to say, then, "How is she handling it?"

"As well as can be expected. She's worried about you, ticked off at me. She went to Norfolk, met with Strayhorn. His father is in Hospice now, unable to talk. He told her his old man confessed after you visited there that he did hire Talton to cover up the accident, but swears that it was only to protect Anna Lee. He was adamant my Dad only drew up a generic document for Talton to sign without knowing the specifics. But they had no idea Talton was planning on trying to blackmail them."

"Scott, give me a break. I searched your house the morning before I left. I found your father's address book in the roll top desk. Steve Strayhorn, my father, Talton—all their numbers were in it. And where in the hell is that key? Your Dad wasn't as innocent as you think."

He groaned in frustration. "Come *on* Andrea. He was an attorney. He was your father's lawyer. Did it ever occur to you that Strayhorn gave my Dad that number when he asked Dad to draw up the agreement? It doesn't mean my father was colluding in the cover up. I told you, he wasn't that kind of man. Besides, even if he opened the safe deposit box, we don't know what it contained. My father was a wealthy man, Andrea. He sure didn't care about the history that much. Said it was depressing. And if there was information about the coffins in it, don't you think they would have surfaced by now?"

She hesitated. He had a point. Her head was beginning to hurt again.

"I'm not sure what I think anymore," she finally answered, her tone bitter. "All I know is that if I'd stayed in Charlotte and hadn't been wooed down here by the smooth-talking Scott McWilliams, none of this would ever have happened."

"Think what you want," he retorted, sullen. "From where I stand, it would have only been a matter of time anyway. Derek would have gone to you, if you didn't come here. He'd been stalking you up there already. He had a plan. He told me so. He charmed you too, didn't he?"

She was speechless. The boy had a spine after all.

"Listen, I have an idea. Where are you now?" he asked.

Trying to decide if I want to press charges against you, she wanted to say, but thought better of it.

"Packed up, ready to leave town."

"Why don't you meet us at the Montrose? I'll run in and get the trunk and the file and bring it out to your car. You won't have to go in the house at all. Could you do that? Mom's here now. I think it will do her good to meet you."

She ignored the comment. "What time?"

She heard a muffled exchange, then: "In about an hour?"

"Yep." Then hung up the phone.

At least she'd get her things. That was something. After this, she would never have to see Scott McWilliams, that house, or this part of the country ever again.

But now she had an hour to kill. What should she do? The hospital social worker said that it was important not to hide from the world. Now was a good a time as any to show her face, though the prospect of facing the public made her stomach do flip flops.

She parked in front of Sound Feet Shoes, walked inside with her head down. Within minutes she'd found a pair of size 7.5 hiking shoes and some Clark sandals, and was out of the store before the girl behind the counter recognized her.

That left her with thirty more minutes to burn. She stepped in the Edenton Coffee House. Again, no one recognized her, though a few local senior citizens hanging out glanced at her quizzically as she headed toward the door. She was okay until she noticed a *Virginia Pilot* wire bin with a stack of newspapers in it. The headline on top read:

"Local Man Recounts Harrowing Story."

There was a picture of Scott. She didn't need to read the article to know what it would say.

So, Scott was a celebrity now? Of course he was. He was a local boy, a darling. And now he was probably being portrayed as a hero who had saved her life. No doubt she would go down in history as the outsider who had brought trouble to town. Is this how the story was going to play out?

Well, local boy, we'll see about that.

By the time she arrived at the Montrose she was about to explode, even more frustrated because Scott wasn't there yet. *Crap.* She pulled out her phone, then realized she'd muted it in the coffee shop so she hadn't heard it beep. A text message popped up.

Scott: *Doctor was late. Running behind. Sorry.*

She typed a message back: *Sorry, but I can't wait that long.*

Scott: *Have a nice life, Andrea. Let me know if you*

need anything.

She didn't answer.

Instead she sat in the car fuming, staring up at the window. The curtain didn't move, thank God. No blood stains on the steps. The clean-up crew must have done a thorough job.

Oh, what the heck. She shot out of the car, bounding up the steps and onto the porch.

But the kitchen door was locked. She tried it again, rattling the old metal doorknob in frustration, door shaking on its hinges. Then it hit her.

Of course it would be locked. This was part of a crime scene.

Well, what difference would one more crime make?

She looked around the porch, spotting a hoe propped up in the corner. Picking it up with two hands she slammed it through the lower right door pane until all the glass fell out, then reached in and unlocked the door from the inside.

She'd leave a note telling him to send her the bill.

Within a few minutes she had scoured the downstairs, even the closets, but no trunk anywhere. Taking the stairs two at a time, she was on the landing in a few seconds. She went straight to the bedroom where Scott had been held captive. Sure enough the trunk was right there.

It was heavier than she remembered, but she managed to drag it out of the room onto the landing by one handle. She was navigating past the spot in front of the window when she slipped, falling against the bureau. Without warning, the portrait of Mary Montrose dropped straight down the wall, behind it. The sound of breaking glass made her wince.

Moaning, she slapped her hands to her head in frustration. *What was it about this house?* One day it was protecting her, the next it wouldn't let her go.

Well, she couldn't just leave it there. Breaking and entering was one thing, but that portrait was a family heirloom. She crawled to the side of the bureau and braced her shoulder, pushing hard, trying to get it to slide forward enough to reach in and pull it out.

But the bureau wouldn't budge. She tried peeking behind it but it was too dark to really see anything but the edge of the frame. Slowly she inserted her right hand, and sure enough, pricked her finger on a shard of protruding glass. When she snatched it out and held it up to survey the damage, blood ran in a rivulet down her wrist, clamping the wound against her mouth. It didn't seem to need stitches, but it sure needed rinsing out. No telling how long that old woman had been hanging up there, what microbes had taken refuge in the dark.

Dizzy, she pulled herself up with her free hand, trying to decide whether to laugh or cry. *Maybe I'm going crazy,* she thought. It sure felt like it. Where were those voices, those dreams and visions when she needed them? Or had her guardian spirits given up on her for good?

Downstairs she found the bathroom, complete with an old medicine cabinet. Inside she spotted a dated bottle of iodine and a packet of gauze. When she closed it, she caught a glimpse of herself in the mirror, wincing. At least she still liked her hair short, but that blonde had been a bad idea. Her roots were already beginning to show.

Where in the hell was Scott?

She looked around, remembering the last time she'd been here. Maybe she could find that file and leave before he got here. The trunk could always be shipped. She began rummaging around in the desk drawers.

And there it was, in the top right hand drawer, right where she had last seen Jennifer's picture, gone now. Well, that was strange. When had he had time to put it away? Hadn't he been locked up the entire time?

Not that Scott's ex-wife mattered to her. It was just creepy, that's all.

She took a deep breath to calm herself, then walked over to the old leather chair and sat down, switched the reading light on and opened the file. Other than a few notes about taxes, a yellowed title to an old car, her father's death certificate and the bill from the funeral home, the only thing that really caught her eye was what seemed to be a copy of a simple will, one of those fill-in-the-blank kinds, no doubt purchased from an old-fashioned office supply store. Scanning it quickly, she read that it named her mother, Celeste Sutton Warren, as the sole beneficiary of the entirety of his estate, and William S. McWilliams as the executor. It had been signed and dated a few months before his death.

Well, that was something. He'd loved her mother enough to make provisions for her. But what had her father owned to bequeath? Nothing but an old trunk so far.

Even stranger was an addendum, typed on a simple sheet of paper, signed and dated a few weeks later.

> *In the event of my death, my remains are*
> *to be shipped to my estranged wife, Celeste S.*
> *Warren, including a key to my safe deposit box*
> *at Bank of Columbia. Enclosed she will find*
> *instructions as to how she is to proceed.*
> *Andrew Warren*

The date on the addendum was three days prior to his death.

That was bizarre. Had he foreseen his own death? It was possible. Or maybe he was frightened of Anna Lee after all. For all they knew, she could have murdered him intentionally. Derek could have been lying about all of it.

Excited now, she sifted through the file again, carefully examining bills, noting a copy of her father's prepaid burial and cremation plan. But there was no copy of a letter to her mother, and no further reference to the key.

What had happened to the key? Had her father died before he could give it to his attorney? Or had her mother forgotten to tell her about it? It certainly hadn't been in her things anywhere. Had it been lost in the mail?

The trunk. Was it hidden in the trunk? Scott mentioned the possibility.

Dropping the file, she ran back upstairs and threw the trunk open, carefully feeling her way over every inch of the lining.

No secret pockets, no telltale bulges.

She sat back on her heels and stared at it, then took a deep breath, gazing around as if answers would conjure themselves up out of thin air. Where could it be?

Next, she picked up the textbooks and thumbed through them. Maybe he had hidden his notes there. But no luck.

Then she picked up the old newspaper. She unfolded it, laid it out on the floor, turned the yellowed pages. Suddenly she saw a familiar picture staring up at her.

Her father. And a story, circled in red pen.

She read the thing without stopping, face flushed. How he'd worked his way through high school, enjoyed amateur archaeology, all the pottery, pipes, bowls and arrowheads he'd found, his plans to go to college. The article had been written because he'd won a scholarship—for good citizenship as well as academics no less—lauding him for his upstanding character, his courage in the face of family difficulty, his love of his Aunt Polly.

She wanted to weep. Her father really had been a good man. Not a man who would have cheated on his wife, abandoned his wife and daughter, passed off fake artifacts. She read through the article again, devouring every word.

Then she heard the slamming of car doors. Folding up the paper and sticking it back in the trunk, she jumped up and ran back downstairs. Steeling herself, she plopped down in the chair and waited. It took a while but she finally heard their voices in the kitchen, talking about the broken glass no doubt.

"Scott, I'm in the study," she called out, dreading the confrontation.

"Andrea, are you hurt?" he called out, sounding

anxious.

When he burst into the study, her first thought was how bad he still looked. One eye was still blue and swollen and a large bandage covered his head wound. His arm was still in the sling. But at least he was shaved. And he smelled good.

The second was the woman following behind him, slight of build to the point of frailty, white-haired, warm brown eyes. She wore a baby-blue cotton sweater set adorned with pearls her own mother would have loved. A Church Lady no doubt, armed and ready to do battle.

Church Lady rushed toward her, enfolded her in a warm embrace.

"My dear child," she began in her soft cultured brogue. "I cannot begin to imagine how horrible all of this has been for you. Please tell us how we can help?" She pulled back, holding Andrea's hands between her own, soft eyes pleading with her, stricken.

Then Scott stepped forward. "You cut your hand! Here, let me look at it." He reached over, expecting her to show him, but she politely pulled away.

"It'll be fine," she assured him. "It's not as bad as it looks."

It was only then that she saw how much Scott favored his mother, and even more disconcerting, how they both looked at her, their tenderness and concern so unnerving she blushed. Seeing the look on her face, Scott beat an exit. "I'll go get the trunk," he offered, heading up the stairs.

"Wait. I need to tell you something first," she blurted. "I didn't cut my hand on the kitchen door. And I'm sorry I broke in. I shouldn't have done that. I cut it trying to move the trunk down the hall. I don't know what happened, but somehow in the process the portrait fell off the wall. The glass broke."

Scott looked puzzled, but didn't say anything.

"It was stupid of me to break in. I should have waited. I don't know what came over me."

But she barely managed to get the words out. The room started spinning. Mrs. McWilliams reached out to her.

"Honey, I think you need to sit down. You're getting pale."

"Really, I'm fine," Andrea protested, wishing they weren't being so nice to her, especially the way she had behaved. *And his mother?* Well, why was she being so damn motherly? And she smelled good too.

Suddenly she missed her own mother terribly. And the dizziness was getting worse. She sat down again, but only because she had no choice. It was sit down or fall.

"That settles it, you are not well and I'm going to take care of you." She turned to her son, "Scott, go make the girl a good cup of coffee and bring in that box of donuts in the car. This girl needs some caffeine and some calories."

"No, please, I'll be fine Mrs. McWilliams." Her protests were weak, whispered.

The look the woman gave her would have been scolding if it hadn't been for the smile. "Don't you think that considering all that we've been through in the last few weeks we can at least be on a first name basis? Call me May. Everyone else does."

"Okay, May it is," she answered, trying to be

pleasant, though the effort cost her. Why was she so incredibly tired?

"Now, that's better. You know, you should smile more often. What a gorgeous girl you are! I can see why my Scott is so smitten."

Andrea tensed. *Smitten?* It was time to make things clear. And she would when she found the energy.

May patted her cheek. "You'll be back to yourself in no time. All we need to do is put some meat on those bones."

She stiffened. "Well, I'll be sure to order plenty of takeout once I'm home in Charlotte. All I need is my Jeep and my dog."

May cocked her head to the side, like an inquisitive bird. "Charlotte? Honey, the shape you're in, you couldn't make it back to the interstate. You need rest and some good home-cooked food. We'll put you up in the guest bedroom."

Lord, the woman was stubborn.

"Well, I'll stay for coffee and donuts, but first I need the ladies room."

"Of course. Right this way," May answered, motioning her toward the hall.

But when Andrea tried to stand back up, she became lightheaded again. She took two steps forward, two steps backward, then passed out cold.

CHAPTER SEVENTEEN

SHE WOKE IN A BEDROOM of some kind but she couldn't quite figure out where. Then her eyes drifted to the bedside chair.

Scott.

She bolted upright, fists clenched, ready to fight.

But when she looked down she realized that, instead of the infamous red dress she had been dreaming about, she was wearing a granny nightgown, certainly nothing she would ever buy. She wiggled her hands and feet. Everything moved. Rubbed her wrists. Thank God she wasn't tied up. Why was she in bed then?

Then the truth came rushing back like a movie, in Technicolor. She threw her head back on the pillow, glaring angrily at the ceiling. "Where in the hell am I?" she yelled out loud.

Startled from his own sleep, Scott jumped up and rushed to her side. But when she kept cursing at him, he panicked and hit speed dial.

"Hey Mom. She's awake. I think you need to come upstairs."

Oh God, not the mother! She pulled up the covers, flopping over on her side away from him, mad at the world. "How long have I been sleeping?" she snarled, voice muffled from under the covers.

"Hmmm, off and on, a couple of days."

Moaning, she hunched down further.

"Andrea, Mom's doctor thinks you were released too soon. They discussed readmitting you, but decided it was better to let you sleep it off here. Your body's way of coping, giving you time to heal."

"I'm coping just fine thank you. Besides, I didn't get hurt that bad."

"I know, but you had already been through a lot before this happened. Let us take care of you. It's the least we can do."

She shot upright. "Damn right it is. And I'm still pissed." She snorted and slid back down under the covers again.

Scott walked around the side of the bed facing her, his face getting harder by the minute.

"You think I haven't figured that out by now? How many times do I need to apologize to you, Andrea? I get that I made a stupid call. I shouldn't have pretended to care about you to get you here. Are you satisfied?"

She shot back upright; glared at him.

"Okay, answer this. Why was my mother's telephone number, *her private number*, on a piece of paper in the kitchen? And don't deny that it was your handwriting. I recognized it from the note you left on the breakfast tray."

He rolled his eyes. "When Derek first contacted me, I thought you were the enemy, remember? He was the one who found the number to your house and gave it to me over the phone. I didn't even remember I had it, I swear."

She crossed her arms, hugged them to her body, not quite ready to concede. She could tell that he had about reached his limit and was tired of defending himself.

Well, too bad. She deserved answers to all her questions, no matter how silly they sounded.

"So how did he get it?"

"He went online, found out where she worked. He was a detective, for Pete's sake. He called the school office, said he was a claims rep. He told them you were the beneficiary to a small life insurance policy left by your old aunt, but he couldn't find your phone number. Here, you can call her yourself and ask." He thrust out his cell phone. She ignored it.

"And what about your mother? Why didn't she come and check up on you?" she whispered.

"He forced me to call her and tell her I was going deep sea fishing and would be gone for several weeks. Trust me, he thought of everything," he added, lowering himself heavily to sit on the edge of the bed, looking worn down.

Still wary, she watched him closely, more closely than ever. She could feel the fire draining out of her, the need to blame. His explanations had been checked and rechecked by detectives. The description of Derek's behavior rang true.

Then why was she finding it so hard to forgive him?

Because Derek is dead.

Is that what she was doing? Taking her anger at Derek out on Scott?

Well, that was just plain wrong. He had been conned too and beaten to a pulp for his trouble.

And considering his history with Jennifer, she could understand why he wouldn't have trusted her. She'd have done the same thing in his shoes.

Of course, she didn't share everything she was thinking, at least not then. Instead she simply reached her arms out and drew him in.

&

It took a few days of rest and eating May's delicious dinners before the headaches went away. Over time they all settled into a routine of sorts. She was moved back into the guest house where she could see the water. At least there she wouldn't be reminded of Derek, content to sit on the front porch rocking, her mind empty. Various friends who'd learned of her story drove down to see her. Scott kept her company, but was careful not to stay too long. May brought supper out every evening for the three of them and they made small talk. They all knew the subject was closed.

The best medicine in the world was her reunion with Henry, picked up in Manteo by a friend of May's and brought to the Montrose.

"Oh my God, Henry!" she exclaimed, running to meet him as he jumped into her arms. He licked her face deliriously and wouldn't let her out of his sight, but then decided he was mad at her. After pouting for several days, he finally warmed back up to her, but only because she allowed him to sleep with her every night.

She finally felt strong enough to wander up to the big house, bored with nothing to do. May was on a women's church retreat, Scott was painting that day, so he handed her a brush and she helped touch up some trim. Afterwards she fixed them some ham sandwiches and set up a small picnic on the front porch. Then Scott left her there to run into town for some supplies, the first time she had been left alone.

She was not afraid. It was rather peaceful sitting on the front steps, the sun shining down on her shoulders, a salamander skittering back and forth. Off in the distance she saw a tractor puttering in a field. Sea gulls dipped and dove into the furrows, looking for worms, seeds and insects turned up by the plows.

She breathed deeply and wrapped her arms around her knees. The rhythms of life here were so calming, so far removed from anything she'd ever known. Henry certainly loved it here. He could dig for moles, chase butterflies, and lift his leg to his heart's content.

Even so, she still needed to think about returning to Charlotte. Her mother's principal had tracked her down, not only to offer his condolences for all she had endured, but to beg her to fill the vacancy.

She told him she'd think about it, but she couldn't make up her mind.

Part of her reticence was leaving this place. And if she were honest with herself, her shared experience with Scott was becoming a tie that bound them together. Who else would ever truly understand the horror they had lived through and how fragile they both were inside?

Not that they were a couple yet, despite May's continual hinting. It was too soon, and they had been through too much. Maybe away from this place she would heal faster. After all, she still suffered nightmares, jumped at loud sounds, found her mind drifting away to that night down in the woods, reliving every harrowing moment.

But was it even reasonable to think she could ever truly go back to her old life again? At least here she never had to explain herself to anyone. And surprisingly, despite all that had happened to her in this house, she felt protected, especially after Scott told her that the picture of Mary Montrose had fallen behind the bureau months ago and had sat there all this time.

Was hearing the glass break only her imagination, or had someone found a way to keep her from leaving too soon?

She chuckled. Who ever heard of a ghost playing cupid?

Maybe she could volunteer at the new dig up on Rocky Hock. She and Phil McMullan were becoming fast friends. She was an archaeologist, for heaven's sake, itching to get back in the field. These days that was more of a real possibility, thanks to Jack, who'd launched a full investigation into Doc, confirming not only his role in the incident in Williamsburg, but years of cover up, sexual harassment, possession of contraband artifacts taken illegally from digs all over the country, mismanagement of funds, the list went on and on.

Surprisingly, she'd gotten a few cards and emails from her old professors, their apologies profuse for not standing behind her. The head of her department offered her a teaching assistant position so that she could start work on her doctorate. They were all embarrassed that they had been conned too.

Chad had the gall to send her flowers, along with a note telling her that he had "forgiven" everything. She threw the flowers in the trash.

But Doc, how had she not seen? Of everything, his part in all this was perhaps the cruelest blow. At least Derek had an excuse for being evil.

Brooding, she was thinking about it all when her cell phone rang. Jack's number popped up on Caller I.D.

"Andrea?"

"Yes"

"I'm sorry, but the nursing home called. Your Aunt Polly passed away last night."

She felt her heart sink. "Thanks for letting me know."

"We'll need to perform an autopsy, so the body won't be released for burial until we get the results back from the state examiner's office. And there's Willie Batts. He's still on ice, waiting to be claimed. Polly was his power of attorney and since you were her next of kin we were wondering if we could send them both back to the funeral home in Columbia when we're done? It's your call."

"I've already talked to Maitland's in Creswell. I'd like to give Polly a decent funeral. It's the least I can do."

"One more thing. We are questioning a young nurse at the nursing home, the one you told us about. Turns out she was Derek's cousin on the Whitlow side. She hasn't admitted anything yet, but the toxicology reports might tell the real story."

She closed her eyes. *So, she hadn't been wrong.*

"Thanks Jack. Keep me posted."

"Sure thing," After that the call ended.

She sat, shivering. Was this nightmare ever going to end? All these people dead, and for no good reason except for some musty old coffins. Maybe they really were cursed, like Willie said. Even now she could hear his voice, see his pointing finger. He had died trying to protect her, even if it had been from the wrong person. That had to count for something. It did in her eyes anyway.

A cloud passed over the sun and suddenly the air turned chilly. Tugging Henry by the leash, she cleared the picnic and trudged back into the house.

☾

Thanks to May, she'd planned a small graveside service, though at first the thought of going back anywhere near the East Lake community made her cringe. Polly had an old family plot there and would be buried alongside distant kin. Evidently the man who had given her the name of Vestal had run off not long after they had married and was never heard from again. They had no children and his name didn't show up on the deeds to her property. Andrea was touched when Polly's lawyer had called her to inform her that Polly had left her household goods and the old trailer to her, advising that the waterfront lot it sat on was now quite desirable. And, oh, there was a small life insurance policy in her name.

Andrea advised him to donate the proceeds and the lot to the town of Columbia for a small children's park and to name it the William C. Batts Memorial Park for Children.

The weather was perfect, huge puffy clouds against an aquamarine sky, grass in the tiny Methodist Church cemetery lush and green. A few of the old-timers in Columbia showed up, including Mildred, to her surprise. At least the old bat had the good sense to act embarrassed. But what the heck, Jack's investigation of her had revealed nothing incriminating.

But that didn't mean she had to like the woman.

Willie had been cremated. As she had expected, no family stepped forward to claim him. She and Scott drove to the Milltail Creek bridge and released his ashes there, saying a quick prayer of thanks for his devotion to Polly, for his efforts to try to save her.

After the service, she walked around looking at the headstones. Hard to believe that beneath these old lichen-covered rocks lay her blood kin. Henry kept pulling on his leash, sniffing at the headstones, leading her to the WARREN family plot over in the far corner.

Her grandparents. Well, Jane anyway. And beside her a small stone, topped by a baby lamb. The only inscription was Infant Warren, not even a birth date. It was the first she had heard that Jane had a baby by Hooch Warren. Stillborn? So much suffering for such a good woman.

But wasn't that the way of the world? So many women through the centuries had suffered so much more than she had, their lives cut short, merciful for those enduring pain and humiliation, like the slave women whose graves no doubt dotted these woods.

But it wasn't just the women of color. Mary Montrose had died delivering twins. Jane had died of breast cancer. Her own mother died too young.

A broken heart? The lives of women everywhere were so hard.

She ought to collect some of those stories and write a book. Maybe one day she would.

"Rest in peace Jane. I'm sorry I never got to meet you," she murmured. Then she gazed at Hooch Warren's grave, but was unable to come up with anything.

She turned to Scott, her eyes moist. "I'm ready," and took his outstretched arm. As they walked across the grass she tried not to glimpse at the flash of shovels in the sun as the gravediggers covered up Aunt Polly.

But they had one more duty to perform. They would take the sailboat out in the Croatan Sound and release her father's ashes.

She was almost feeling joyful as they crossed over the Virginia Dare Bridge onto Roanoke Island. No wonder old John White had been entranced by the place.

Who could blame him? The view of the sound was truly breathtaking, especially when a Great Blue Heron rose and flew next to them for a few brief seconds, then it veered off, rising in an arc before diving down into the marshes. So beautiful and majestic, its flight alongside them like a benediction after the horrors they had been through. Andrea looked at the hawk tattoo on her wrist, thought about the irony of the owl they'd seen in the woods. Death for Derek, but wisdom for her and Scott. Now a Great Blue Heron, the messenger from heaven.

She had lost so much—her father, her mother, her trust in the world. At least she had learned the truth, and that went a long way. She might have been denied her father all these years, but at least now she could honor his memory by spreading his ashes close to his beloved Roanoke Island.

They loaded their picnic basket (compliments of May) onto the sailboat, along with blankets and sundries, Henry going ahead on deck to check things out for them. Finally, all settled in, Scott unfurled the sails, then carefully steered the boat away from its moorings out into the main creek. Within a quarter of a mile or so they were out in Shallowbag Bay, overlooking Pirate's Cove and the Virginia Dare Bridge, endless blue sky and water arching overhead.

Their plan was to sail up to where the three rivers converged—the Roanoke, the Chowan and the Alligator—into the Albemarle Sound, where the icon was found on the map, and the Dare Stone was supposedly discovered. If all went well they would make a full circle, coming back to Roanoke Island and the Outer Banks, picnic in the boat off-shore at Roanoke Festival Park, then call it a day by twilight.

They would disperse the ashes last.

So far all was going smoothly, a perfect day for sailing, not a cloud in sight. A slight breeze flapped the sails, titanium white against a blue sky. Henry stood on the bow, wearing the little doggie lifejacket she'd bought him the day before. She laughed as she watched his tail wiggle and his nose sniff the breeze, but she had to shush him to stop him from barking at the boats that passed as if he owned the coastal waterways.

Finally, as the day began to dim, Scott anchored

the boat and made his way to where she sat. Gently he took the urn from her hands.

Sunlight dappled her face; danced on the waves. She breathed a silent prayer, letting peace wash over her, balm for the soul.

But then her eye caught a movement. "Scott look!" she whispered, pointing toward the shore. Down by the edge of the water, a white doe, nibbling grass. Startled at the sound of their voices she froze, gazed at Andrea for what seemed like an eternity, then turned, gracefully bounding off into the woods behind her, vanishing like a ghost.

Andrea closed her eyes to keep from weeping at the beauty of it all, the moment too sacred and special to trivialize with words. She closed her eyes, took a deep breath, and reached into the urn. She pulled out the bag holding her father's ashes, then stood up. Holding it high, in one swooping movement she upended it into the breeze. A slight gust of wind came out of nowhere, suspending the particles in a cloud of grey smoke, then dispersed and disappeared, dust in the wind.

And like that, her father was gone.

She gazed at the shore where she had seen the white doe, unshed tears rimming her eyes. Had Virginia come for him after all? She would like to think so.

Scott stood beside her, his arm around her shoulder. Even Henry was quiet, standing on high alert on the bow. Gulls cawed, a fish jumped out of the water in the distance; a fishing boat chugged by.

"Goodbye Daddy," she managed to murmur. "Fly home to mother." She turned to Scott, burying her face in his chest. He rocked her in his arms for a few minutes until she pulled away, gazed up at him and smiled.

It was done.

As Scott manipulated the sails and drew up the anchor, Andrea watched, letting the sunlight bake her shoulders. With every day, including this one, she was beginning to realize just how strong and good a man he truly was. Maybe one day she'd get up the courage to tell him about her dreams and visions, the "gift" Willie had told her she had. But the time wasn't quite right, not yet anyway. She was still too tender and raw.

She gazed down at the urn, empty now. What should she do with it? She certainly didn't want to keep it. She couldn't toss it in the water. Probably best to give it back to the funeral home. Maybe someone else could use it.

She peeked inside one last time. Surprisingly, there was a piece of tape on the bottom. As she reached in the urn and pulled it out, her mouth dropped open.

"Scott! Come here. You're not going to believe this."

When she opened her hand, a small brass key lay in her palm, sparkling in the sunshine.

EPILOGUE

COPY OF PRIVATE LETTER FROM Andrew Warren to wife, Celeste Warren, found in a joint safety deposit box in the Bank of Columbia.

September 1, 1985

My dear Celeste:

Please forgive me for not telling you I was ill and sending you away like I did. Please believe me; it wasn't because I didn't love you. When I suggested that you move back to live with your parents I thought it would only be until I finished graduate school. I never dreamed it would be forever.

By now you should know that the cause of my death was pancreatic cancer. I was diagnosed shortly after you left. I knew if I told you, you would insist that I get treatment, and rush back to my side. But I was not about to let you spend the rest of your life paying off debt for a disease I will not survive. When I was a child I watched my mother die of cancer. I couldn't do that to you.

*Since you are reading this I assume you
have the key, my remains have been dispersed,
and you are in possession of the contents of the
safety deposit box.*

*The package contains remnants of what I
believe are a letter from John White, found in
one of two riven coffins both set apart about
100 yards from where the original coffins were
supposedly buried on an incline in 1950.
Because they were sealed in pitch and under
water, they were protected from exposure. They
appear never to have been disturbed. I suspect the casket inside the first coffin where the
papers were stored is one of those White buried
on Roanoke Island, but that is pure specu-
lation. The other coffins I took pictures of are
fragments of those reburied in 1950, which I
found again. Anything in them was long gone.
The remaining pictures I took are in the safety
deposit box, which I'm sure you've seen by
now.*

*Knowing I won't be around long enough to
secure their safety, and not having the emotional stamina to deal with such a historical
find, I decided it was best not to reveal the
news while I was still alive. I removed the
parchment fragments inside the box, along with
some of what appear to be fragments of drawings of a young white woman wearing Indian
clothing rolled in parchment and deerskin. I
am certain these are John White's drawings of
Virginia Dare. I labeled each fragment and
placed them in the archival bag, along with the
drawings that you have in your hands now. As*

for the box itself, I resealed it, put it back in the empty coffin, wrapped it all in plastic, and reburied it along with all of the other shards of wood. They shouldn't be difficult to find.

I believe that the largest coffin may contain the skeleton of John White. I did not open it because it would start decomposing if exposed to air, as you know. There may be other coffins in the area too, but I ran out of time.

The only thing my attorney, Bill McWilliams, knows is that I am dying. I have instructed him to put the key at the bottom of the urn, seal it with my ashes, and put it in the trunk and ship it to you. I figure no one would think to look for the key in the urn. No one knows what's in this safety deposit box but you.

Please take everything to Dr. Phelps as quickly as possible. He will know what to do. The coordinates are in the field notes that are attached and shouldn't be difficult to locate. I removed them from my journal in case they should fall into the wrong hands. The journal itself was in the trunk, as you know by now.

I suppose you are wondering why all this subterfuge. It's a long story, but Anna Lee is going off the deep end and I don't trust that she won't do something stupid. Steve, well Steve is too weak and greedy. I cannot trust him with a find this important. Both suspect something is wrong with me, but I have told them nothing. I couldn't bring myself to tell Aunt Polly either. It would be too hard on her. But I know I must when the time comes.

You were right about Anna Lee. She is unwell. She has even gone so far as to try to convince me that she had my child after she went to New York, but put it up for adoption. I don't believe her of course. I even asked her for proof, but she has none. When I told her that even if there was a child I still loved you, she didn't take it well. After I'm gone, I doubt you'll ever hear from her. I hope so anyway.

I am only telling you now because I didn't want you to think she had anything to do with our separation. That is far from the truth. I just wished I had listened to you when you told me you didn't trust her.

If you are wondering, I have made my peace with God. I can only ask for your forgiveness. It gives me comfort knowing that you and Andy will never want for a thing. Even so, if I could trade my life with you and our child for that worn out old box full of John White's secrets, I would gladly set it to flames.

No doubt you found your wedding ring too. I always thought I'd see it on your hand again one day. Now I ask only that you give it to our daughter, as a symbol of my enduring love for the both of you.

   Love forever,
   Andrew Warren

The crowd was enormous; press credentials everywhere: *The Wall Street Journal*, the *National Geographic, Washington Post*, even a special agent sent by the good Queen of England herself. The click and pop of cameras flashing was like fireworks on the Fourth of July.

Andrea and Scott stood side by side at the podium, along with their spokeswoman from the N. C. Department of Cultural Resources, speaking on their behalf.

"We'll take the first question from over there," she announced, pointing to a young man wearing glasses down on the front row, hand jerking up and down like a hyperactive first grader.

"When will the results of the testing become public?" he asked.

"Not for a few months," she answered, already pointing in another direction.

"How about the parchment?" another called out from across the room.

"We have to confirm its authenticity, but it seems to be a journal entry written by John White, the Governor of Roanoke, and a signature that matches those on earlier documents. It appears he knew he was dying. We should be able to publish the results of our findings in a few weeks." The crowd sucked in a breath.

"Did you find his remains?" shouted someone from the back of the room.

"We are not sure yet. In order to establish the identity of the skeletal remains discovered in one of the coffins we would need to compare it to a known living relative in England, but so far none has stepped forward." There was a collective moan. Another hand shot up.

"Yes," the spokeswoman said, nodding in the girl's direction.

"I'd like to direct my question to Ms. Warren. Rumor has it that you've had a DNA test and might be his descendant. Is that true?"

Andrea smiled and stepped forward. "We're working on it," she quipped. "And I know you are going to ask this so I'm going to go ahead and answer. No, we haven't found Virginia. However, the letter contains references to her and there are a few sketches of a white woman in Indian garb that may be her and other scenes of the Secotan village where they lived. Based on names on the frag-ments we are conjecturing she may have become the first wife of Wanchese and that she may have given birth to living children."

Pandemonium broke out; questions shouted from multiple directions.

"Go do your own research," she laughed, having to speak loudly to be heard above the fray. More shouting, a flurry of questions, and still, the ques-tions kept coming. It was like the world couldn't get enough of Virginia Dare.

Finally, Scott and Andrea were hustled off the stage and into a waiting car, whisked away from the Museum of Natural History down Hillsborough Street. Their next stop would be the Governor's office, where a reception had been planned in their honor.

"Whew, that was interesting," Scott laughed, helping her slide in.

"To say the least!" She smiled, glad to see him happy. It had been a rough haul.

He turned to her, took her hand. "So how does it feel to be a celebrity?"

She shrugged, smiling. "Actually, a bit overwhelming. I think we're going to have to hire an assistant to handle all the invitations and requests that are pouring in." Then she frowned a bit. "I don't mean to sound ungrateful, but you know that I'd rather be out digging. It's going to be hard to wait until next spring."

Scott smiled. "I know a certain Airstream that is empty down at the beach. I think if you hired that assistant then maybe we could get away, at least for a week or two anyway, get that little red heart tattoo you promised yourself. Right there…" he pointed at a spot just above her breast and grinned.

Her mouth dropped in mock surprise. "Why Scott McWilliams," she teased." Then, more seriously, "I forgot to tell you. Loretta sent me a text. It's for sale."

"I'll bet I know what you're thinking." He chuckled, then kissed her on the cheek.

"Yep, we're going to need an Airstream out in the field."

They locked hands, her mother's wedding ring shining on her right hand.

Andrea leaned her head against Scott's shoulder, closed her eyes, and dreamed.

Up high in the clouds above the city, a hawk circled round and round.

JOHN WHITE'S FINAL JOURNEY ENTRY

(Dated Spring, 1607, translated from the original written in Elizabethan English on fragments found in the coffin with skeletal remains. First published in The Journal of Historical Archaeology, Fall, 2017, presently on permanent loan to the Smithsonian, in Washington, D. C.)

I, JOHN WHITE, GOVERNOR OF ROANOKE, do write this last entry for the sake of Posterity, that one day, God Willing, the World may know the Truth that I did, a fortnight ago, finally return to my beloved family, having waited for such a time whence I would be free of hindrance from Patron, Prince, or Queen, and would be granted the great fortune of booking passage on a trade ship out of the Caribbean that would eventually bring me here.

Rest assured that had it been in my powers, I would have found my way to this fair isle long ere now, and did in truth attempt so many times. Yet, Circumstance was such that I was forced to live without benefit of wife or child, sustained only by my hope and belief that my own dear Elenor was safely hidden away in New Eden, living in great peace and contentment, and giving Glory to Our God.

Alas, it pains me sorely to say that, in this too, I was indeed greatly misguided.

My only hope is that her Sacrifice was met with favor in the eyes of Her Lord, and that her suffering was not prolonged, although I fear that, once again, I am deceived by my own selfish yearnings. My one solace is my sweet Virginia, in whom all Hope for the Future now resides. I leave her now in the safekeeping of Wanchese. I pray that their child will be a glorious testament to the Grace and Mercy of God and that when my appointed time comes to leave this God-forsaken earth that, despite my great Pride and Arrogance and my many grievous Sins, my Lord and Savior will welcome me Home.

John White, Governor of Roanoke

❦

VIRGINIA DARE

1607

I AM METAQUESUNNAUK, QUEEN OF THE
Secotan.

Not really, for I jest. Everyone knows I am not
in truth a Queen except to my husband, Wanchese.

My name means "little red pear" in English
because my hair is a coppery red, like the ripe pears
he so loves. It was given to me at the naming ceremony last year during the Festival of the Green
Corn.

The ceremony is forever burned in my heart.
Three virgins in the middle, men and boys dancing around us at a fever pitch, black eyes glittering,
bodies glistening in the bonfire. Even now I see the
wild henna designs on their faces, tattoos encir-
cling their arms and legs, and the sweet pungent
odor of their sex. It is a wild cacophony of color
and sound, everything and everyone in a frenzy,
even the old women covered in shells, beads and
feathers, hammered discs of copper and silver,
dancing to the beat of the wild, wild drum, the
priests and conjurers praying in strange tongues,
throwing uppowoc into the holy fires, breathing in

the drunken fumes.

Throughout it all he stared at me, the look in his eyes making me glad and afraid all at the same time. My heart thumped wildly, and under the deerskin coverings and copper girdle lightening shot up in my belly, all gifts given to me by him. By the time he finally claimed me I could hardly breathe, especially when he took me by the hand, running with me, blushing and giggling off onto the banks of the great Pamlico, where he finally laid me down.

Now at night when he comes to me, he laughs and teases me, pinches my nipples, telling me that I have this name because my flesh is pink like the pear; sweet and juicy. Of course, when I am out of favor with him or when it nears my bleeding time he calls me his little Kewa, because I try to rule over him like the little god of childbirth that sits on a shelf in our lodging, flat chest, round at the hips.

The other wives are jealous and long for his embraces but he is especially pleased with me now. My bleeding time has come and gone and there is no show of blood. The mothers tell me that this is because I have a child growing inside of me. She will be born in the summer, like I was. In my heart I know it will be a girl child and that no matter what happens I will never leave her or forsake her.

I still remember the stories, stories about the Great Ship that brought us all from England, me still inside of her, like my child is growing inside of me now. The winds blew, the storms came, and we had no food. My grandfather sailed to England to get help for us. But he never returned.

And now, after all these years, he is here. But alas, he is too late for my mother. She and my father and a few steadfast friends sought shelter upriver in the old fort built long ago, hoping to start over again. I have not seen them or heard from them since she gave me to Wanchese when I was a child. Though I am sad for her, I am grateful she loved me enough to leave me behind, for would I not have suffered her same fate had she taken me with her?

Wanchese was not glad to see the white men return. He was afraid they would come in great numbers, take me back and make me their Queen. Did he not witness my baptism and the crowning of Manteo as Lord of All of Roanoke when I was a child? Did not England make Elizabeth their White Queen, and I named after the Great Virgin?

That is why he wooed me away, to protect me from their terrible plans. He has been to England, told me of his travels; the great towering lodge houses made of hard earth, metal, and stone. Gold and silver so bright, the dishes, the rings and necklaces, hanging from even the horses they rode. Wanchese hates England, hates everything about it—how they dressed him up in strange clothes, tried to make him learn to walk like a woman, kneel before their White Queen. And the stink of their bodies, piss and shit, like the wild pigs his men hunt in the swamps, men rutting their women in the halls where they think no one can see.

Secrets, lies, and filth.

The thought of being taken away from here frightens me.

Grandfather is ill. He will die here I think. My herbs and potions cannot cure him. For guilt and a broken heart there is no cure.

He does love me I know. Out of gratitude for his

care of me he presented Wanchese with the silver cup, the one given to Wingina by the man named Grenville.

Grenville was an evil man. He lied and claimed that Wingina had stolen it, then chased him down and cut off his head, the Great Weroance of the Secotan People. I hope he travels into the sun when he dies, burns in Popogusso forever. Perhaps if he had been less greedy and ambitious things could have been very different in our worlds.

But then I might not be the wife of Wanchese, a powerful werowance himself now. I would not be giving birth to a princess.

The truth is that even if Wanchese had not come for me, eventually I would have run to him. And how could I not help it, he as beautiful as the Great Blue Heron gliding through the marshes at sunset. In our language, the name Wanchese means to take flight off water.

The Secotan are my people now, their language is mine. I will weave our mats, make our bread from the coscushaw, and help the other wives with the harvest of our beans and corn as I wait for our child to be born.

I feel her stirring underneath my breast even now.

Perhaps I will name her Sarah, Sarah of the Secotan, English and Indian, first child born with blood from both worlds. Our priest will baptize her with the silver cup and the holy waters of Mother Ocean, Father God.

I will teach her that the cup is precious, to be hidden from the world, and she will pass it down to her daughter and all the daughters of the future so they too will remember who they are and where they come from, and how much they are loved.

A NOTE FROM THE AUTHOR

PART OF THE FUN OF being a historical novelist is the privilege of being allowed to create hypothetical outcomes to real unsolved mysteries. But along with that comes risks that what is intended solely as entertainment will somehow be confused with the factual story, and thus take on a life of its own.

The Legend of the Lost Colony is a billion-dollar industry. Countless television and radio shows, books, plays, and poems have dealt with the subject since the early 1900's. *The Legend of the White Doe* was one of the first, along with the outdoor drama *The Lost Colony* that is produced every summer down in Manteo since the 1937. Lately interest has resurged even stronger with new archaeological discoveries and advances in technology in the field. It is interesting to watch scientific efforts converge.

By and large this story is fictional but, to the extent that is possible, I have tried to keep the science sound and the historical references as accurate as possible.

Here is what we know:

Though there are new findings recently that point to the possibility that some of the Roanoke colonists may have survived and intermarried with the local Indians in various coastal regions of North Carolina, nothing has been discovered that proves that theory conclusively. There are several ongoing archaeological digs being conducted as this is written, primarily on Hatteras Island, another on Salmon Creek (in Bertie County on the Chowan River near Avoca Farms) and in the Rocky Hock area (across the river from Salmon Creek in Chowan County) outside of Edenton, N. C. At this point, there are no digs being conducted in the old Beechland area of mainland Dare County as that is a National Wildlife Refuge, and getting permission to dig is a long, complicated process unless there is definitive proof of cause.

Artifacts have been discovered in all various digs that do prove an English presence, but since there were several voyages to what was then known as lower Virginia within a few decades of the Roanoke settlement, it is difficult to conclusively link those artifacts to them, though there are a few who claim otherwise.

Everyone wants to be *the* archaeologist who finds the Lost Colony.

The Dare Stone does exist, though its provenance has been in question ever since it was claimed to have been discovered by a traveling salesman from California in 1937, passing through the Rocky Hock area near Edenton, on the Chowan River. Unfortunately, in response to the sensationalism that find triggered, scores of fake stones surfaced in the following years. But in 1941 the authenticity of all the stones was debunked by the Sparks Report, which appeared in the *Saturday Evening Post*.

However, recently there have been new scholars and archaeologists looking at the first stone again as apart from the decidedly fake stones that came after. This new effort has been the recent subject of several History Channel programs such as *America Unearthed* and *The Search for the Lost Colony*. It does indeed look much different, the writing seems more authentic, and there is some archaeological evidence that the place it was found was the site of a major Algonquin Indian village, and the home of a great *werowance* (Algonquian word for *king*) who could have sheltered the Dare family long enough for Eleanor to have scratched the message on the stone.

Brenau University in Georgia, which owns that Dare Stone, has launched a full-scale investigation into its authenticity.

I must admit I am a skeptic, largely because I do not want the tragic message on the stone to be true. But for the purposes of this book I suggest it as a believable ending to Eleanor's journey, except that I had to figure out how to get around the fact that the stone clearly states Virginia died and was buried with Ananias at age four. For that reason, I chose to portray Eleanor as mentally unstable, fear driving her to give up her child, so ashamed that she'd rather John White think Virginia dead than to have him believe she was capable of trading off her child, even if it was to save her life.

We do know that the real Eleanor gave birth to a boy who died when he was a year old, a year before she left England, though there is no hint anywhere of what caused it, not uncommon given the times, when so few children survived to adulthood. (By the way, *Eleano*r is the modern spelling, but *Elenor* was often used back then, particularly on the Dare Stone.)

There is no record she was "gifted" in any way, but it makes sense to me that she may have been somewhat of a religious fanatic. Why else would she bring her unborn child to such a hostile place unless she believed God was on her side?

In defense of Ananias, there is no record of the kind of husband he was in real life. If I have portrayed him as a weak bully and I am wrong, then I hope he doesn't haunt me.

John White poses a dilemma for me. I cannot fathom a father who would ask a pregnant daughter to accompany him on such a dangerous journey. We know from his sketches he was a gifted artist and very intelligent, and we all know creative types can be very charming and manipulative. I don't think it is too much of a stretch in imagination to believe that narcissism, grandiosity, and an inflated since of religiosity and self-importance might have driven John White to choose fame over the welfare of his family.

But again, I may be wrong. The colonists may have chosen to leave England because it had become intolerable for those of a devout, religious nature. Overcrowding, filth, and corruption made it a hard place to live. There also may have been considerable financial incentives.

There is also a good possibility that White's journal entries were falsified to prevent his competitors from figuring out the location of the colonists or to thwart piracy. We know he directed them to go "fifty miles into the main" if necessary, which could mean he knew where they were but didn't have the resources to go to them on his return journey, at least not at that time.

However, for whatever reason, it is widely accepted that after John White left Roanoke Island, he stopped searching for Eleanor and returned to England for good, retiring to a cottage in Ireland where he stayed for eleven years. No mention is made of further voyages and there were no journals found. In fact, a last journal entry alludes to his being happy in the knowledge his daughter and her family are safe, but doesn't say why he believes this to be so, or where he thinks they might have gone.

In Ireland the trail goes cold. There is no record of his death and no mention of any surviving family. To this date, it is true that no living descendants have been found. The problem is complicated because we do not know who Eleanor's mother really was. Some scholars theorize that White could have been afraid that without the Queen's protection and with no money of his own, he only returned when it was safe to do so, without anyone's knowledge. It was reading about this part of the mystery that inspired me to write this novel. What if there were more journals written, but we simply don't know where they are?

This provided me with a very plausible ending to my story, one based on precedent. When John White departed from Roanoke Island the first time he buried his papers and drawings in caskets. Upon his return, he discovered that the caskets had been vandalized and everything in them ruined. Since there was no mention in his journals as to what happened to them afterward, it was reasonable to me that he may have kept one of those he rescued, then buried it with him upon his death, especially if the location of his grave was intended to be kept secret. Where John White lies is an enduring mystery to this day.

Of course, his final "letter" to the world is totally a fabrication. One could only dream of such a find. To make sure it's discovery wasn't too farfetched, I consulted Dr. Charles Ewen, Director of the Phelps Archaeology Lab, who explained that the only way such a document could survive for three hundred years was if it were in a total anaerobic environment, sealed with pitch and airtight. In the swamps that would mean under the water table. So that is what I devised.

Yes, it is theorized that seven of the colonists (two men, four boys, and a young woman) were taken captive and forced to work in the copper mines, probably up near the Virginia/North Carolina border in the piedmont region. There have been reports from various reliable sources through the years, particularly Captain John Smith, from the Jamestown Colony, commissioned to go in search of the missing colonists. He also reports that the Powhatan claimed to have massacred the rest.

But who knows? The Powhatan may have simply wanted to frighten future settlers. If you really want the back story, read *Roanoke: Solving the Mystery of the Lost Colony* (2000) written by Dr. Lee Miller. It is the best source to learn more about the actual history.

As for my personal theories, I think it makes perfect sense that at least a handful of colonists survived, intermarried, and stayed hidden in the deep recesses of the inland areas. The population of Tyrrell County reads like the roster of the good ship Tiger, and yes, many families do claim they are descendants. Mary Wood Long wrote a fascinating study about surnames titled *The Five Lost Colonies of Dare*. It can be ordered online.

I also think there is more to the story than meets the eye. Stress tends to do one of two things: it either brings people closer together, or drives them apart. The people who made up the Roanoke colonists were a closely-knit group of family and friends, many of them business partners. Imagine leaving everything you had ever known to follow someone you trusted to the ends of the world, only to be left stranded in an alien environment without enough food or fresh water. I can see the possibility that after three years of suffering and starvation (there was a terrible drought and hostile Indians) they would direct all that fear and anger toward Eleanor and Ananias and even force them out. Perhaps they, and a group of loyal followers, found their way to Salmon Creek. But again, that is merely conjecture.

Whatever happened, everyone desperately wants to believe Virginia grew up to live a happy life, including myself, so that is how I chose to portray her story.

In real life Phil McMullan, Jr. is the author of *Beechland and the Lost Colony*. It was his graduate thesis in the history program at N. C. State University. He believed so much in his research he enrolled at the age of eighty. In real life Phil is very much as I have portrayed him. At the writing of this both he and his wife, Norma, are alive and kicking and very much involved in the ongoing search, not only for the coffins, but for the second Dare stone. You can find his book on Amazon.

You might also be interested in Judge Whedbee's book, *Legends of the Outer Banks*. He was the first to write about the discovery of the coffins. And yes, coffins were found by a dredge operator, then lost again. Many believe that the coffins are still there, very near to where I describe them, though I have played fast and loose with the geography of the area, mainly to discourage would-be seekers who would dare to dig without permission. Be advised that laws are very stringent and could result in years in prison, fines, not to mention encounters with bears and snakes, both in great abundance, and all very lethal.

Some say truth is stranger than fiction. The truth is there really *was* a Bear Lady of Tyrrell County. Her name was Kathryn Grayson. She modeled briefly in New York, but left it behind to create a bear refuge on almost a thousand acres in Tyrell County almost forty years ago. She lived in an old mobile home on her property devoid of electricity or running water for many years. Her sole commitment in life was to the protection of bears, often harassing the known illegal bear hunters, complaining to the authorities, and confronting locals setting traps. There is no reference anywhere to children born out of wedlock or ties to murders. I have no desire to besmirch her good name.

Her story caught my imagination for many reasons. I love exploring the Wildlife Refuge in Dare County (and you can too), often photographing the bears there (albeit from behind the safety of the hood of my car and a good long-range telephoto lens – and never, ever feed them!)

We do know that against all advice otherwise, Kathryn trained bears to feed from her hands, allowed them in her house, even slept alongside of them, and taught them survival skills (like how to climb over barriers and avoid traffic). But there is no evidence that her training included attack on command. That is solely my creative invention, as is the bear named Wingina.

Sadly, Kathryn's body was found in 2014 on a logging path not far from her home. She was in her mid-sixties at the time of her death. The damage to her body was consistent with mauling by a bear, though an autopsy could not confirm if death was the result of the mauling, or came after the fact. I like to think her heart simply gave out, she fell asleep, and one of her friends was trying to wake her.

I wish to thank Kathryn posthumously for having the courage and bravery to live as she desired, though it saddens me to wonder what might have disenchanted her so with humans that she would feel the need to do so.

Rest in peace, Bear Lady.

Willie Batts is loosely based on a real character, Tommy Tucker, who is an awesome guide and explorer living down in the wilds not far from Beechland. If he has ever had a problem with alcohol I have no knowledge of it. He does know a lot about the history of moonshine and mayhem as well as hunting for artifacts in that part of the woods. I would trust my life with him, as many have.

As for Derek, he is a terrible example of love gone awry, twisted by the cruel hand of fate. And totally a creation of my own imagination as are all remaining characters.

Of course, I have my own life story propelling my fascination with early North Carolina history. As a direct descendant of the old Quakers who settled the Albemarle region (and lived on land where the historic Newbold–White House sits now) only a couple of generations after the Roanoke Colony was founded, my love for the stories that abound in this area is ongoing.

Though some may find my subject matter heavy, it is my belief that exploring dark themes is cathartic on many levels, especially for victims like myself. My brother committed suicide in 1990 at the age of twenty-six. The impact of that experience profoundly affected my health and outlook on life, as well as shaping my career direction. I am grateful that for the last fifteen years I have been able to parlay that experience, albeit painful, into a deeply satisfying career not only as a therapist, but as a corporate crisis specialist. To date I have responded to over four hundred corporate accidents, robberies, murders, suicides, and deaths of co-workers, all traumatic events for those working in those companies. I know all too well how important a compassionate response is to those involved.

As the rates of suicide seem to be escalating at an alarming rate across the world, I think we need to be talking more about the way suicide impacts the lives of the hidden victims left behind. I have chosen the art of storytelling as one way of doing so.

And yes, writing has been cathartic for me.

There is a Montrose Plantation in Louisiana, though I have not modeled my Montrose after it. Not long ago I found an obscure reference to a plantation by that name in existence up until the mid–1800's somewhere along the Roanoke River, though I've yet to identify its true location. The interesting thing is that I adopted the name long before I knew about the others. The Montrose of Edenton is fictional but modeled after many such homes still standing in Chowan County.

By the way, Henry the Wonder Dog is based on my own beloved Henri, an Australian Silky Terrier who has been my faithful companion throughout the writing of this book.

At present I am working on a sequel to *The Coffins*.

If you would like to sign up for my email list please visit:
www.deborahdunnbooks.com

ACKNOWLEDGEMENTS

THERE ARE MANY WHO HAVE lent their expertise and support to the writing of this book. I would first like to thank Phil McMullan for writing his graduate thesis and opening my eyes to the possibility that the Lost Colony was never really lost. Thank you for your friendship, faith in me, historical research, and early manuscript approval.

I would also like to thank Dr. Charles Ewen, Director of the Phelps Archaeology Lab and Professor of Anthropology at East Carolina University for his willingness to read my manuscript while it was still crusty and unpolished so that I could avoid making crucial errors in the science early in the writing. His help and encouragement have been invaluable.

I would also like to mention Dr. Stanley Riggs, professor of Geology at East Carolina University and founder of NCLOW (North Carolina Land of Water, a nonprofit) for telling me about seeing a white doe on Roanoke Island when he went camping there as a young father with his family.

There are many who have lent their expertise, mainly the writers like Lee Miller, David Quinn,

Michael Oberg and others I've referenced in this book. I've never enjoyed doing research so much in my life! I would also like to give a shout out to Brent Lane, Director of the Carolina Center for Competitive Economies and former board member of the Lost Colony Foundation for his friendship and willingness to share insights about his discovery of the icon that led to the dig at Salmon Creek. I would also like to thank self-proclaimed "rogue" archaeologist Fred Willard, Director of the Center for Lost Colony Science and Research for early direction as well as various National Park Rangers, particularly Rob Bolling, for his knowledge of the Roanoke Indians and their language, and the staff at the Outer Banks Research Center for answering so many of my questions.

Next I must give a nod to my agent, Jen Kaersbeck, for reading and editing the first crude draft. Jen, you will never know how your faith in me has a writer has helped me find the courage to move forward in my craft. I hope we can work together again someday.

Every story needs readers. Authors need early readers who will give them honest feedback. For this I must thank my dear friends, Sherie Lewis, Kimberli Buffaloe, Ava Thompson, my sister Teri Matheson, my niece Erin Matheson Barr, Norma McMullan, and Lamb Basnight, another of my amateur archaeology buddies. And to my nephew, Nick Wilson, you will never know how much you mean to me.

Then there are those who polish. For this I thank Debi Elramey, Sydney Edwards Dunn, and Becky Mitchell. Kind words, a keen eye, knowledge of the craft and a willing spirit—these are the attributes of a good editor. All three of you have these things in abundance.

I am truly a woman who is blessed. Without such a loving husband who puts up with a wife who likes to hang out in the swamps, I doubt this book could ever have been written. Thank you, my Rick, my Rock. And no mother has ever had such wonderful cheerleaders as I have in my two children, Lee Dunn and Greyson Briere and their respective spouses, Sydney Dunn and Michael Briere. They read my books, encourage me to keep writing, and tell me I am wonderful even when I'm not.

To anyone I may have forgotten, I promise to catch you on the next round!

Made in the USA
Columbia, SC
22 July 2017